Sherlock Holmes
and
The Whitechapel Vampire

Dean P. Turnbloom

Paperback ISBN 9781780921235
ePub ISBN 9781780921242
PDF ISBN 9781780921259

Published in the UK by MX Publishing
335 Princess Park Manor, Royal Drive,
London, N11 3GX
www.mxpublishing.com

Cover design by www.staunch.com

Grateful acknowledgment to Conan Doyle Estate Ltd. for the use
of the Sherlock Holmes characters created by Sir Arthur Conan
Doyle.

For Alexander and Aiden, always reach for your dreams.

Contents

Chapter 1

FRESH HOPE

Her arm dangled as he lifted her from the bed. A single drop of blood remained on her still warm pillow, a silent witness to her last moments. Cradling her body, he carried Marguerite from her room above Le Chat Noir down the back stairway to his awaiting coach. Mademoiselle Dubois, he knew, would not be missed for several hours. To avoid discovery he would deposit the young prostitute's remains in the one place he knew she would not immediately be found, the Seine River.

Running through the center of Paris, the Seine was ideal. Not only was it a convenient receptacle that would not immediately give up its secrets, but it would also corrupt her body to beneficial effect disguising the true nature of her attacker.

The blood he'd so recently ingested would sustain Baron Antonio Barlucci during the long trip back to his villa outside Milan. It was from there he administered his affairs as one of the wealthiest financiers in Europe, known internationally as the Pope's banker. But before leaving Paris, he directed his driver to the Academy of Science where a young American doctor was about to give a lecture that piqued the baron's curiosity.

His carriage ambled along Le Quai du Tuleries, the clacking of the horse's hooves against the cobblestones clinging to the humid night air. Movement near the water's edge caught the baron's eye; he watched as two policemen, their trousers rolled up their legs, worked to pull a body from the river. "Mon dieu!" The cry echoed up from the river giving it a disembodied quality, "She's like the others."

The coach passed a police wagon parked near the water. Two detectives stood beneath a gas lamp. A second voice, addressing the detectives, called out, "Her throat's been cut

1

nearly through."

Settling back in his coach the baron smiled, confident his latest victim would not be found till he was well on his way back to his villa.

This centuries' long game of fox and geese he played with legal authorities across Europe was one he could not afford to lose. At the dawn of his affliction, eluding even crude law enforcement agencies proved a challenge. As time wore on, the agencies became more adept, but fortunately they lacked the sophistication to effectively incorporate lessons learned the way the baron could. His intellect and patient observation allowed him to stay two steps ahead of detection. The immense fortune he amassed down through the centuries, further insulated him from suspicion. One advantage of being a vampire in this modern age was the reluctance of law enforcement to believe in him. Tonight as he watched the detectives and police officers discover the refuse of his appetites, he knew not only would he not be held accountable, but also his involvement would never be suspected.

When he arrived at his destination, he strode unnoticed into the lecture hall. The baron's fashionable but modest dress allowed him to blend seamlessly into the elite assemblage of Europe's scientific community. With dispassion he took his place in the rear of the hall.

Curious but cynical, the baron watched and listened to the charismatic speaker at the lectern deliver his discourse titled "Dispelling Folk Lore with Science". As the young doctor spoke, describing his methods and the success he'd achieved on the Dark Continent with a variety of blood disorders, the baron's interest became more acute—an interest soon to have a crucial influence over both their destinies.

With every word, the baron became increasingly convinced that this was the young man for whom he'd been waiting. As he watched, he thought about how patient he'd been for this moment to arrive. He thought back to his awakening in the early thirteenth century when the Inquisition would have burned one such as he at the stake. Unaware at the time just how long this curse would last, he watched as the world around him marched forward with inexorable sluggishness. He watched and waited as the world crept from the dull nescience of the dark ages, through the renaissance of enlightenment, and ultimately into the modern industrial age. Finally after six centuries, it appeared science had freed itself from superstition, attaining the dimension necessary to liberate him from the burden he'd so long carried.

The baron exited the hall with guarded exuberance before the lecture was over. The journey back to his villa in Milan was a long one and he was anxious to return. He would need time, time and research, in order to put into action the plan now formulating in his mind. As he climbed into the back of his coach, he had his driver stop in the middle of the deserted Pont Neuf on his way out of Paris, one final bit of business to tend to.

The overcast Parisian sky conspired to conceal his actions as the baron removed the lifeless body of Marguerite from her temporary crypt. Effortlessly he carried her to the edge of the bridge. Without ceremony he lifted her over the stone railing. Pausing only long enough to ensure no one would see or hear he relaxed his grip, allowing her body to slip into the black water of the Seine. His dark business concluded the baron retired to the back of his coach for the journey home.

Chapter 2

ACCUSATION

Carlino Gaetano and Vittorio Martinez first met when they were six and nine-years old. Vittorio rescued the younger Carlino from three bullies who were trying to steal his hat. The two soon discovered they had a connection born of tragedy. Each of them had lost a brother to the cholera epidemic that swept through central Italy in 1873. They came to feel they had somehow been brought together, each filling a need of the other. Their shared grief created a bond between them stronger than blood and a loyalty that would last a lifetime.

From that day on they were inseparable.

At twenty, Carlino, dark and swarthy along with Vittorio, with reddish hair and ruddy complexion, twenty-three, left their small village of Portovenere to seek their fortune in England. They arrived in Genoa near the end of July to gain passage onboard the White Star Line's ship *Manchester*. Finding her manifest full, they scoured the docks looking for another ship readying to make the crossing. At last, fate delivered them to the cargo ship *Lira*. It was small and outfitted for cargo, but the word on the dock was they also carried a limited number of passengers.

With crew members busily loading the *Lira*, readying her for the voyage, Carlino busied himself watching the activity on the pier, while Vittorio, always the more practical of the two, set about finding someone with whom to discuss passage onboard the ship. Carlino lagged behind as Vittorio approached a group of rough-looking sailors, "Excuse me, Captain," he said, addressing the one who appeared to be in charge. "We would like to book passage to England aboard your ship."

Turning on his heel to face Vittorio, the sailor responded, "What's that ye say?" Carlino watched the grizzled sailor's manner soften as he eyed the two young men before him. He could see the man taking his measure of Vittorio, then asking, "What can I do for you, then?"

"Passage, sir. My friend and I would like to book passage on your ship to England."

The sailor looked from Vittorio to Carlino and back, then stepped around him. Carlino saw him wink to his mates when he thought he was out of view of the two boys. They looked on with amusement. "Aye, then, I'm the Captain of the *Lira* all right, but passage ain't cheap. You got money?"

"Yes, how much?"

As the sailor stood before Vittorio, feet apart and hands on his hips in a show of bluster, Carlino saw a quiet figure approach him from behind. When the other sailors noticed, their amusement waned and they began to disperse in haste. The figure, standing directly behind the "captain", listened to the exchange.

"Twenty lire," announced the "captain".

The ire of the quiet man was evident in his eyes and it was clear to Carlino the "captain" was a fraud. Now Vittorio looked past the imposter to the figure, who was now laying his hand upon the "captain's" shoulder, "Beggin' your pardon, *captain*!" he said, biting off the word as he placed a rough hand on his shoulder and spun the sailor around to look at him. "I think the bilge is awaiting your inspection, if you please, sir" he said, shoving him toward the ship, "and I'd better not hear o' you playin' capt'in no more, you whale slime."

"Yessir, Mr. Brady, I mean, no sir, I won't, I promises," the would-be captain scurried away, tripping over his own feet as he went.

Vittorio now came under the glare of the mysterious figure who struck such fear into the group of coarse sailors. But his face now took on a peaceful look with a spark of genuine humanity as he said, "You'll have to excuse them. They really meant no harm, but I fear you're an easy mark for vermin of his kind. You were looking for the Captain?"

"Yes, sir, would that be you, sir?"

Smiling, he extended his hand, "No, not the captain. I'm

5

William Brady, First Mate on the *Lira*."

Shaking his hand, Vittorio replied, "I'm Vittorio Martini and this is my friend, Carlino Gaetano. We hope to buy passage to England on your ship."

"Aye, I see," he said as he released Vittorio's hand. "You'll find Captain Madison just down the pier, there," he said as he motioned toward a large man inspecting cargo. "He's the only one can grant you passage."

"Thank you, sir," answered Vittorio. As he and Carlino made their way to where the Captain stood, Carlino spotted a young woman on the deck of the ship. Gianetta Rossini looked down from beside an older couple, her parents, thought Carlino. When Gianetta's eyes met his, Carlino's heart leapt in his chest. Never had he seen a woman so beautiful. Her chestnut hair, tousled by the wind, shimmered in the glare of the noonday sun. Even at this distance he could tell her eyes were green, sparkling like two emeralds as she smiled at him.

From the look on her face, it was obvious she was equally attracted to the young, dark, ruggedly handsome Carlino. His clean-shaven face beamed when he caught her eye.

Just as obvious was her parents' disapproval of their daughter's attraction. They pulled her away from the rail as soon as they noticed her smiling at Carlino and the three of them disappeared inside the skin of the ship.

Captain Josiah Madison grimaced as he checked cargo against his manifest. A menacing presence, the ship's captain was of average height but broad of back, exaggerated by the cut of his deck coat, with a thick black beard and bushy eyebrows that nearly touched above his vulpine nose.

"Captain," Vittorio called when he was close enough for the ship's skipper to hear, "my friend and I seek passage to England aboard your ship."

Busy with his inspection, the captain ignored Vittorio. As Vittorio again opened his mouth to speak, Captain Madison cast a gaze in his direction hard enough to pierce solid oak. "You have money?" he snarled around the briar pipe clinched between his teeth.

6

"Yes, we have money," Vittorio replied, then asked, "how much for the two of us?"

Without blinking the Captain replied as he dislodged the pipe, "Twenty-five lire. Each." He punctuated his proposal with a mixture of tobacco, smoke, and saliva deposited in the direction of Vittorio's shoe.

Vittorio took a step back, "Fifty lire?" he asked, out of range of the captain's spittle, "passage on the *Manchester* is half that amount."

"Then take passage on the *Manchester*," the captain said as he snapped the pipe back into his mouth, turned his back to Vittorio, and returned to his cargo inspection.

"Their manifest is full," Vittorio replied.

The captain repeated the price, without looking back, "Then it's fifty lire, take it or leave it."

Fifty lire was well more than half of what the two had between them and they would need a stake once they got to England. Vittorio turned away, disappointed, but Carlino grabbed his arm, pulling him closer to speak into his ear without the captain overhearing. "Vittorio, we have no choice," he pleaded with his friend, fearing he might never again see the young beauty onboard the ship.

"But Carlino, it is nearly everything we have," Vittorio reasoned.

"We can earn more when we arrive in England. It will cost us more than that to stay in Genoa long enough to find another ship with only a hope of finding a cheaper price."

Accepting the truth of his friend's argument, Vittorio turned back to Captain Madison. "Very well, Captain. Fifty lire."

The Captain turned to face him as Vittorio counted out fifty lire in silver from a small bag. "You can stow your things in steerage. You've got the last two bunks onboard." Smiling as he took the coins, the Captain counted them again. "We sail at dawn," he barked as he turned back once again to the cargo.

As soon as he was onboard, Carlino began to inquire about the young woman he'd seen from the pier. He discovered her name was Gianetta Rossini, and she was on her way, accompanied by her parents, to England. There she would marry a wealthy businessman. Disappointed, he could still not get her out of his mind.

He left the cabin he shared with Vittorio late that evening to get some fresh air on deck as the activity around the ship's imminent departure settled down and few were up and about. He saw her as he approached the bow of the ship. She sat on a bollard, gazing up at the waning quarter moon. "Good evening, Signorina," he said as he approached her.

She turned toward him, startled at first, but her surprise dissolved to delight as she recognized Carlino, "Good evening," she replied, then coyly turned back again to gaze up at the moon once more.

"I saw you earlier, when I first arrived," he said, not knowing what else to say, hoping to spark conversation.

"I know," she answered without looking back.

After an awkward silence, he offered his hand saying, "My name is Carlino Gaetano."

She turned to look at him, accepted his hand, and said, "I am Gianetta...Gianetta Rossini." Her green eyes appeared to glow in the moonlight.

"I know," he answered with a smirk, "I asked about you from some of the crew."

"Oh?" she asked, seemingly surprised, "and what else did they tell you about me?"

"Only that you are engaged and that you travel to England to marry," he answered honestly.

When she heard this, she sighed, saying, "Yes, it is true. My parents have arranged for me to be the wife of Lester Armbruster." at the sound of his name she made a disagreeable sound, "Hmmph! Gianetta Armbruster. It sounds simply horrid, does it not?"

Nodding in agreement Carlino ventured, "Then you are not in love with him?"

She looked at him with piercing eyes, "No!" she said, "I barely know him."

"Then why do you marry him?" Carlino asked in earnest

8

wonderment.

Casting her eyes down and away, she replied, "I do it for my parents." She stood and walked to the rail of the ship. Carlino followed. The words came slowly at first, her voice barely a whisper as she related how her parents had fallen onto hard times. When she spoke of the gift of dowry offered by the Armbrusters, she spoke more quickly, her voice taking on an edge that surprised him. She recited how the gift would make her parents solvent as tears began to fall down her cheeks. "Do not look at me that way," she said turning away from him. "My parents are good and loving people. They need me to do this for them," she said as the tears rolled down her cheeks. "How can I not?" her eyes pleaded for an answer.

"Your parents' fortunes are their own affair," Carlino told her, thinking of his own father as he spoke.

"That is easy for you to say, you are a man."

"You think I speak lightly? You think I do not know what it is to have your parents plan your life for you?" His voice sharpened. "My father wanted me, expected me to take over his business."

"And so you have run away from home?" she said, allowing the bitterness in her heart to wash through her words, despite her tears.

"I left, but I did not run," showing no humor as he spoke. "But before I left, I told my father his way was not mine, that I wanted something more than to be a merchant in a small fishing village."

"You make it sound so easy, but you do not know my parents," she said softening.

"I know it is not easy. My father refused to even look at me the day I left." As he spoke, he turned toward her, his pain showing in his eyes as he grasped her arms. "It is not about your parents. It is about you, what is in your heart." Thinking about the arguments he had with father leading up to his departure and the bad terms on which they'd parted, he continued, "The plans they made for you should not bind you when your heart does not desire it."

Gianetta looked up at him. "That is what I told my Mama," she said through her tears, "but she said she and Papa know best."

Carlino put his arms around her shoulders pulling her closer as he comforted her. She rested her head on his shoulder, droplets falling as she cried without giving voice to her tears. Standing close to her in the moonlight, feeling her warmth, Carlino wanted to take her in his arms and kiss her, but he was too timid. Once her tears subsided, he looked at her and whispered, "Tomorrow I will talk to your parents. I will tell them it is not up to them who you marry. That is the old way."

"No, you must not," putting a finger to his lips to quiet him. She continued, "if you speak to them, they will not let me out of their sight. We will not..." she stopped.

"We will not?" he asked, feeling emboldened. "We will not, what?" His voice expectant, he asked, "Do you mean you wish to see me again?"

She turned away, her cheeks flushing as she answered, "Yes, I would." Turning to face him she said, "I would like that very much." Looking up at him, her green eyes twinkling like the stars over their heads she cautioned, "but if they suspect we have even spoken together, they will not allow it. They will keep us apart."

"If they are so determined, how will we meet?"

"Just as we have tonight, silly," came her reply, flirtatious as she smiled and walked her fingers up his chest. "My parents would not approve my being out of our cabin even tonight," she paused, flashing a delightfully devious smile, "but they sleep very soundly. I have only to pretend to slumber. Once they fall asleep, I can easily sneak away for a midnight stroll alone...or with you," she said, smiling once again.

"Then we will meet every night, just as tonight," he said, his voice barely a whisper as he gazed into her smoldering eyes in the moonlight, "until I have convinced you to stand up to your parents." She returned his gaze, standing close and looking up at him.

Neither noticed the gilded four-wheeled coach as it

10

approached the brow of the ship, not until its passenger was half-way up the gangway. Gianetta shivered.

"You are cold," said Carlino.

"No…no, it is not that."

"What is it, then?" he asked.

"There, that man coming onto the ship…" she pointed toward the gangway, "he is evil." She blurted out the words without understanding why. As she did, she stepped back into the shadows as if she were afraid of being seen.

By the time Carlino turned to look, he was nowhere to be found. "I do not see anyone." Spying the carriage, he added, "but whoever he is, he must have come in that coach," indicating the heavy black landau that turned around on the pier and drove slowly away. Looking back toward Gianetta, he took her in his arms, pulling her shivering body closer, "Why do you say he is evil? Do you know him?"

"No, I…I do not know why I said that…I just feel it. You…you don't think he heard me, do you?"

"Do not worry," he said smiling down at her, holding her tightly, "I will protect you."

#

After the ship set sail for Southampton, Carlino tried in vain to get the attention of Gianetta. She would not even look in his direction. He was unsure whether this was done for the benefit of her parents, to dissuade them from thinking there might be an attraction, or she had merely been teasing him the night before. As the day wore on, he finally gave up. Instead, he tried to interest himself in other pursuits.

Naturally gregarious, Carlino made it his business to meet each of the other passengers. He first made the acquaintance of Milo and Cristina Magdalena. They were an elderly couple on their way to visit their son in St. Albans, just north of London. Milo had recently retired from the banking business, and he and his wife were going to meet their only son's wife and new baby. They were a quiet, kindly couple who kept to themselves.

The Rossinis were his next stop. When Carlino

11

approached them at dinner that evening, Gianetta excused herself feigning seasickness. Carlino hid his disappointment, and proceeded to try and get to know her parents. Somewhat suspicious of his motives, Paolo and Anna were less approachable than had been the Magdalenas. He did learn that they were from a noble lineage in Italy. They took great pains to let him know this, also ensuring he knew their daughter was betrothed and on her way to be wed.

The eighth passenger did not show himself; he remained in his cabin all day. When the First Mate sat down to join the others for dinner, Carlino inquired, "Who is it that is staying in the Captain's cabin?"

Looking around the table at the passengers' expectant faces, the Mate told him, "Just another passenger on his way to England." Smiling, he added, "He is quite well known in some circles." He appeared to revel in their curiosity as he looked around the table at the other passengers coveting the secret he held.

"Who is he?" asked Anna Rossini.

"I am afraid I cannot tell you. His wish is to remain anonymous and undisturbed. He has paid us well for our discretion," he said with a grin. Seeing they were still curious, he added, "But I can tell you this. He is recuperating from a great tragedy. His father recently died and his mother shortly before. He is on his way to England to settle his father's affairs."

"The poor man," sympathized Cristina.

"Indeed. The shock and grief of losing both his parents in such a short period has put his health in jeopardy. For this reason he is in need of rest, which he hopes this voyage will provide." Before he continued, he looked each of the other passengers in the eye, then said, "I implore you, should you see him about the ship, give him wide berth."

Soon after the ship put to sea, Vittorio had gone looking for the First Mate to inquire whether he and Carlino might be able to work as deck hands and earn back part of their passage. After dinner that evening he informed Carlino of their good fortune. He was able to secure positions that would earn each of them ten pounds by the time they reached Southampton. It was exhausting work, but Vittorio and Carlino were young and strong. Besides, as he explained to Carlino, he preferred it over having nothing to do to occupy his time.

"The First Mate has agreed to return nearly half of our passage in exchange for our honest labor," Vittorio told him, his excitement brimming over.

"But Vito, we are not sailors. Besides, I have other plans."

"Do you not understand, Carlo, we will earn back enough to see us through till we can find work in England. The Rossinis, I am sure, know your 'plans' and have some of their own. Forget her, Carlo, she is trouble for you."

Carlino, wishing the conversation to end so that he might go on deck to meet with Gianetta, relented. "Very well, Vito," he agreed, "we will work. Now, I am going to sleep. We can speak more tomorrow," he said as he climbed into his hammock. Before rolling over he added, "But you are wrong about Gianetta."

Pretending to sleep, Carlino waited until his friend had closed his eyes before he made his way on deck to seek Gianetta. He found her in the same location where they had met the night before. He rushed toward her, but she playfully kept him at a distance. "I thought from the way you behaved today, perhaps you had changed your mind about seeing me," he told her, his voice tinged with mock sadness.

"No," she said. Her hand lingered on his arm as she brushed by him to stand at the ship's rail. Eyes seaward, she said, "But if I fooled you, then perhaps I fooled Mama and Papa as well," then she turned to smile at him.

"You were quite convincing," he assured her. As he moved closer, once again he felt the urge to kiss her.

She moved away. With a coquettish look she asked, "Are you trying to kiss me?"

Confused, Carlino asked, "Do you wish me not to kiss you?"

Laughing, Gianetta replied, "Oh, Carlino, I did not say

13

that, but we barely know each other. What would you think of me if I let you kiss me so quickly?" Upon saying this, she twirled away from him. Her lips pouted, she teased him with her eyes as she moved down the rail toward the ship's longboat.

Carlino accepted the game and followed her. He caught her by the arm as they slipped beneath the davit securing the boat. Pulling her toward him, he answered, "I would think you are the most beautiful girl I have ever seen." Taking her in his arms, he looked down at her smiling face and as she closed her eyes, he kissed her.

Each night of the voyage, Carlino and Gianetta met on deck after her parents were asleep. Together, they walked the deck of the ship, falling deeper in love. Each day, Gianetta pretended not to know Carlino existed, though she yearned to be in his arms, just as he yearned to hold her. As the ship progressed on its journey to England, their romance also progressed, from the playful flirtation of two young people enjoying each other's attention to the passionate and prolonged kissing of two young lovers. All the while Gianetta's parents were blissfully unaware in their cabin. Shortly before the ship reached its destination, just four days before landing in Southampton, Carlino held Gianetta in his arms and together they pledged their love for one another.

Hand in hand, they made plans to be together as soon as Carlino could find work in England. As a token of his devotion, Carlino gave Gianetta a ring. It had belonged to his father and his father's father and bore his family's crest.

Gianetta told Carlino, "But I have nothing to give you in return, my love," then began to cry as she kissed his hand, rubbing her cheek against it.

He held her close to his chest, telling her, "Do not cry, it is not important; I know how much you love me. I do not need anything to prove that." They stood together in the faint moonlight as he stroked her long hair with gentle hands. While doing so, one of her combs fell loose in his hand.

Gianetta took the comb from him. Looking at it, she reached up to kiss Carlino's lips. "Carlo," she said almost in a whisper, "accept this comb as a token and pledge of my love.

14

These belonged to my grandmother." As she removed the other comb from her hair she told him, "I am her namesake. She gave these to me when I was a little girl. Look," she said as she held up one of the combs in the pale moonlight, "the golden scarab has my initial engraved upon it."

"But Gianetta, how will you manage with only one comb?"

She pressed the comb into his hand. Looking up at him, she said, "Carlo, while we are apart, the comb will be as I am, useless and lost without you. Once we are together again I will have both to wear, my love."

"Then I shall keep it very safe, my darling," he whispered. "I will treasure it even as I treasure your love." Taking her in his arms again, he kissed her. Overcome with the passion of young lovers, they concealed themselves within the empty longboat covered over with canvas. It was here, on this night, that they consummated their love.

All the following day Carlino walked the ship in a daze. He held the memory, replaying it over and over in his mind, unaware it would be their last night together. For the following night Gianetta would disappear.

As Carlino prepared to go topside to meet his lover, Vittorio detained him below decks to warn him of the rumors being passed among the crew and that Gianetta's father and mother were becoming suspicious. He pleaded for Carlino to break off their relationship before he was caught and something bad happened.

Meanwhile, Gianetta waited near the longboat for Carlino to arrive. As she waited with tortured patience, she failed to notice a stranger watching her from the shadows. He approached her, asking in a low voice, "Are you out alone this evening, Signorina?"

Startled, she turned. Some trick of mind caused her to see Carlino for just a moment, but his eyes looked different—they seemed to burn into her. Then she realized it was not Carlino, but instead the same stranger she'd seen come onboard the ship on the night she and Carlino met. An icy finger down her spine caused her to shiver involuntarily. Unnerved, she wished to cry out, but instead only answered, "No, I am waiting for someone."

"Ah, I see...your young man. Are you sure he is coming?" the stranger teased with a smile that was as menacing as it was alluring.

"Of course he will come," she answered feeling less sure than she was just the minute before. She felt ill at ease, yet unable to walk away. She felt drawn to him, as the moon draws the tide.

"I am only teasing you, little one. Of course he is coming. In fact, I sent your young man a message to meet you," he said, looking about the deck, "but not here."

"You sent him..." the words fell dully from her lips as her mind searched for clarity. With a sudden apprehension she asked, "Where? Where is he to meet me?"

"I sent him a message to meet you in the Captain's cabin," he answered. Continuing, he explained, "You see, I am a hopeless romantic. I've watched the two of you together, nearly every evening of our voyage. It's quite evident you are in love, as it is equally evident your parents seek to keep you apart."

She looked into his eyes. They were deep and as she looked she had the sensation of falling, the little thrill in the pit of her stomach. He smiled at her with killing kindness. She felt herself beginning to trust him, wanting, needing to trust him.

"Come. We will go to my cabin and await your young man. Carlino is his name, no?" As if in a dream, she took his arm and they walked to his cabin. "I've watched the two of you; it is quite obvious you belong together." His voice was velvet. "I only wish to offer you a night of uninterrupted privacy before the ship arrives in port." As she gazed into the stranger's dark eyes, listening to his soothing voice, her last lingering suspicions disappeared, much as an early morning fog dissipates beneath the warmth of the sun. As he held the door open, she released his arm and they entered his cabin unobserved.

The following morning, Gianetta's parents were inconsolable as they searched in vain for their missing daughter.

By 9:00 a.m. it was obvious she was no longer on board. Vittorio was just outside when Gianetta's father found the Captain in the wheelhouse, "Captain, I must insist a search be made. My wife is most distraught. We must know what has happened to our daughter."

"We've turned the ship around, Mr. Rossini, but I'm afraid there's not much more we can do. If she's fallen overboard during the night, the chances of finding her are one in a million."

"Fallen overboard? Nonsense," Paolo Rossini barked at the Captain. "It is far more likely she was thrown overboard."

"What are you saying, Mr. Rossini?" Thrown over? By whom?"

"Do not pretend you do not know, Captain," Paolo complained, his voice tinged with acid. "I have heard the rumors as I am sure so have you. It is that boy, Carlino; he is the one who has done this."

"What possible reason..." the captain questioned.

"Reason? Why, the oldest reason known to man! Jealousy!"

"Explain yourself, sir," the Captain demanded.

"My daughter is to marry when we arrive in England. Her husband is very wealthy and well connected. Gianetta is young, but she knows her duty," Paolo said, steel in his voice. "This Carlino must have become enraged when Gianetta told him she could not see him again, enraged to the point of murder." Paolo's eyes widened as his voice rose, "Arrest him, Captain, I demand it."

"Arrest him? What if you're wrong, sir?"

"I am not," insisted Paolo.

Realizing Mr. Rossini could be right, and seeing he was most certainly too upset for the captain not to do something, he instructed his First Mate, "Search the ship. Look for anything that might provide a clue as to what happened to Miss Rossini."

"Aye, Captain," the First Mate replied.

"And," the Captain continued, "start your search with young Gaetano's quarters."

"Aye, sir." The First Mate left the Captain and Paolo in

the wheelhouse. Vittorio raced to find and warn Carlino, but it was too late. It wasn't long before the turquoise comb was discovered in Carlino's room, hidden in his steamer trunk.

The Captain and First Mate surmised Paolo Rossini had been correct all along. The entire crew knew that Gianetta, although engaged to be married, had been seeing Carlino secretly at night. Guided by the assertions of the Rossinis that Gianetta had every intention of marrying her fiancée when they arrived in England, it wasn't difficult to believe she would have tried to break off their relationship with the voyage nearing its end. From there, it followed that Carlino would have become jealous. With the additional evidence of the comb, it appeared clear the two must have fought, with Carlino murdering the girl in a fit of passion. Having seen what he had done, he would naturally have disposed of her body at sea.

Carlino, despite his protestations of innocence, was placed in irons and put in the forward hold of the ship. There he would await the inquiry of the maritime authorities in Southampton.

The night before the ship was to arrive in port, after the excitement had quieted down, the Captain called on the stranger occupying his cabin. "Excuse me, sir, the ship will dock tomorrow in Southampton. Is there anything you require?" asked the Captain as he entered.

"Yes, Captain..." his guest replied, "I wonder if you might have my belongings taken to this address." He handed the captain a slip of paper adding, "I'm afraid the dreadful business about the young woman's murder has left me a bit unnerved."

"Of course, sir."

"I'm sorry to say I may require your quarters a bit longer than I'd originally intended, until tomorrow evening, if it's not too much trouble." Noting the Captain's slight hesitation, he continued, "I'm prone to headaches and the bright sunlight only serves to exacerbate them." As he laid a small bag of coins on the table between them he added, "I would appreciate it if I weren't disturbed by the authorities. I really don't believe I can add much to their investigation and my nerves are quite unsteady."

The captain's eyes opened widely as he picked up the bag of coins, "It's no trouble at all, sir. I shall see to it your things are delivered as you wish," he answered, opening the bag. Seeing the gold coins within, he added with a sly smile, "...and I believe I can arrange the paperwork in such a manner the authorities won't even know you were onboard."

"That would be most satisfactory, Captain. Yes, most satisfactory indeed."

With the additional bonus in hand, the captain was not inclined to question his instructions, regardless their odd character. Neither would he later mention to the authorities the blood stains he would soon discover in his cabin—blood stains that might save an immigrant printer, wrongly accused of murder, a trip to the gallows.

Chapter 3

ALLIES, OLD AND NEW

"Ah, Watson, nothing can quite compare to a summer's day in Paris, don't you agree?" commented Sherlock Holmes while he and Dr. John Watson were sitting at a small sidewalk table sipping espresso at the Café de la Paix.

"I prefer London regardless the time of the year, myself," answered Watson as he ruffled his newspaper in annoyance, peering over the corner at his friend.

"Please, old boy, don't get me wrong…for residential purposes I hold England, in general, and London specifically in the highest regard, but there is something to be said nonetheless for a holiday in Paris," Holmes remarked. Watson noted a wistful look in Holmes' eye as he continued, "And while it's true one can't get a good cup of tea in the whole of France, these fine espressos and cappuccinos are appropriate compensation, even you must admit." Taking a sip, he persisted, "They're quite stimulating. Enough so to forego the needle, at least temporarily, don't you think?"

"I suppose that might be a point in their favor," admitted Watson with a sigh. He considered his companion's propensity toward cocaine distasteful and was grateful for any distraction that obviated his need for the needle. "I still prefer a good strong cup of tea to this new drink fad."

"Good old Watson," chided Holmes, "faithful to the end."

"Yes, I suppose I am," answered Watson, feeling a bit piqued. "I must say I find it most peculiar of you to extol the virtues of a country with which your own has had such strained relations down through our history—a country so fickle in its constitution that it changes its governance with a frequency more akin to a lady and her hats than a civilized nation," Watson chastised, and then added, "I find it most peculiar indeed, and you might do

20

well to remember the words of the philosopher, 'When a man is tired of London, he is tired of life; for there is in London all that life can afford.'"

As he concluded this homily, he noted the corners of Holmes mouth curling ever so slightly with a mirthful look in his eye, signaling he'd been purposefully provoked. In a huff, he turned slightly away and murmured to himself as much as to Holmes, "I suppose you find it quite amusing to raise my ire. I should think a man of your abilities could find other ways in which to amuse himself."

"Come, come, old boy, don't be cross," Holmes cajoled, "I am actually quite surprised you were the least taken in by my little jest. I doubt there is a man in all England more profoundly proud of his country than I."

Softening, Watson admitted, "Yes, you're right there, or at least I'd always thought it." Then, smiling, "I can't imagine what Mrs. Hudson would say should she hear you carrying on so." A small chortle escaped his lips.

"There's a good man, Watson," cried Holmes as he clapped his friend on the arm, "but let's not tell her, shall we? That's not a kettle I'd care to set a-boil." Looking up toward the street, Holmes noted, "Ah, I do believe this must be Chief Inspector Renard coming now," rising to meet the inspector who had stepped from his coach.

"Mssr. Holmes, I presume?" asked the inspector as he stepped up to the table occupied by Holmes and Watson.

"Yes, and this is my friend and associate, Dr. John Watson. You are Chief Inspector Renard?" inquired Holmes as he gave a momentary glance at the credential the inspector held out for his inspection.

"That is correct, Mssr. Holmes," he replied. "May I sit?"

"Of course, Inspector," answered Holmes, pulling out a chair for the inspector while returning to his own seat "and congratulations on your recent promotion. May I get you something?" Holmes asked as he gestured for the waiter.

Waving the attentive waiter away, the inspector replied, "That's quite all right, Mssr., thank you," with a quizzical look on his face. "Tell me, how did you know my promotion to Chief Inspector was recent, Mssr. Holmes?"

"Élémentaire, Inspector," Holmes replied, smiling at Watson. "I pride myself on noticing the small things most people ignore. For example, I notice the heels of your shoes are turned over, yet the top leather appears to be relatively new, suggesting a good deal of walking. The Chief Inspector takes a coach."

"That's a bit of a stretch, Mssr. Holmes."

Agreeing, Holmes continued, "Indeed, and I wouldn't base my deduction on that exclusively, Inspector. But I also noticed your badge is quite new, not yet showing the wear one would expect when carried in your hip pocket inside a leather case. Also, your official identification says you are Inspector First Class Louis Renard, not Chief Inspector Renard. Thus, a recent promotion is the only possible answer."

"Qu'est-ce que c'est? You noticed all that in the time in which you glanced at my credentials? I'm quite impressed," he took a deep breath. Letting it out slowly, he said, "Your reputation is not exaggerated, Mssr. Welcome to Paris."

"Merci, Inspector. I hope you don't mind that I asked you to meet us here. When I received your wire at my hotel, I thought it would be more advantageous. You see, Dr. Watson and I are on a short 48 hour holiday in Paris before engaging in a small matter somewhat south of here, in Arles. We preferred to spend the short time we have until our meeting there sampling the fresh air and cuisine of your fair city."

"Perfectly understandable, Mssr. Holmes," answered the inspector. "Then you are on your way to Arles?"

"Yes. We're to meet with a young Dutchman whose acquaintance I made while he was teaching in London. He has since turned his hand to art, although it's doubtful you've heard of him. His name is Vincent van Gogh and he's asked us to come to Arles to investigate a case of forgery involving his work."

"No, I'm afraid I have not," said the inspector showing little interest in the art escapade. "Actually, I was hoping you would be staying in Paris a bit longer."

"Oh? And what appears to be the trouble, Inspector?"

"I'm not quite sure, Mr. Holmes. You see, we had a nasty bit of business a little over a month ago when we pulled four young women from the Seine; each one had her throat cut. They were all about the same age and certainly of the same occupation, if you understand my meaning."

"If I do, Inspector I would also imagine women of that ilk would from time to time incite great passion and their violent demise might not be too unusual in a city the size and reputation of Paris," Holmes replied stirring his espresso.

"Quite so, Mr. Holmes, but these women were a bit unusual in one other respect in particular."

"Oh?" Holmes asked. He held the spoon still in his coffee as he asked, "In what way?"

"Well, Mssr., they appeared to have had all the blood drained from their bodies."

"I see," stirring once more, "...and you don't believe their throats being cut is sufficient enough cause for this, er, abnormality?"

"Mr. Holmes, I was once a military investigator and it's been my experience a wound of this sort would certainly cause a lot of blood to be spilled, but once the heart stops pumping, the loss of blood to the rest of the body ceases. At this point it begins to, what is the word, collect, pool..."

"Yes, hypostasis."

"Oui. There was no *hypostasis* evident in these women." The inspector gave Holmes a most serious look, "No, not even a body thrown in the river would likely lose as much blood as that."

"...and your investigation has turned up nothing to explain this?"

"In each case, the young woman was identified and her residence was searched. And in each case only the smallest drops of blood were found upon each woman's pillow. The extent of their injuries were somewhat masked by the time they spent in the river, but I do not believe their wounds, however grave, fully account for this lack of blood."

"You say you've had four such cases, Inspector? When

23

was the last one?"

"That's just it, Mr. Holmes. We found four corpses, a week apart, with the last discovered the first week of July and we've had none since."

As he listened, Holmes sat turned toward the inspector with one leg crossed over the other at the knee, resting his elbow on the table and his chin on the base of his palm while tapping his cheek with his forefinger. When the inspector had finished, Holmes said, as if to himself, "That puts it well over a month ago." Settling back in his chair and pulling his pipe from his jacket pocket, he commented, "I'm afraid with so much time gone by and with the women having been found in the river, I doubt there is very much I can do, Inspector. I'm terribly sorry."

"I understand, Mssr. Holmes. I thought as much. But if I can be so bold as to trouble you further, there is something you might confirm for me."

"If I can be of assistance, I'd be most happy to, Inspector."

Leaning forward, Renard said, "I have a suspicion the culprit may be a visitor to Paris, rather than a resident."

"What leads you to that deduction, Inspector?" he asked as he lit his pipe and sent billows of smoke into the Parisian air.

"First of all, we had four cases in as many weeks and none since. During that same time there was a gathering of sorts at the Academy of Science. Shortly after it was over, the murders ceased."

"Although titillating, I'm not sure one can be precisely tied to the other, not without more to go on. Correlation is never conclusive evidence of cause and effect."

"There is a bit more, though it might be, how do you say it, dubious."

"Go on, Inspector," Holmes said with interest.

"About fifteen years ago, there was a similar spree of murders in the same area of Paris. It was shortly after the establishment of the Third Republic when confusion abounded. At the time, over twenty such women were found in the Seine. A general panic struck the city."

"That's strange," remarked Watson, "I don't recall ever hearing of such a spate."

"I do remember a string of murders," Holmes admitted, "though not the particulars as information was sorely wanting, but I had no idea there were so many victims."

"Ouí, though the Gendarmes, who were in charge of the investigation, were very close-mouthed about it. The newspapers were forbidden from writing accounts of the murders. I only know the particulars, as you call them, from reading the official records."

"And these murders were similar?" asked Watson.

"As far as I can tell, they were identical. Young women, all from the Montmartre district, all prostitutes, throats cut, drained of their blood to the last drop. Even their residences…in almost every case a bit of blood was discovered on their pillows, but nothing more."

Holmes sat puffing on his pipe, blue smoke dancing in the light summer breeze, "I agree, Inspector, all this would certainly lead one to the logical conclusion the murderer was not a resident, but a visitor, an occasional visitor with an appetite for the macabre."

With a look of relief, the inspector smiled, "Thank you, Mr. Holmes, I was afraid I was losing my mind."

"Losing your mind? I don't understand," Watson interjected. "It seems perfectly logical to me."

"Yes," agreed the inspector, "but I'm afraid I misled you on some of the facts. The twenty murders in 1873 were an exaggeration."

Holmes listened as Watson replied, "Nevertheless…"

The inspector cut Watson off in mid-sentence, "At least, it was an exaggeration for that particular spree. You see, there were only a handful of murders then, though the Gendarmes' records weren't clear on the exact count, but there were other murders some time before…"

"Before?" asked Holmes, "How much before?"

"The twenty murders I just described to you actually occurred not in 1873, but in 1793, during the time of the First

Republic," concluded the inspector.

For a moment Holmes and Watson sat silent. Watson was stunned as he calculated the time span. At last Holmes smiled and said, "Come now, Inspector. You surely don't believe your recent murders to be the work of the same man. He would necessarily have to be over a hundred years old."

"Oui, of course I know. This is why I was hoping you would be visiting Paris for a longer time. It is puzzling, N'est-ce pas?"

"Curious, yes, but reason tells me you have someone imitating the original murderer, for purposes unknown, nothing more. The ordinary is infinitely more difficult to fathom than the extraordinary. Yet even that is interesting."

"I knew you would find it so, Mssr. Holmes. Will you extend your visit to Paris?"

"I'm afraid it's out of the question, for now, Inspector. I've given my word to young van Gogh. But I will contact you when we arrive in Arles as to where we're staying. Should you encounter another murder, don't hesitate to contact me at once. By train, I can be here in less than a day."

#

August 17, 1888

With its gray lichen covered walls, located half a block from some of London's meanest docks, the Anchor Pub was not what one would call a family establishment. Rather, it was meant to separate a thirsty laborer from his hard earned money. The first watering hole a dock worker with a week's wages in his pocket would likely find, the Anchor Pub was often where that same docker would spend a good portion, if not all, of those earnings.

From his table in a dark corner, the baron watched as the towering man entered the pub and made his way to the bar. Earlier the baron had spoken to Abner, the bartender, inquiring if there might be someone with a strong back interested in earning some extra money. Abner mentioned there was someone who might fill the bill by the name of Garrett. He told the baron he'd

26

known Garrett for years, as did many of the pub owners along the docks. Garrett kept to himself and was, for the most part, quiet and peaceable. But Abner knew it hadn't always been so with him and described for the baron the evidence the big man wore of a more errant past—a prominent nose showing multiple breaks, and a long white scar running vertically from his forehead, across his pale blue, askance-looking right eye, and down his cheek. Abner recounted for the baron the bar fight in which Garrett received that little memento, a scuffle with a band of smugglers that had nearly cost Garrett his life.

He also mentioned Garrett had lost his family some eleven years past. His wife and a daughter he would never know died in the act of childbirth. Since that time, he'd lived in a small tenement building close to the docks.

"I'll have a pint, keep," ordered Garrett. Standing six feet four inches tall, he was an imposing figure. He kept his prematurely grey hair cropped close to his scalp and appeared to be in constant need of a shave.

"'Ere you are, mate," Abner said, pausing to fill the big man's glass before wiping down the bar with his filthy rag.

"Quiet night," Garrett remarked as he sat the glass back down after swilling half its contents.

"Go easy, mate, there's plenty," Abner cautioned, again filling his glass. "Mostly regulars here tonight."

Deep lines crossed Garrett's leathery face, worn into it from years of hard labor working as a longshoreman. His job, physically demanding without much pay, satisfied his basic needs. A stevedore's pay supplied him with enough money to live in a couple of clean rooms as well as enabled him to purchase the meager meals he required with enough left over to allow him to drink as much as he liked, and Garrett appeared to like his drink very much.

According to Abner, the large and formidable Garrett had a reputation as someone not to be trifled with, and seemed content to sit alone at the bar, and get slowly and solemnly numb. Abner supposed he'd earned the right to drink in solitude without being disturbed and did so, most nights.

Unfortunately for Garrett, this was not most nights. Tonight would bring Garrett some new scars, a new occupation, and a new employer. It would launch a new beginning for Garrett, the beginning of the end.

While he minded his own business having a pint of bitters, a stranger, a small runt of a man, roughly pushed his way up to the bar alongside him. "Pardon me," said the little man as he made a display of spreading his elbows out on the bar, "my gov'nor tells me you've pinched 'is purse."

"What's that you're saying?" asked Garrett as he looked at the intruder through bleary eyes, "aww, go on wi' you," and dismissing the intruder, he turned back to his drink.

"Hey," the undersized adversary persisted as he turned toward Garrett, catching his arm, "mind your manners, bloke, I'm talkin' t' you."

With menace in his voice he said, "Go away, little man, before I stuffs you in that 'toon yonder," indicating the brass spittoon at the end of the bar.

Abner, who'd been watching and listening all along, could no doubt see where this was leading. He leaned over the bar raising a cricket bat above the edge so both Garrett and the interloper could see, "I'll have no trouble in here," he said, nodding toward the pacifier in his hand, "take your disagreement outside if you must have it."

Grumbling his reluctance, Garrett stood off his stool. "Keep my drink fresh, Abner, this won't take long," he said with a wink, and turned to follow the little man through the crowd. Out the door they went, to the corner and around the side of the pub into what Garrett thought was a deserted alley way. Once there, he discovered the alley was not as deserted as he'd believed. He'd been drawn into a trap.

In the dark passage between the pub and an empty warehouse three men were waiting. "Get 'im, boys," cried the runt and with a confusion of fists, feet, and fury they set upon him. As the trio of ambushers held Garrett, their smaller compatriot began to beat him unmercifully.

"Aaarrghhh…" moaned Garrett. With great effort, he

managed to pull one arm loose. With it he hurled his closest aggressor into the wall. The others countered by knocking Garrett's legs out from under him, kicking him in the head, back and shoulders, heavy boots pummeling their victim with abandon. "Kill the bloody bastard!" one of them shouted. In desperation, Garrett latched onto a pair of legs. Struggling to his knees, he propelled their owner into the other assailants knocking all three into a can of rubbish. By this time the first attacker, having recovered, found a length of shoring. Crying, "Try this on for size, mate," he broke it across Garrett's back as the big man was trying to find his feet. A stunned Garrett staggered about long enough for the others to rally, setting on him once again. The match continued for some time with Garrett holding his own, but the disparity in numbers began to take its toll.

Unseen by Garrett and his assailant, the baron had followed the two out of the pub. Waiting in the shadows for just the right moment, when it was obvious that Garrett would not survive much longer, he stepped in. The baron's blade, drawn from the handle of his walking stick, gleamed in the moonlight as he came upon them. With quick slashes he gave two of the young toughs superficial cuts, "Aaaghh, blimey, what the..." cried one, who upon looking into the eyes of his attacker ran screaming into the night as if the devil himself were chasing him. His partner's wound proved painful enough to convince him of the wisdom in cutting his losses and beating a hasty retreat, leaving his two remaining compatriots to whatever fate awaited them.

These last two the baron peeled off Garrett as if they were so many leeches, flinging them against the brick wall of the pub with such force one of the two fell dead on the spot, his skull fractured. The other, though stunned, took flight as quickly as he could get to his feet.

The baron helped Garrett to his awaiting brougham. "Come, you've had a hard time of it," he said in a soothing voice. "My estate isn't far, I'll dress your wounds and you can rest there." Not waiting for a response from the nearly unconscious Garrett, he drove straightaway to his residence near

Hyde Park, where he nursed the big man's injuries.

So far as a grateful Garrett knew, when the stranger stepped in to save his life he acted out of simple charity. But charity was an emotion the baron had long ago discarded. His intercession on behalf of Garrett was a carefully orchestrated maneuver to secure a servant who would have the undying loyalty as well as the physical stature required to protect him, especially during the day when he was most vulnerable.

Unknown to Garrett, it was the baron who arranged the attack that nearly took his life. By deceiving the attackers into believing Garrett possessed fifteen pounds of the baron's money, which he promised them if they would teach the big man a lesson, along with an added inducement of an additional ten pounds, the baron made them an offer too tempting to refuse.

Now he manipulated the ill-fated and unaware Garrett, turning his feeling of gratitude against him. He took Garrett's earnest appreciation for an act perceived as kindness and used it to forge a powerful bond between himself and his unsuspecting pawn.

The baron was no ordinary stranger coming to aid a man in distress, but a creature of extraordinary abilities. His unusual condition equipped him with certain equally unusual talents. It was the malleability of Garrett's mind along with his massive size and extraordinary strength the baron was after. Those traits made him perfectly suitable to the baron's needs.

This same basic scenario had played itself out in countless similar situations through numberless years. Garrett was the latest entry in the long list of physically capable yet easily beguiled victims of the baron's ruthless designs.

He promoted a profound feeling of gratitude in Garrett, an emotion he knew would be totally foreign to him. He knew it was impossible for Garrett to guess this supposed altruist had manufactured his feeling of indebtedness out of whole cloth. Not only did he put Garrett's assailants up to the attack, but through a perverse trick of the mind he also influenced, deepened, Garrett's response to his supposed kindness using a form of mind control, a by-product of his aberrant condition.

30

As a mere victim, Garrett was more fortunate than he would have been as an object of prey. The baron's prey were doomed. The fortunate ones, such as Marguerite and Gianetta, were dead. Others became wholly dependent upon their predator to the point of obsession, making them unsuitable for any role beyond a ready source of blood for the baron. Those who survived his initial bite became addicted to it, utterly submissive to the baron's will. This addictive subservience made them unable to focus their attention on anything other than the baron and their all-consuming need for his "kiss". It was a circumstance quite unlike the simple mind control he exercised in the case of Garrett. Rather than bending the wills of these wretches, his bite destroyed them, driving them insane, making them unsuitable to perform the tasks for which he needed Garrett. Some of the baron's least fortunate victims still resided in Europe's asylums, hopelessly awaiting his return.

Within a day or two of being rescued, Garrett was up and around. Although no conversation ever took place, a silent agreement arose between them, with Garrett immediately taking on the role of man-servant, driver, butler, gardener and whatever else his master required. Even though he felt strangely uneasy in the baron's presence, from all outward appearance Garrett gave his new master complete and total devotion.

On a future occasion, when a guest at one of the baron's many dinner parties asked him how he came to work at Darthmore, Garrett answered almost involuntarily that he owed his life to the baron. What would be left unsaid was that Garrett would one day be required to repay that debt, a fact of which Garrett himself was most probably unaware.

Chapter 4

DESPAIR

Carlino stood trembling atop the wooden crate. Teetering on his precarious perch, he looked down at the ribs and planks of the ship's hold where he'd been held captive these last three days. Sweat dripped from his face, disappearing in the shadows below. With quiet deliberation he fashioned a crude noose with a portion of the cargo net and slipped it around his neck.

The surrogate brig in which Carlino had been kept prisoner was a small compartment in the forward part of the ship where the pitching is most exaggerated. Carlino's last days onboard the *Lira* were unbearable. His father, he thought through bitter tears, would have been much amused at the irony. The ship in which he had sought freedom, freedom from his father's dominance, had now become his prison.

Used to store grain during the ship's last voyage, the hold had become home to a family of rats who still foraged for remnants within its framework. The stale, fetid air, the sound of the rats scurrying about in the darkness and the constant pitching of the ship kept Carlino awake and unable to eat during his imprisonment.

The rough manila line making up the cargo net chafed his neck as he steeled his nerves. Taking a deep breath and closing his eyes, Carlino kicked the crate from beneath his feet.

Carlino dreamed of Gianetta and their last night together. He could hear her breathing, smell her skin. Gently, she stroked his hair and kissed his cheek. He could feel the warmth of her body caressing him, as his own warmth returned to his extremities. He heard her call his name, "Carlino..."

Opening his eyes, he discovered Vittorio applying a compress to his cheek, a look of grave concern on his face that brightened into a smile when he saw his friend's eyes open.

Confused, he asked, "Where is Gia..." stopping as the

reality of the last few days and all that was happening came flooding back. The pain of losing his love all over again was almost too much to bear and the knowledge he was being accused of her murder only served to compound his misery. Since that night on the ship when they first kissed, Carlino felt his heart beat only for her.

"You should have left me, Vittorio. Better to die by my own hand."

"No, Carlino, no. I will get a lawyer, the best in all England. You will see."

"And how will you pay for him? No, Vittorio, I am not a man worth saving. My life is worth nothing without my Gianetta."

"No, Carlino. If I thought you could have killed this girl, then I would have left you for dead without a thought. I know you did not do this thing. But do you not see, if she was murdered, the one who did it will never be caught if you should die. Be a man, Carlino. You owe it to Gianetta to live long enough, at least, to see her true murderer hanged."

These rough words, roughly spoken by his friend struck a chord with Carlino causing him to slough off the dry husk of self-pity into which he'd wrapped himself. Vittorio's words made him see his current predicament differently. He must fight the charges brought against him, for Gianetta's sake—but how?

While they awaited the return of the Master-at-Arms and Third Mate, Carlino and Vittorio discussed plans for Carlino's defense. Vittorio again vowed to get him the best lawyer in England. Although he knew his friend's words were well intentioned, Carlino also knew they could not pay for a lawyer. When Vittorio told him he would wire both their fathers to get money, Carlino said nothing. Having left Italy against his father's wishes, he knew it was unlikely his own father, a domineering and vindictive merchant, would be forthcoming. While they were still talking, the door opened and in walked the Third Mate and Master-at-Arms.

"I see you are still alive, guinea," the Master-at-Arms said to Carlino, dragging out the slur as he spoke, showing his contempt.

Fists clinched, Vittorio rose but Carlino caught his arm, "No, Vito. We don't need you in irons too," he said, smiling at his friend as he stood before the men, presenting his wrists in submission. After securing manacles on his wrists and chaining these to leg irons, they roughly pushed him out the door to take him to the office of the port commissioner, where the Admiralty officials were waiting.

Approaching the office, they saw the parents of Gianetta Rossini coming out. Anna Rossini, Gianetta's mother, spat on Carlino as he was led past, "Murderer!" she cried.

Paolo put his arm around his wife, pulling her to him as she buried her face in his chest. When he led her away, Carlino heard Paolo say, "Don't worry, Anna, he'll hang, this I promise you."

Having already spoken to the parents of the missing and presumed murdered girl, as well as the ship's crew and Vittorio, the minds of Mr. Todd and Mr. Barrington, the Admiralty agents for the port of Southampton, were all but made up. Vittorio was made to wait outside the office while his friend was interrogated.

"Bring the prisoner forward," Mr. Barrington ordered the guards on either side of Carlino. Barrington and Todd were seated behind the dockmaster's desk, which was on a raised dais, stretching nearly the width of the small office.

"You may sit," Mr. Todd told Carlino, gesturing to a plain wooden chair placed directly in front of the dais. Carlino sat, but the chains made it too awkward for him to gain any position of comfort.

"Now then, we understand you were meeting with Gianetta Rossini while the *Lira* made passage from Genoa to Southampton. Is this true?" asked Mr. Todd.

"Yes, Signore, but…"

Holding up his hand to silence Carlino, Mr. Todd continued, "This fact has been corroborated by the ship's crew as well as your own friend and traveling companion. I don't believe there can be any question as to the truth of the matter," he said, passing a glance toward Mr. Barrington. "Did Miss Rossini's parents know the two of you had been meeting in this manner?"

"No, they would not…"

Again, Mr. Todd raised his hand to stop Carlino from continuing. Mr. Barrington, seizing on the obvious, announced, "So you admit you were meeting with Gianetta Rossini, without her parents' knowledge or permission, every night from Genoa to Southampton. Is that correct?"

"No, sir, the night before she was discovered missing, we did not meet."

"How convenient," commented Mr. Todd with a smirk as he glanced in the direction of Mr. Barrington, "that on the very night Miss Rossini disappeared, you claim there was no meeting." Mr. Todd and Mr. Barrington exchanged a knowing smile as Mr. Barrington opened the ledger in front of him scribbling down some notes.

Without looking up, Mr. Barrington said, "I think we have all we need here," as he continued to scribble for some time. Finally looking up at Carlino, he said, "Carlino Gaetano, you are hereby formally charged with the willful murder of Gianetta Rossini aboard the *Lira* while it made transit from Genoa, Italy to Southampton, England. Murder on the high seas is an offense punishable by hanging and your guilt or innocence is a matter for the Admiralty Court to decide. You are, therefore, hereby ordered to remain in custody at Newgate Prison, in London, until your trial." Closing his ledger, he gestured to the guards to remove Carlino, "Take the prisoner away."

"But I am innocent…" Carlino rose from the chair and began to protest when one of the guards clipped him on the chin, sending him reeling backward.

Carlino realized that in the eyes of Mr. Todd and Mr. Barrington, his guilt was clear. He admitted meeting secretly with Gianetta Rossini. The ship's captain, crew and even Vittorio, best friend, corroborated these secret liaisons. This in itself was quite damning. When added to the testimony of the parents, who declared Gianetta Rossini was engaged and looking forward to being married, it was more than sufficient to convince them of his guilt.

The guards roughly carried Carlino out of the office into an awaiting police wagon. In a cruel jest, one of the guards recited a perversion of the prayer given by the bellman at the Church of St. Sepulchre Without on the nights prior to executions, "You prisoners within, for wickedness and sin, St. Sepulchre's bell will surely do you in." With a nudge and a wink, they slammed shut the wagon door, laughing at Carlino all the while.

As the police wagon carried Carlino to Newgate Prison to await his formal trial and certain eventual execution by hanging, Vittorio vowed to do all in his power to save him.

Tears rolled down Carlino's cheeks as the wagon rolled down the cobblestone street. He wept for his good friend, whom he knew had no real chance to save him. He wept for his beautiful Gianetta, lost in the vast, cold ocean. And finally he wept for himself, for whom the insult of being accused of Gianetta's murder only added to the pain of losing her. Through the barred window in the back of the police wagon he watched as Vittorio grew smaller in the distance. Eventually, Vittorio disappeared, swallowed up by the mass of people in the street going about their daily lives along the docks of Southampton, oblivious to Carlino and his pain.

Chapter 5

A CHARMING SPIDER

The ballroom sparkled with light and laughter as the masters and matrons of London's high society enjoyed cocktails, delicacies, and exquisite treats at this most lavish affair. The occasion was a celebration of the end of the triumphant tour of Dr. Alan Tremaine as he travelled Europe speaking at the most prestigious medical and scientific establishments the continent and England have to offer. The host was none other than Baron Antonio Barlucci. There were champagne fountains and tables laden with a variety of hors d'oeuvres from America, Britain and France, as well as fresh fruit. A full string chamber orchestra was commissioned for the occasion to entertain the guests who numbered in the hundreds. Many of London's wealthiest and most powerful families were represented, all in their finest attire.

Baron Barlucci was stunningly handsome as he greeted his arriving guests. At over six feet tall with wavy jet black hair and a pencil-thin mustache, he stood out wherever he went. Tonight, he looked even more magnificent than usual, supervising every aspect of the evening's affair. He toured the kitchen, dining room, and hall, ensuring all of his meticulous instructions had been carried out by the hotel staff to perfection. His attention to detail bordered on obsession, but it was his wish this affair be flawless in every respect. He'd been planning this evening since Paris.

Soon after his arrival the baron became a fixture in London society's night life. Whether giving a dinner party at his impressive Victorian mansion, going to the theater, or attending a lecture, Baron Barlucci was always in the public eye and always in the company of the very toast of London society. He explained the reason he was never seen during the day was due to a skin condition that made him extremely sensitive to sunlight. His family name was well known, having been associated with banking and finance for centuries. Rumors of his enormous personal wealth, of his Italian aristocratic descent, and of his somewhat eccentric behavior, all combined to make him an exotically interesting and highly desirable guest at the most glamorous of social events. With charming good looks as well, he was considered to be an excellent catch by many of London's debutantes.

At last satisfied with the arrangements, he took his place in one of the balconies. From this high perch he could survey the grandeur in order to get its full effect. His blue eyes, so pale they appeared grey, scanned the room admiring the finery of his guests. He watched as they enjoyed the visual and culinary splendor he had provided. Standing high above the floor of the ballroom, he was the first thing his guests saw as they entered the hall. The finely trimmed mustache, the classic profile with its chiseled features along with his broad shoulders made even the most reserved women of London's upper class giddy as schoolgirls whenever they caught his eye.

The music chosen for the evening was a mixture of Mozart, Beethoven and Vivaldi. Of these, the baron most preferred Vivaldi. Perhaps it was because the composer was Italian, or perhaps it was because some of the works chosen for this evening were commissioned by him from Vivaldi himself. These pieces in particular put the baron in a good frame of mind and tonight he wished to be at his very best, his most charming. It was tonight for which he'd been waiting a very long time. This night he would meet and engage with a man who had the knowledge and the talent to relieve him of the chronic affliction from which he suffered.

He had arranged this extravaganza in the Alexander Hotel's Grand Ballroom as a contrivance to meet a certain Dr. Tremaine, brilliant American hematologist. The doctor had gained the notice of the scientific and medical communities through his amazing work with blood disorders on the Dark Continent. With London as his final stop before returning to America it seemed the perfect choice for a congratulatory party for the doctor.

He'd chosen the Alexandra Hotel as the venue tonight specifically because it was one of the most expensive and exclusive in London. Overlooking the park at Knightsbridge, he hoped it would suitably impress his guest of honor.

From high above the ballroom floor, the baron watched the array of elegantly dressed women consciously parading for each other. They paraded for their male escorts as well, but most especially they paraded for the baron. This lurid form of mating dance never failed to amuse. It reminded him of the colorful Hoopoe bird of his native Italy. Ever aware of the women around him and his effect on them, he consciously and pointedly remained charming, but aloof, allowing the hope but not the promise of some future tryst.

As a collateral consequence of his condition, the baron possessed the ability to gauge a woman's interest by sensing subtle changes in her respiration and body temperature. His powers of observation were most acute and served him well. It was impossible for a woman to portray herself to him as something she was not, nor could she lie about her feelings toward him. He found this to be a great advantage.

Late in the evening, while assessing the festivities, the baron heard the strangely familiar sound of a young woman's laughter. It was a laugh that transported the baron to another time and place. He thought he would never hear such a laugh again, not since the death of his adored Maria, but it was unmistakable.

It reminded him of the delicate patter of water as it flows over the pebbles of a cold mountain spring, just as Maria's had. His eyes darted about the crowded ballroom scanning the direction from which it came. As he moved about the enormous hall in search of its origin, his thoughts went back to that other place and time.

~~~

He recalled in bittersweet memory the first time he heard the sound of that laughter, more than a century and a half ago in Milan. He had been invited to the home of Pietro Agnesi, a wealthy silk merchant, to dine with Pietro along with an assemblage of philosophers and teachers from the highest ranks of Milanese society. Pietro's daughter, Maria, was twenty years old and said to be a prodigy of sorts, who spoke regularly with such men, engaging them in deep philosophical discussions.

The baron was invited in the hope this young woman would impress him enough that he might favor her father with membership in the merchant's guild. Guild members enjoyed access to a larger market and, more importantly to Pietro, a higher class of clientele. Membership would increase Pietro's stature in the society of Milan.

Before the evening ended, it was evident Pietro's plans had borne fruit. The baron was quite taken with Maria and she with him. Maria had touched his heart in a way he didn't think possible. In spite of himself, he fell in love and more than anything it was the sound of Maria's laughter that brought a smile to his heart, a heart without feeling for five centuries.

As time passed, they became engaged and it was as they were planning their wedding the baron decided to tell Maria his darkest, most guarded secret. Walking in the garden of Maria's home just after midnight, the baron bade Maria sit on a large rock, while he summoned the courage to confront her with the truth tormenting him. He knew too well what he had to tell her might make him abhorrent in her eyes, but he loved her too much to keep such a terrible secret from her.

The substance of the baron's revelation was never disclosed by Maria to anyone, save her confessor. Her aunts, Coletta and Angelina, discretely observing from a respectable distance, could see only that there was a serious discussion between the two. But when after an hour they at last kissed, the aunts drew a relieved breath, tittering between themselves, believing whatever trouble had been discussed was now resolved. Then, abruptly, the baron arose putting on his hat. Without a word, he left the garden. He was never again seen in the Agnesi household. The following week, Maria informed her father she was joining the order of the Blue Nuns, devoting herself to charitable works.

The baron saw Maria only once more, many years later, as she lie close to death. She had sent for him, asking that he keep the promise he had made to her as she had kept hers to him.

As he approached her in her rooms at the Pio Albergo Trivulzio hospice in Milan, he was moved to tears.

She saw him as he entered her room. Smiling, she said, "I've kept my promise, my Tonietto," using the nickname she'd given him so many years before.

"I know that you have, my love," he said as he kneeled beside her bed and kissed her cheek. "And now, I have kept mine, my love…my Maria."

"You are still the most handsome man in Milan, Tonietto," she said, laughing quietly.

"As you are the most beautiful of women," he replied in a tone so loving and sincere she could not doubt he meant it, despite her seventy-one years.

"I wanted you here, Tonietto; my time is short and as I go to God, I wanted you here that he might see us together, that he might grant my prayer for you."

"Maria, save your prayers, don't waste them on a…"

She interrupted him by placing her finger to his lips, "Grant an old woman her dying wish and sit with me as I pray for us both, my love."

Baron Barlucci sat there beside Maria far longer than he was comfortable as the dawn approached. Tenderly he held her hand in his. She died, just before dawn on that cold January morning in 1799.

~~~

Now, almost ninety years later, he heard the sound of that laughter again. He felt his heart thump in his chest, though he knew this was impossible. Still, his spirit was elevated as he searched about the crowded hall in an effort to find the source of that laughter.

Moving easily among his guests, greeting them as he went, he spied the tall slender figure of Sir Charles Warren. It was the elegantly dressed young woman at Sir Charles's side from whence came the laughter.

Sir Charles was an old acquaintance of the baron's. It was from his father, Sir Charles, Senior, who upon his retirement from the military was appointed to the banking commission, the baron had gained an interest in the Bank of England. A lucrative business arrangement for both, it cemented a lasting friendship. Sir Charles, of course, had always assumed it to be the baron's father with whom his own parent had business dealings.

"Ah, Sir Charles, my old friend, how good of you to come," the baron warmly extended his hand toward the distinguished looking gentleman with the flowing gray mustache.

"How good of you to invite me, Baron," he said smiling broadly, grasping the baron's hand firmly, "allow me to introduce my niece, Abigail Drake."

As he introduced her, Abigail, who at twenty-two years was both beautiful and intelligent, turned to the baron, lowering her dark brown eyes in a charmingly affected way, and gave a small curtsy.

"How delightfully charmed I am to meet you, Signorina Drake," said the baron, taking her hand.

"A pleasure, Baron," Abigail replied.

As her eyes rose to meet his, there appeared a glimmer of recognition, then, it was gone. Or did he imagine it, wondered the baron.

"The two of you share an interest in music, Baron. Abby plays the piano and her favorite composer is Vivaldi, as is yours I believe, sir," said Sir Charles a contented smile on his lips.

"Is that so, Signorina?" asked the baron as he bowed at the waist to kiss her hand. "We must attend a concert together sometime."

"That would be most delightful, Baron," laughed Abigail, in the self-conscious way a young woman laughs when she receives an unexpected compliment. The music of her laughter again took the baron away, for just a moment, back to Italy and to the arms of Maria.

It was while he was still engaged in small talk with Sir Charles and the charming Abigail that a very intense looking young man with dark curly hair and a much too serious expression, approached the small company introducing himself, "Pardon the intrusion, Baron, but my name is Dr. Alan Tremaine and I…"

"Dr. Tremaine, no need of an introduction," taking his hand, pumping it with enthusiasm, "and you aren't intruding at all." After introducing his guest of honor to Sir Charles and Abigail, the baron continued, "I can't tell you how much I've enjoyed your lectures, Doctor. I hope you are enjoying yourself at this small celebration of your success."

A bit embarrassed by the attention, the doctor continued, "Yes, I am, very much, Baron. I wanted to thank you for your generosity in hosting this in my honor. I had no idea it was to be so grand," he said as he looked about at the impressive display of opulence.

"Nonsense, my dear Doctor, a man of your accomplishments should be celebrated." Taking the doctor by the arm, he turned giving a curt bow and said, "Sir Charles, Signorina Abigail, I hope you will excuse us. Please enjoy yourselves." With that, he slowly ushered the doctor away, engaging him with small talk and flattery, displaying what Tremaine found to be an astounding familiarity with his work.

He led the doctor across the floor, into a quiet alcove in which there were two overstuffed chairs. Inviting the young doctor to sit, Barlucci asked, "Now then, Doctor, tell me how it is that a young man such as yourself has accomplished so much in his life?"

"Baron, you flatter me."

"Not at all. To accomplish what you have in so short a time, you should be most proud…most proud indeed."

"Well, I…I don't know what to say, Baron, I…"

"Doctor, I apologize, I'm embarrassing you. Tell me, how long do you expect to remain in England?"

"Actually, I'm arranging my passage back to America in three weeks."

"So soon. What a pity."

"Well, you see, I'm engaged to be married and I'm quite anxious to return."

"Ahhh…congratulations, Doctor, congratulations! Did the young lady accompany you on your tour?"

"Oh no. You see, her parents are very provincial. They would never have allowed it, prior to our nuptials."

"Hence your impatience to return. I don't blame you, old man. I should wonder why you tarry so long."

"It's purely due to business, I'm afraid. My agent is still on the continent."

As the two got to know each other, the doctor found the baron to be an extremely charming host. They chatted for over an hour about art and music, as well as his work.

Shortly after 1 a.m. the baron excused himself for the night, "Please forgive me, Dr. Tremaine, but I'm afraid I've found our conversation so engaging that I've neglected my other guests; now, regrettably, I must say goodnight, as a pressing matter requires my attention."

"I too have enjoyed our chat, Baron; you are a most gracious and interesting host."

"Now it is I who am embarrassed. Nonetheless, I must be going," he said rising. "If you'll forgive me," giving a curt bow, the baron turned and began to walk across the floor. Before he'd taken two steps, he turned back to the doctor as if something had just occurred to him. Once again addressing Tremaine, "I wonder, Doctor, would you be interested in having dinner with me, say, next Saturday? I would be very much disappointed if you were to return to America before we've had a chance to get to know each other better."

"Next Saturday? I'd be delighted, Baron."

"Splendid," the baron said, handing him a small card, "here is the address. It's near Hyde Park and is called Darthmore Hall, I'm sure the cabbies in the area are familiar with it. Shall we say 8 o'clock?"

"That would be fine, Baron."

"Excellent. Then I shall see you Saturday night," he concluded, bowing once again. Turning, he walked away across the crowded floor.

Before leaving, the baron conferred with the hotel staff, ensuring the party would continue until the last guest had retired. He then excused himself, bidding his guests to continue enjoying his largesse throughout the night, and departed.

The air had an unseasonable chill to it as the baron stepped out under the grand portico at the entrance to the hotel. Climbing into his brougham, parked to one side of the tree-lined semi-circular drive, he directed Garrett to take him to the East End of London, into a district known as Whitechapel.

Chapter 6

GRISLY CLUE

August 31, 1888

Mary Ann Walker had a bright future in which to look forward. Born in London, she was perpetually cheerful and optimistic, earning the nickname Polly, as her mother said she was prone to "chatter like a parrot". The third of six daughters, she always had the loving support of a large family while growing up and her father Edward made a good living as a locksmith.

When she was twenty-two, Mary Ann married William Nichols in St. Bride's Church, a landmark on Fleet Street with its distinctive spire designed by Sir Christopher Wren. Her husband William worked as a machinist in the south of London and made a decent living wage. But the pressures of raising a family, a family that grew to six children by the time she was 35 years old, proved too much for Mary Ann. She developed a weakness for alcohol and that weakness drove a wedge between her and her husband. They began drifting apart. As the years wore on, Mary Ann's dependence on the bottle grew ever stronger. The Nichols' stormy relationship finally ended in 1881 when Mary Ann deserted her husband, along with her six children, for the final time.

While life in Victorian England wasn't easy for a woman alone, it was especially difficult for a woman prone to abuse alcohol. Penniless, she drifted from workhouse to flophouse, earning her drinking money through prostitution.

Tonight, just four days after her forty-third birthday, Mary Ann had once again been turned out of a common lodge for lack of four pence to pay for her bed. She quipped to the lodging-house deputy, "I'll soon get my 'doss' money..." as she left in search of a customer for her decidedly fading *charms*. "Just see if I don't," she muttered to herself as she staggered down the dark alleyways of Whitechapel.

By 2:00 a.m., Mary Ann had made her doss money twice over. But it was thirsty work and she soon spent what she'd made on a bottle of rye. A half-hour later found Mary Ann, a bit unsteady, on her way to the corner of Brady Street and Buck's Row, a common meeting place for street dollies and their customers, off the beaten path but with a street lamp that provided light enough to transact their business.

Singing a bawdy tune, she stumbled past Court Street. A sudden chill, as if she'd stepped into an ice house, caused her to stop short and look about her. "Brrr...blimey, it's cold," she whispered to the wind, her white breath blending into the sudden fog. Wrapping her sweater more tightly around her, she hurried on. Then she heard it. A regular tap, tap, tap, as of something striking the cobblestones behind her, drawing closer with each tap. "Who's there?" she called into the fog. Her response was silence.

Shaking with fright, she turned.

A dark figure stood directly behind her. He wore the tall hat of a gentleman, the collar of his great coat turned up covering his face. He said nothing, but from his eyes spoke Death.

She drew in her breath to scream but before the sound could escape, he grasped her by the throat. As he pulled her closer, he pinched off her windpipe, lifting her from the ground. The only sound she could manage was a hoarse whisper.

Before she lost consciousness, she felt his teeth pierce the flesh of her neck. The last sensation Mary Ann Nichols felt on this earth was that of an ecstasy more palpable and more pleasurable than any she'd ever found in the bottom of a gin bottle. She smiled grotesquely as the life drained from her body.

All of this occurred a scant fifteen minutes before Police Constable Neill happened upon Mary Ann's lifeless remains lying in the entry way to Brown's Stable Yard early on Friday morning.

Having just passed this way less than thirty minutes prior, Constable Neill was surprised when he nearly tripped over the corpse in the darkness. "What's this?" he asked the night as he pushed the lifeless form with his toe. Now realizing it was a body, Constable Neill struggled to find his whistle, blowing it furiously to alert others in the vicinity that trouble had been discovered. Police Constable John Thain was the first to arrive on the scene. "'Ere, Thain, run and get Dr. Llewellyn," cried Neill, now kneeling beside the body. Dr. Rees Ralph Llewellyn maintained a surgery close by on Whitechapel Road.

"What's on, Neill? What's happened?"

"There's a woman dead 'ere," shining his light on Nichols pallid face, "looks like she's had her throat cut."

"Blimey, I'll fetch 'im straight away," he cried as he ran off in the direction of Dr. Llewellyn's surgery.

The overcast sky offered Neill no assistance in his examination of Mary Ann's lifeless body. With the nearest gaslight at end of the row, at Brady Street, Neill was left with only his torch to illuminate the scene.

By this time, Police Constable Jonas Mizen from adjoining 'H' Division happened upon the site. Neill motioned him over with his lamp, "'Ere, Jonas, hold my torch while I examine the body."

Taking the light, Jonas directed the weak beam onto Nichols head and shoulders area, "Bloody 'ell, is she dead?"

"Of course she's dead, what do you think?"

As he examined the body and the surrounding area, Neill was struck by the fact there did not appear to be an over abundance of blood at the scene, while he could plainly see her throat had been cut cleanly from ear to ear. "Look 'ere, Mizen, 'er throat's cut, but the blood don't add up."

"Yeah…'ardly more than a lady's teacup full," added Constable Mizen.

"Maybe she was murdered somewheres else and dumped 'ere," Neill proffered, but subsequent investigation of the scene would show blood splattering on the cobblestone beneath the body, indicating she was murdered on the spot where her body was discovered, despite the scant amount of blood in the vicinity. "She's still warm," Neill noted, looking up at Mizen.

"She's not long dead."

"No, not long at all."

The air was unseasonably cold for late August as they waited over an hour for the doctor to arrive on the scene. At this time of the morning, 3:45 a.m., Buck's Row was deserted. Even the sound of a police whistle didn't rouse many nearby lodgers from their warm beds.

"Jonas, you'd better go for the ambulance, then round up some of the boys to 'elp, there's sure to be a crowd." Soon the streets would be filled with carts and merchants carrying their wares to the various markets as the city awakened to a busy Friday morning. "One more thing, Jonas," Neill called as Constable Mizen turned to leave, "ring up Inspector Abberline. He'll want to see this."

Constable Neill had patrolled Whitechapel for nearly thirteen years. Assigned to 'J' Division of the Metropolitan Police, he had seen his share of the kind of violence one individual can perpetrate on another, but this murder was decidedly different. Never had he come across a woman whose throat had been cut in such a savage manner before, so violently her head was nearly severed from her body.

Judging by her manner of dress, where her body was found, and the fact she was out on the streets at this time of night, Neill was quite certain she was a prostitute, belonging to that class of woman known as an "unfortunate" who earned money for her bread and lodging, as well as a bottle, by selling her favors in the dark streets and alleys of Whitechapel. Unfortunate was certainly the word for this poor creature, Neill thought, to meet such a gruesome end.

By the time Dr. Llewellyn arrived the first stirrings of life began to show along Buck's Row. Before he'd completed his cursory examination, a small cadre of curious onlookers were milling about. As he concluded the exam, he placed his notebook, calipers, and other utensils back into his black bag, drawing a soiled sheet over the body in an attempt to preserve the victim's remaining dignity.

"You'd best call for the Inspector, Constable" the doctor ordered as he stood up, "her throat's been cut so deeply as to nearly decapitate her."

"I could see that for meself, Doctor," replied Neill, with a pleased smile on his face that the doctor hadn't told him anything he didn't already know for himself. "I've already sent for Inspector Abberline, I expect he'll be along smartly."

"There's more, you know," the doctor confided in a low, nearly inaudible tone, careful not to be heard by the curious onlookers, "her torso's been split open like a Christmas goose."

Neill's smug smile slid from his face, "Lord..."

\#

September 3, 1888

London's Metropolitan Police Force has its Executive and Criminal Investigations Division (CID) offices located on a small stretch of road between Northumberland Avenue and Whitehall Place. The name of the road, (Great) Scotland Yard, has become synonymous with the force itself.

Scotland Yard, as the Metropolitan Police is most commonly known, is a separate entity from the City of London Police. The City's jurisdiction is restricted to the limits of the city proper, comprising approximately one square mile. Scotland Yard's jurisdiction ranges over an area contained within a fifteen mile radius from Charing Cross, excluding the City's one square mile. The total area is approximately 700 square miles. Scotland Yard employs over 13,000 full time constables in twenty-three divisions. In addition, another 760 men patrol the five dockyards, about the same number of men on the entire City of London Police payroll.

The headquarters of the Criminal Investigations Division's Central Office (CO) is located in the same building as the Office of the Commissioner. Inspector Frederick (Francis) Abberline had made the trip up the three flights of stairs to the Commissioner's office three times since he'd been in CO and it had never been good news. When the news was good, the Commissioner came to see you.

"Look at this!" Sir Charles Warren, Commissioner of the Metropolitan Police, pointed to the morning edition of *The Times* spread across his desk. He read aloud, "'The Metropolitan Police have made no arrests and from all reports have no prospects to do so in this most heinous series of murders in the city's East End..."" As he paused, Abberline could see the vein in Sir Charles's forehead growing larger. He continued with his voice rising in a crescendo, "Do you have any idea how this makes the Metropolitan Police look, Inspector? Like bumbling IDIOTS!" Sir Charles slammed both palms down on his desk as he rose, pacing behind his chair in front of the palladian windows that looked out over Great Scotland Yard, "Inspector, this is the third such attack in the East End in as many months, each worse than the last." Sir Charles voice boomed as his fist crashed down upon the corner of his desk, "It must stop! The newspapers are having an absolute field day with this, calling us incompetent, questioning our tactics."

Standing behind his ornate desk of Sapele mahogany from West Africa, inlaid with ivory in intricate detail, a memento from his time in colonial South Africa, Sir Charles's eyes peered out from beneath his bristled eyebrows, looking down his long patrician nose as Inspector Abberline approached to speak.

"Sir Charles, we believe these recent murders to be the work of a gang of ruffians who've..."

"Ruffians?!" As he spoke, his deep baritone caused the windows behind him to rattle in their casements. "Of course they're ruffians," cried Sir Charles, his long white mustache quivering as he spoke, small droplets of spittle forming along the edge, "who else would soil their hands with creatures of this ilk. But why has no one been arrested?" Again, slamming his hand down on the desk for effect, "Results, Abberline! Nothing less!"

"Yes, Sir Charles; of course, Sir Charles," backing his way toward the door, "will there be anything else, Sir Charles?"

"Yes, Inspector, I'm seconding you back to Whitechapel until these murders are solved. I want you to capture this villain before I have to read anymore of this drivel in the papers, do you hear?! Now get out!"

As he reached behind his back to open the double doors, Abberline replied, "Yes, Sir Charles, right away, sir," then slipped through the opening, closing it again in front of him.

Adjusting his tie, Abberline turned to walk across the outer office. On his way to the door, he stopped by to see Agnes, Sir Charles's much too attractive secretary, "May I say you are looking quite lovely today, Agnes?"

"Mind your manners, Inspector, what would your wife think you talking that way?" Agnes asked. She was actually very fond of Abberline, but in a fraternal way. A close friend of Abberline's wife, she knew the two were very much in love and his seeming flirtatiousness was completely innocent. She could not imagine the proper and somewhat stodgy Abberline ever getting out of line. Despite his being one of the top investigators at the Yard, he had the appearance and demeanor of a banker.

"I expect Emma would agree with me, I do," answered Abberline, "then she'd give me a right smart on the kisser," he said smiling, rubbing his chin.

"Good on her," Agnes said, then beamed as she pointed to a conspicuously large diamond on her left hand, "Besides, I'm engaged."

"Engaged? Congratulations, Agnes," he said with genuine good humor. "You're going to break a lot of hearts around here, you will. Who is the lucky piker? Are Emma and I invited to the wedding?"

"You wouldn't know him, I'm sure, and I'm not so sure I'd want you to," she said, winking at him. "We haven't set a date yet, but I'll be sure to let Emma know when we do. By the way, Mr. Monro asked that you stop by his office before you leave."

"Monro?" Abberline snapped out of his flirtatious revelry, "Thank you, Agnes," as he hastened towards his mentor's office, "and best wishes."

"Thank you, Inspector."

Abberline hurried on to Monro's office. It had been a while since he'd seen him, not since his recent resignation as Assistant Commissioner.

Abberline was much indebted to Monro. It was Monro who recognized the talented young, and at the time recently married, policeman as having real potential. It was he who was responsible for Abberline's rise in the department, taking him out of Whitechapel as an inspector where he was in charge of the local Criminal Investigations Division, having him transferred to Whitehall, Division A, then on to CO (Central Office) where he was subsequently promoted to Inspector, First Class.

James Monro had been Assistant Commissioner of the Metropolitan Police as well as the chief of the Detectives Division when Sir Charles succeeded Edmund Henderson as Commissioner in 1886. From the start it was obvious he and Monro would be at loggerheads for most of their tenure together. Sir Charles, formerly Major-General Warren, Knight Commander of St. Michael and St. George, was of the old British patrician mold. Born into a proud military family, he was tall, very thin with an aristocratic stature, bushy eyebrows and flowing mustache. By contrast, Monro was a policeman's policeman, having served Her Majesty as Inspector-General of Police in India. He returned to Britain in 1884 and rose through the Metropolitan Police Department on his own merit. Physically, Monro was rather short and squat, sporting a smaller, more contemporary mustache.

When Sir Charles took over the reins as Commissioner, Monro's dual roles made matters between the two men somewhat awkward. As Assistant Commissioner, he worked for and reported to Sir Charles. As the head of Detective Services, he reported directly to the Home Secretary, Henry Matthews, to whom Sir Charles also reported. The resultant situation of having a subordinate with direct access to his own superior was a constant source of irritation to Sir Charles. He was always more than a bit suspicious Monro was angling to replace him as Commissioner.

Monro found the arrangement no more palatable. He considered his position as co-equal to Sir Charles, and made no bones about saying so. The situation was rife with conflict, fomenting resentment and professional rivalry between the two men.

The friction finally came to an official end early in the month of August when Sir Charles, growing frustrated with the independence of CID, began taking his case to the newspapers. He attacked both Monro, for what he termed "rank insubordination", and Home Secretary Henry Matthews, for tacitly condoning the actions of his Assistant Commissioner. Monro resigned his post as Assistant Commissioner, unable to work for Sir Charles any longer under these circumstances, but retained the position as Head of the Detectives Division.

When Abberline arrived at Monro's office, the door was standing slightly ajar, swinging open as he knocked. Piles of folders and loose papers were stacked upon every horizontal surface, in stark contrast to the punctilious order of Sir Charles's office.

Monro sat with his back to the door, inspecting some documents as thick rings of smoke from his Meerschaum rose above his head, hanging like a cloud.

"Come in, Francis," he bellowed without looking up, "I was hoping you'd stop by."

Abberline approached his desk, "You wished to see me, sir?"

After a few moments of silence, Monro turned. Smiling as he looked up at Abberline, he asked, "What do you make of these Whitechapel murders, Francis?"

"Well sir, we believe them to be the work of a gang of young toughs who've been extorting money from the prostitutes in the East End, sir. We've questioned a few but so far we've been unable to get any actionable information."

"Yes, yes…very well, I see," he said. The smile faded from his lips as thoughtful puffs of smoke rose in the air above him. After a period of somewhat awkward silence he continued, "This last one, though" rustling the newspaper on his desk, pushing aside the clutter to make room, "this Mary Ann Nichols…singularly grisly, I understand."

"Yes, sir," answered Abberline, unsure where the conversation was leading. "The attack was so violent her head was nearly detached from her body. Also, her abdomen was opened side to side with her intestines pulled from the cavity."

"Horrendous…" he grimaced, then his eyes rose from

the newspaper to meet Abberline's. "Not exactly the usual sort of thing you'd expect from those young toughs, eh?" blowing a cloud of smoke in the air between them, "...a madman, perhaps?"

"Perhaps, sir. It *is* more gruesome than what we've seen by several degrees." As he stood in front of Monro's desk, Abberline began to think perhaps there was more to this case than he had first believed. James Monro was well known as a police officer with uncanny instincts about crime. He made a mental note to go back and review the details of the Nichols case.

Puffing again, Monro went on, "Yes...indeed. I understand Sir Charles is loaning you back to Whitechapel for a while. No one better for the job, I'd say." Once again smiling, he concluded, "Well...please keep me informed of your progress."

"Of course, and thank you, sir." As he turned to leave he noticed Monro was already absorbed again in the document he'd been examining as Abberline arrived. On his way back to his office, Abberline went over in his mind the facts of the case as he knew them, deciding to have another look at the corpse of Mary Ann Nichols.

Chapter 7

DECEPTION

The reserved home of Sir Charles Warren reflected the man himself. Located on London's western fringe, the remote wooded area surrounding it served to screen the house and property from neighbors, making it appear even more secluded than it was. Garrett drove the brougham up to the front entryway while the baron anxiously peered from the window. Although he'd seen the house and the estate many times before, this was his first visit with Sir Charles as the occupant. Sir Charles inherited it, along with most of his wealth, from his father, Sir Charles Warren, Senior. In spite of his familiarity with the estate and notwithstanding his disciplined self-command, he was still quite eager to arrive, unable to admit to himself what the reason might be. The baron was hoping to see the young Miss Drake again.

His interest was less romantic than pragmatic. Being the niece of such a respected member of London society as Sir Charles, would work to his advantage were he to take her as a wife. The baron had learned long ago that a corollary to the adage of *guilt by association* is *innocence through affiliation*. The aristocracy rarely looks with too fine a lens at its own, making it imperative for the baron to maintain a certain level of association. Marrying into an impeccable bloodline had served him well in the past. Once the nuptials had been performed, the bride would slowly decline in health, accompanied with a false pregnancy, until at last she died, usually during *childbirth*. The fiction could be carried further with a conveniently stolen baby, cared for by a loving nanny. When the child was old enough to be sent to a distant school, it as well as the nanny could be disposed of. When the time came, the baron would assume the role of his own son. The reclusiveness for which he was renown in his home country aided him in carrying off this illusion.

The house appeared dark but for the flicker of a firelight in the front bay window. Garrett stopped the coach, descending to open the door for the baron. Barlucci stepped out wearing an elegant black suit with a velvet collar, black topcoat and a silk-lined velvet cape to match. The top hat he wore accentuated his already unusual height. As Garrett drove the coach to the rear of the house to await the baron's need, Barlucci rapped on the door with his walking stick, an accoutrement he was rarely without.

A servant answered. Handing him his hat, coat, and walking stick, the baron introduced himself, whereupon he was led him into the drawing room. Sir Charles awaited his arrival seated by the fire with a warm brandy in his hand.

"Baron, old boy," Sir Charles rose to greet the baron in an uncharacteristically familiar manner, brought on no doubt by his third brandy, "how good of you to come," he said, shaking the baron's hand.

"How good of you to invite me, Sir Charles," replied the baron playing upon their last greeting.

"Eh what? Oh, yes, very good. Call me Charley, old boy," Sir Charles returned as he clapped him on the shoulder.

"Very well then, Charley," he said, smiling at his host, "you have a most charming home. I'm flattered you've seen fit to allow me to visit."

"Nonsense. Our families have been associated for so long, you are like a member of my own family—a cousin, perhaps, what?"

"Nonetheless, it was a thoughtful gesture, Sir...er, I mean Charley," the baron insisted, smiling his most engaging smile.

"Here," taking the baron's arm, he led him to a comfortable chair near his own, "take a seat by the fire. When was the last time we saw each other? I've been trying to remember."

"I believe it was at your father's funeral. I arrived shortly after he passed on an errand for my own father."

"Ah, yes...a sad time," Sir Charles paused for a moment, a strained look on his face. Then, smiling, "You know, of course, my father spoke very highly of yours. He was quite impressed with the man."

"You are too kind, Charley, but I must confess, my father was also very fond of yours. He was quite upset when he heard of his passing. He would always tell me that of all the British he had met, your father was the most trustworthy, and in business, trustworthiness means much."

"As in all things, my dear baron, as in all things," as he spoke, his eyes took on a wistful look as he remembered his beloved father. After a moment, he came back to himself. Continuing, he said, "I remember my father writing me of your father's interest in my findings in Palestine while I was assigned there. Quite the historian, was he not?."

"History was a passion with my father, a passion that he passed on to me. Speaking of Palestine, my father told me it was you who discovered the means by which the people of the old city of Jerusalem could attain fresh water, even while under siege. Indeed it's called the 'Warren shaft'[1], is it not,?"

"Yes, yes, or I should say the excavators under my charge discovered it, though I got the credit—along with the namesake."

"Ah, but you were the man in charge of the expedition."

"Quite so, but what I found even more interesting was the series of tunnels uncovered beneath the Temple mount itself. No one knows what their origin or use was, but they are quite extensive."

"I don't believe you were the first to discover them, Charley. If you don't mind my saying so, it might be more correct to say you *rediscovered* the tunnels. I recall they were originally discovered by the Knights Templar, were they not?"

"Ah, you speak of the Templar legends. Very good, old boy, I'd quite forgotten what an authority your father was on the Templars. Quite an interesting sect they were, I believe; soldier priests, eh what?"

---

[1] the "Warren shaft" runs from within the old city of Jerusalem to the Gihon spring

"Yes, Charley, soldier priests…legend has it they were the keepers of many secrets, as well as the bankers to both Europe's royalty and the Church. In fact…" the baron was interrupted as the door to the drawing room was opened and Abigail entered.

"Excuse me, Uncle, but Aunt Maggie sent me to tell you that dinner is quite ready."

Rising quickly, the baron gave a curt bow in Abigail's direction, "Signorina Abigail, you are looking very lovely this evening, as always."

Blushing, Abigail managed a shallow curtsy, accompanied by "Why thank you, Baron," before a nervous bit of laughter escaped her lips.

Sir Charles also rose, noticing the way the baron's eyes lit up when Abigail entered, "Ahem, very well, Baron, this way," extending his hand toward the open door, "Abby, please escort the baron to the dining room."

With a slight blush on her cheek, Abigail led the way to the dining room, the baron at her side. Sir Charles, smiling, followed closely behind.

The baron sensed Abigail's interest through a slight increase in both her body temperature and her heart rate as they walked down the hall together. As he was escorted to his chair, he extended his hand across the table, "Lady Margaretta, a pleasure to meet you at last. Your husband has spoken of you often. Now that I see your beauty, I don't wonder he hides you away, here."

"Oh…" Lady Margaretta laughed, "and I can see for myself your charm and good looks have not been exaggerated."

"Sir Charles is too kind…"

"Oh, I didn't mean I'd heard of it through my husband…" Lady Margaretta said, inclining her head toward Abigail, who was now turning crimson as she pretended to examine the silverware, "but please, sit down," she said as she took her seat, cuing the rest of the company to also be seated, "and please, Baron, I'm not so formal as my husband. I insist you call me Maggie."

"Only if you promise to call me Antonio," he answered smiling.

A bit impatiently, Sir Charles interrupted, "As I recall, Baron, your father took his meat extremely rare. Are you of the same habit?"

"I'm afraid so, Sir Charles, my digestion is an inherited trait, which makes meat that is too well cooked difficult to digest."

"Beastly. Ah well, I believe you'll find the rarity of the beef in the platter on your right to your liking," he said, gesturing with his fork. "I must have my beef cooked through and through, don't you know."

"Uncle," Abigail said in a scolding tone, "you'll embarrass our guest."

"What?" Sir Charles said looking up, "Dear me, quite so. Pardon me for prattling on so."

"Not at all, Sir Charles, it's quite all right," answered the baron as he skewered a small piece of underdone beef, "I'm aware that my peculiar habits in the area of cuisine preparation are a bit at odds with normal custom."

"How long will you be in London, Baron?" asked Lady Margaretta, hoping to change the subject.

"I'm afraid only a month or two this visit, Lady Maggie, and then I shall be traveling to America."

"America?" asked Abigail.

"Yes, I have some business there, as well as some personal matters to attend to."

"Abigail is taking a voyage to America soon too, aren't you dear?" offered Lady Margaretta.

"Why, yes, I'm visiting my mother's family, in New York. Aunt Maggie is going to go with me."

"Ah, then perhaps we will see each other. I'm destined for New York myself," the baron smiled charmingly. "It's good that you are not traveling alone, Signorina Abigail. A strange city, especially one as large as New York or London, is no place for a young woman alone."

"Why, Baron," answered Abigail, "I'm surprised one as

cosmopolitan as yourself would hold to such old-fashioned notions."

"Signorina," the baron said smiling, "you would be surprised just how old-fashioned I am,".

"So," Sir Charles interrupted, "tell us how you've been spending your time in London, Baron."

"Oh, I'm afraid business matters have been keeping me fairly busy, Sir Charles. But I have managed to combine business with a bit of pleasure, which I think you may find quite interesting."

"Oh? How so?" Sir Charles asked around a bit of well done beef.

"I've just invested a tidy sum in a company that makes what they call a *phonograph*," he said with more than a modicum of satisfaction.

"Phonograph? What the devil is a phonograph?"

"It's a device that can record sound to be played back later," the baron answered proudly.

"You don't say," said Sir Charles, a bit disinterestedly. "Can't say I see the usefulness in that."

"I believe I've heard of that. It sounds extraordinary," offered Lady Margaretta.

"It is, quite extraordinary. In fact, Sir Charles, I have a recording of a musical composition by Arthur Sullivan. A piece for cornet and piano."

"Truly?" asked Abigail, "It can record music?"

"Yes," answered the baron, "Sir Charles, you should come by Darthmore for a visit, I'd be delighted to play it for you."

"I'm afraid I'm not much for gadgets, Baron, but it appears Abigail might be interested," he said, once again gesturing distractedly with his fork in his niece's direction before hastening to cut another bit of meat, devouring it ravenously.

Surprised, but nonetheless pleased, at the suggestion, the baron asked, "You don't think it would be improper for Signorina Abigail to be unescorted in my home?"

"Nonsense, old boy, you're practically family."

Turning to Abigail, "Well then, would you be interested, Signorina? I'd be most happy to play it for you. Perhaps you would, in recompense, do me the favor of playing something on the piano. Your uncle tells me you are quite a virtuoso."

"My uncle flatters me, Baron, but perhaps we could play a duet, if you've brought your bow. Uncle has told me you are quite an accomplished violinist."

"Your uncle is far too kind, I'm afraid, and," smiling his most engaging smile, "apparently quite free with his compliments," pausing as his host and hostess chuckled, "but it would be enchanting in the attempt, I'm sure, Signorina. I shall consider it a date then. Shall we say Saturday evening? I have a later engagement, but if you could come by at six, it would give us quite enough time to both listen and perform."

"Saturday? I'd be most happy to…that is, if Uncle and Auntie wouldn't mind."

"Of course we wouldn't mind, dear, it was after all, my idea," Sir Charles beamed.

"We can have you driven there at six, my dear. Your uncle can pick you up on his way home." Turning to her husband, Lady Margaretta cautioned, "You won't forget, will you dear?"

"Of course I won't forget, my dear. It's settled then."

Yes, thought the baron, it's settled, knowing he would need to sate his "predilection" before Saturday, if he were to keep both his appointments for the evening and still maintain his charming demeanor.

#

September 7, 1888

Baron Barlucci relaxed comfortably in his box seat at the Lyceum Theatre. The music of Sir Arthur Sullivan floated up to him, incidental to Henry Irving's production of Shakespeare's *Macbeth.* The baron smiled, thinking what a vast improvement over the music accompanying the performance when first he'd seen it. That performance, in a theater not far from the Lyceum, featured the playwright in the title role.

63

His thoughts drifted along with the music. He began to think about what a fortuitous choice London had been as an intermediate stop on his journey to New York. The hunting here proved to be good with the prey easily culled from the flock.

This city was literally teaming with life and all life has to offer a man with the baron's particular needs. He knew, of course, that in such a metropolitan environment he would need to curb his appetites and he made his best efforts to do so. Subsistence level was how he viewed his *harvestings*. He took what he considered small game, venturing only where he felt his actions were sure to draw little official attention.

Although he knew his victims would be discovered, he was confident the true nature of their demise would go unnoticed. Any investigation would be in keeping with conventional police methods, which through long experience he knew to be somewhat inept and no real threat to a man of the baron's intellect. An additional fact working in his favor was that the area in which he took his prey was the lowest level of London society where violence was well established. As always, he'd been meticulous in his study of his chosen hunting ground.

London was a city of great contrast. Affluence and poverty rubbed up against one another daily, creating a nearly ideal environment in which the baron could satisfy his needs. While the area surrounding his Darthmore residence was affluent, with crime nearly non-existent, there were other areas of London in which crime and violence were all too familiar. It was always best, the baron learned, to confine one's baser practices to those areas in which they would be least likely to stand out, as it were, from the prevailing atmosphere. Just such a place was Whitechapel.

The Whitechapel District of London's East End was on balance the poorest district in the city. All manner of vice and corruption, from pickpockets to prostitution, were commonplace and found there in abundance. Death was a daily occurrence within its confines. Despite this, or perhaps because of it, it was not uncommon for wealthy gentlemen to frequent the area. Whether looking for illicit gambling or illicit sex, the danger inherent in Whitechapel provided these privileged patrons the thrills they sought. Their presence in the area, after respectable folks had retired, was well known, as well as tacitly accepted, or ignored. This made it ideal for the baron's purposes. His presence in Whitechapel, for the most part, went unnoticed. But tonight, at least while he watched the play, he tried not to think of his Whitechapel activities. Despite knowing he again would soon need to slake his thirst, the baron sat back biding his time, enjoying the performance.

Gazing out over the audience full of fine ladies and gentlemen, the baron tried not to see them as potential prey. He was well aware that as the hunger in him grew stronger, if it remained unsatisfied, he would be unable to see them in any other way; he would no longer see their humanity if he did not feed again—and soon.

The knowledge of how the hunger could consume him was ever present in the baron's mind. He had learned to keep it at bay through periodic feedings; otherwise, he would be powerless to stop the orgy of ingestion that would result.

He thought about how powerless he had been in that small village outside Budapest. Early in the last century, as a test of his will, he had delayed feeding to a point well beyond any past experience. The result, a village whose entire population was decimated in a single night, haunted him to this day. Fortunately, in recent decades, he'd been more successful at tempering the hunger by feeding only at intervals of about ten days, sometimes a bit more.

In a previous era he'd kept a multitude of women as virtual chattel slaves. He satisfied his hunger by feeding in small amounts from them, each in their turn. Because of the difficulty in gauging how much he could consume from a given woman, this method had taken much time and patience to develop. Even more difficult was stopping, once the feeding started, resulting in a periodic need to restock his stable. In the modernity of present times, this chattel method was wholly impractical. It was much more difficult task today to spirit away a village's virgins without reaping the ire of the villagers.

His current modus operandi was arrived at through trial and error down through the interceding decades, proving to be the best medium course between allowing the hunger to rule him, feeding at will, and endeavoring to resist it entirely until it burst forth in an orgy of blood and desire. He'd long ago come to the conclusion the best he could do was to minimize the carnage he wrought. More than capable of feeding every night, perhaps even twice nightly, his conscience was unable to bear the human toll, once the hunger was sated.

By feeding only sparingly he was able to minimize the number of deaths to roughly one per week, perhaps fewer if the blood was rich enough and of sufficient quantity. He considered this an acceptable amount of devastation. To that end he had learned he could sometimes increase the quantity, if not the quality, of the blood he consumed by also feeding on the offal of his victims such as the heart and uterus, where blood naturally accumulates even after he'd drained the body through a major artery—that is, if there was enough time in which to harvest these organs.

Along with refining the methodology of his actions, the baron had developed a philosophy wherein he was no more culpable for the deaths of his victims than society as a whole was for the deaths of the poor and indigent. In many cases he believed he was doing both his victims and society a service. On the one hand, he ended the daily suffering of a destitute and hopeless victim. On the other, he reduced the excess population of society's refuse. In this way, he concluded he was doing both a public and a private service.

During his voyage to England he had only needed to feed once, and was fortunate enough to have found the perfect victim, as well as an unwitting accomplice. The *Lira*'s captain, Josiah Madison, had shown himself to be of a reliable sort, ensuring the baron's "special needs" for privacy were scrupulously respected. The victim was chosen for her duplicity in being one man's betrothed, while another's whore.

Now, sitting here, he felt things were going along very smoothly.

~~~

The applause from the appreciative patrons after the final scene of the fifth act brought the baron out of his reverie. As he looked out over the audience, already beginning to rise from their seats, he had good reason to be pleased with himself, recalling all he had accomplished in his short time in London, knowing his plans were coming together so nicely. He was to have dinner with Dr. Tremaine the following evening, which he hoped would lead to a new beginning or rather an end to his long search for a cure to his condition. He was extremely confident he could enlist the doctor's assistance being totally unconcerned about what it might cost. And of course, there was the charming young Abigail Drake. He was strangely drawn to her, but to what extent and to what end he had not yet decided.

As he left the theater, he climbed into his coach and directed Garrett, his driver, to again take him to Whitechapel, which he'd already come to think of as his private little game preserve.

Chapter 8

PUZZLE

A week and a day passed since the discovery of Mary Ann Nichols. The next victim in Whitechapel, Annie Chapman, was found just before six o'clock in the morning by a porter in Spitalfields Market, John Davis, as he was preparing for work. Crossing the yard behind his residence, he noticed something lying in the passage from the backyard to the street. As he approached, the sight of Annie's cut throat with her entrails draped across her body sent Mr. Davis flying to the police station in Commercial Street.

Inspector Abberline had just arrived at the Central Office of Scotland Yard when a telegram from the Commercial Street Police Station announced the circumstances of Annie Chapman's murder. The wire, sent sometime after the preliminary examination by the division doctor, said the body was being removed to the mortuary on Old Montagu Street for a more thorough autopsy. Abberline grabbed his bowler and overcoat then took a cab to the mortuary, where he could examine the body himself.

The city was crowded and bustling as the Hansom made its way to Old Montagu Street. The air was brisk and the sky overcast on this Saturday morning. The inspector could see his breath as he traveled in the cab toward the mortuary, the air as cold as the dismal business awaiting him. He was anxious, though, to examine Annie Chapman's remains. He wanted to see if there were any "peculiarities" with her that were also present with Mary Ann Nichols.

After his chat with Monro the previous Monday, Abberline had re-examined the Nichols corpse before she was buried in the county cemetary, noting anything he might have missed on his first exam. This would be a chance to compare and contrast what he'd found there against what appeared to be another victim of the same fiend.

Old Montagu Street was at one time lined with well-kept, expensively attractive homes. As London grew, however, the neighborhood around Old Montagu began to deteriorate leaving now only a few dilapidated houses containing only the memory of their former glory. The mortuary building on Old Montagu was one of those homes, formerly grand, that survived specifically to fill a municipal need to house the remains of those too poor for a more elaborate or dignified burial than was afforded by the state.

As Abberline entered the building that served as the mortuary, the putrid odor of rot and decay assaulted him. Inside was Robert Mann, the caretaker. Mann was a resident of the Whitechapel Workhouse whose duties included working in the mortuary when the need arose. A strange little man, he was a perennial "guest" of the nearby workhouse who repeatedly volunteered for the grisly work at the mortuary, a task for which there were few takers. Something in his manner caused Abberline's skin to crawl. Although he'd never been caught doing anything untoward, there were persistent rumors he had an unnatural interest in the dead bodies he attended, particularly the women.

"Where is Dr. Phillips?" Abberline directed his question to Mann.

"Come and gone, sir," replied the caretaker, not bothering to look up from his sweeping as he hummed a tune from a child's rhyme.

"Has the doctor completed his examination?" Abberline snapped his question.

At last looking up, he recognized Inspector Abberline, "Yes, Inspector, he left some time ago. Is there anything I can help you with?"

"Yes, I'd like to see the victim."

"Of course, Inspector, she's laid out in the next room. I've cleaned her up a bit, as she was left quite untidy," he said with a comically wide grin that appeared out of place in these surroundings.

Abberline ignored what he took to be an attempt at humor, or worse, entering the room where the body lay. As he opened the door, he covered his mouth and nose with a handkerchief against the stench he'd been aware of in the outer room, but which only grew stronger and more gut-wrenching as he entered.

There were three bodies in the windowless room that in past days served as a formal dining room; Annie's was on a table in the middle beneath a cord dangling from the ceiling at the end of which a single naked bulb illuminated the table where the body lay. The table itself was made of copper with a three inch lip all around. It was fitted with scuppers in each corner that channeled any liquid down to a drain on the floor. Abberline approached the table, drawing down the sheet covering the body in order to thoroughly examine the victim's wounds.

Upon completion of his examination, Abberline drew the sheet over Annie's body and again entered the outer room. He found Mann standing by the door. Although he had a broom and dust pan in hand, the inspector suspected he had been watching the examination of the corpse. "Everything meet your satisfaction, Inspector?" he grinned.

Stifling his gag reflex while wiping his eyes on his handkerchief, he said, "Yes, thank you. Tell me, have they identified the victim?"

"Oh, yes, sir, 'er name is Annie Chapman, identified by several what knew 'er. She's quite well known locally, Annie is, at the work'ouse and in the lodging 'ouses and such. Lately, I understands, she'd been at Crossingham Lodging 'ouse, Dorsett way," Mann replied as he moved toward the door, opening it for Inspector Abberline. "Will there be anything else, sir?" he asked with one hand at his waist, palm up.

If he'd been expecting some gratuity for his services, he was sorely disappointed as Abberline walked brusquely by him with a terse, "No, thank you."

Abberline shivered as he climbed back into the hansom he'd had waiting for him outside the mortuary. It was more his contact with the odd little man in charge of the mortuary than the cold that caused his discomfort.

After leaving Old Montagu, Abberline went directly to the hospital where Dr. Baxter Phillips, the H Division surgeon who first examined Chapman's body, was Chief Examiner. Entering his office without knocking, Abberline inquired, "What did you make of it, Doctor?"

Formalities between Abberline and Dr. Phillips had gone by the wayside long ago. Physically, Phillips was rotund and culturally he was rather crude for a doctor. His outward appearance gave the impression of sloth and his bearing was a bit casual, but Dr. Phillips was highly professional when it came to his work and the inspector knew it. He had known the doctor for many years—since the time he was walking a beat in Whitechapel. He respected him professionally, and despite his manner or perhaps because of it, he liked him on a personal level.

"What's that?" Dr. Phillips said, looking up. He was enjoying a mid-morning snack of sausage and hard cheese when Abberline fairly burst into his office, startling him.

His cluttered desk bore not only stacks of reports yet to be filed, but also the wrappings of today's lunch, and from the look of things, several lunches prior. "Ah, Inspector, pardon…I wasn't expecting you," Phillips said as he cleared away a small portion of the clutter before him. "Ghastly! That's the word for it, all right," he replied, "perhaps the most savage murder I've ever seen," as he worked to swallow the mouthful of food he'd been enjoying. "She must have died instantly, thank God, or nearly so," he managed to sympathize between bites of sausage.

"Did you see the marks on her neck?"

"My God, man, of course I did," spitting small bits of cheese in the air between them. "Her head was nearly cut off."

"No, no…" Abberline paused, eyeing the cheese morsels on his jacket, and then fixing his gaze back on Dr. Phillips, "I meant the puncture marks."

"Puncture marks?" Dr. Phillips asked as he sucked the greasy residue of the sausage off his chubby fingers, raising his eyebrows to punctuate his question.

"Yes, puncture marks," the inspector indicated their approximate position by placing his index and middle finger on his own throat, "on the right side of her neck. They were partially obscured by the slash that killed her, but they were there, nonetheless."

"Well, now that you mention them, yes, but I must say I didn't really make much of them at the time…" Dr. Phillips had pulled his notebook from his desk drawer and his pudgy hands were busily thumbing through it. "Aha! Here it is." Reading from his notes, "'…two small semicircular indentations of approximately 3/16 inch diameter in the flesh through which the knife apparently passed – possible puncture wounds or postules – about 2.5 inches apart, signs of ecchymosis present'." Looking up from his notes, "Yes, I saw them, but they appeared superficial, probably caused by some disease, as the flesh in the area was blackened, as I recall." Looking from Abberline to his notes, then back to Abberline, belching, "There you have it. But I can't see how these small wounds could possibly be of any value in your investigation, Inspector. After all, she died from having her throat slit."

"Mary Ann Nichols had the same, identical marks on her throat."

"So? It could be bug bites or some other parasites. Living in the horrid squalor of the East End, I'd be surprised not to see evidence of such pestilence."

"Yes, doctor, you are undoubtedly correct," replied Abberline, rising to leave, "thank you for your time, Doctor." Then as an afterthought, Abberline asked, "Tell me, did you observe a large amount of blood present at the scene?"

"Well, let me see," the doctor scratched his head, "No…no, I don't believe I did, come to think of it. Curious, now that you mention it. There was precious little remaining in the body. Very odd."

"Once again, thank you very much for your time, Dr. Phillips," Abberline said as he departed.

On the ride back to Whitehall, he thought about the marks on Annie Chapman, marks nearly identical to the ones on

Mary Ann Nichols. He couldn't shake the feeling he'd seen similar wounds before, but was unable to recall the case. The doctor was probably right about them having no special significance, but it struck Abberline as odd that so little blood was found at both scenes plus the fact that in each case the slash wounds appeared to originate at or very near the point of these small punctures, as if "…camouflage", he mumbled to himself.

Chapter 9

COLD COMPASSION

September 8, 1888

In anticipation of his guests's arrivals, the baron made meticulous preparation. The first to arrive was to be Abigail Drake.

He'd been enchanted by her since they first met at the gala he'd thrown for Dr. Tremaine. Quite used to having a female companion around him, both to do his bidding when he was otherwise indisposed, as well as acting as his concubine, he found himself somewhat torn. In the past, in order to create a veil of normalcy, he would present such a woman as his wife. Through this masquerade, he was able to fashion the fiction of his own succession, aided by his penchant for reclusiveness.

A part of him wanted Abigail to fill that role. This predatory part of the baron knew it would be easy to arrange such a role with just a kiss and determined to make her his this very night. But another part of him—one that had lain dormant within him for nearly a century—wanted something more. Abigail had awakened in him feelings he hadn't known since the death of his beloved Maria.

In the baron's view, he existed alongside the hunger he considered to be almost his alter ego or doppelganger, not exactly part of him but not entirely independent. He felt this side of him always to be in opposition to his true self. He had, over the years, come to terms, learning to live with it. In point of fact, he thrived.

Perhaps it was true. Perhaps he was two beings; perhaps his affliction was a strange sort of dualism not dissimilar to the Manichean dualism that was at the root of the heresy he'd helped to extinguish so very long ago. Or, perhaps, he was only deceiving himself, with these thoughts being a mere fabrication to allow him to cope with the unholy destruction he'd caused over the centuries.

74

Whichever it was, tonight the evil was upon him and he meant to bring Abigail under his power, whether he wished to admit it to himself or not.

"Ah, Signorina Abigail," the baron effused as he opened the door to greet his guest, "I'm so happy you could make it. Please, come in," he said, taking her hand and bussing it lightly with his lips. He could feel the warmth of her life's blood pulsing through her hand as he smelled her scent on the air, warmed by her skin. Even though he'd fed the previous evening, the proximity of such a fresh supply of blood heightened his senses.

"Thank you, Baron, I wouldn't miss the opportunity to see and hear the device you described at dinner," flushing slightly as his cool breath gently brushed the back of her hand. The baron removed her wrap as he breathed in the fragrance of her hair above the bare nape of her neck, handing the wrap to Garrett, who had just appeared from the corridor.

"Yes, please come this way," leading her past Garrett down the hallway. "I've redecorated the drawing room as a music conservatory," he said escorting her into a brightly lit room with a grand piano on one side and a desk on the other. Atop the desk was a large wooden box with an even larger, white cone-shaped device attached. At the tapered end of the cone was a metallic disk out of which protruded a needle poised above a white cylinder.

"Is that it, there?" Abigail asked excitedly as she moved toward the odd-looking box on the desk.

"Yes, here, let me demonstrate for you," and the baron began turning a small crank on the side of the box. As he did, the cylinder began to turn, slowly at first, but then more rapidly until the turning speed became uniform. After a few more turns of the crank, the baron took the disk between his thumb and forefinger, delicately touching the needle to the end of the cylinder.

As they waited in anticipation, the baron, feeling the beast rising within him, watched the pulsing in Abigail's throat. How easily it would be, he thought, to have her now.

Even a small bite would place her in his power, but he knew it wouldn't stop there, eventually, once bitten, he would consume her. What a pity that would be, of course, but it was inevitable. He moved closer. He felt the urge to possess her push aside his more benevolent side.

At first, there was only a rushing sound with occasional pops and hisses, but then a voice coming from the large end of the cone announced the title of the music to be played along with the name of the composer, Arthur Sullivan. With the voice breaking the silence, Abigail's eyes lit up as she laughed excitedly.

The angelic laughter issuing from Abigail's lips broke the spell the baron had allowed himself to fall under, touching the vestigial part of him that still served as a soul. Then the music began. Abigail, showing obvious excitement, grasped the baron's hand in her own and squeezed, saying, "Oh Baron, this is wonderful."

For a moment, the baron saw his Maria in Abigail's eyes. The urge to strike, which only moments before had been so strong, passed over him like a summer cloud. He patted her hand, "Yes, it is wonderful, Ma...my dear." Holding her hand tightly in his own, he fell silent as they both listened intently while the music played.

The entire recording lasted barely two minutes. When it concluded, Abigail clapped excitedly, "Play it again, won't you?"

"Of course, my dear," he answered as he began turning the crank anew, returning the needle to the start of the recording.

This time, they both stood silently as the recording played. When it concluded, the baron turned to Abigail, "Would you like to hear it again?" The inner conflict within him had completely subsided as the baron looked at Abigail lovingly.

Looking up at him with tears stinging her eyes she answered, "No, not just now."

"My dear, you're crying, what is the matter?" fearing she may have sensed something amiss in him.

"You'll think me such a silly girl, Baron. It's nothing," she said looking away.

"Not at all, I could only think good thoughts of you,"

cupping her chin with his forefinger while turning her face back toward him. "I've become very fond of you in the short time we've known each other."

Her eyes glistening as she spoke, "You have?" A smile broke through the clouds of her despair.

"Yes," he replied, realizing the surprising truth of his words. "Now tell me. What was the reason for the tears, little one."

"It's nothing, really. I mean," she hesitated, "the music was so sad, and it made me think that I will be leaving soon for America and..." her voice trailed off.

"And...?" he asked.

Smiling, shyly, "And I may never see you again." She abruptly pulled away. "There, now you know and must think of me as a silly empty-headed girl."

Laughing softly, "Not at all. Why are you so sad? As I told your uncle, I too am planning a journey to New York."

"Yes, but you will be busy, and New York is a very big city."

"As is London, Signorina, and I have met you here. Besides, I could never be too busy to see you."

"But that is because you know my uncle."

"And now, I know you. I'm sure we will see each other in New York, if that is what you would like."

Her face brightened, "Truly?! Yes, I would like that very much. When...when will you be going?"

"My plans are not final, but by the end of the year, surely, Signorina."

"Oh please, you may call me Abby. We must be familiar, don't you think? Especially if we are going to see each other in New York."

"I would like very much to be more familiar, but for now, I shall call you Abby only when we are alone. We must not be too familiar or we will invite the wrong kind of talk, my little Abby. Especially if we expect your Aunt Maggie to allow us to see one another in New York," the Baron paused, affecting a concerned look on his face.

"What's the matter? Your face looks so serious."

"It's nothing, only…" he stopped, slyly enticing her into further inquiry as to his thoughts, orchestrating hers as easily as he played the violin.

"Only? Only what, Baron?"

"It's only that when we were dining together at your Uncle's home, I had the impression your Aunt wasn't feeling well," working to plant the seed that Lady Margaretta was suffering from some ailment.

"She was probably only tired; I'm sure she isn't ill." Her brow furrowed with worry as she continued, "Oh dear, that would be most distressing."

"It is probably nothing. Let us not worry about it," the baron insisted, even as he probed her mind, influencing her to inquire after her aunt's health. From his intuition concerning Lady Margaretta's character, he felt assured she was like other women of means. Grown spoiled and comfortable, they were easily influenced by suggestion, particularly if that suggestion was introduced by someone close to her, in whom she trusted.

"Very well, I'll not worry," Abigail said, even as the concern cemented itself in her mind. It would be too disappointing if Aunt Maggie were unable to accompany me, she thought, knowing it might cause her to have to postpone her voyage.

Forcing herself to smile, while putting her aunt out of her mind for the moment, "If you are to call me Abby, what shall I call you? Baron seems so stuffy," she asked as she walked around the room, coyly running her fingers over the baron's furnishings.

Let's see," the baron pretended to contemplate as he followed behind her, then offered "why not call me, 'Tonietto'?" The words came out of his mouth before he'd even realized their implication. This was the name by which Maria had called him, his Maria. No one had called him that either before or since, yet it seemed right for Abigail to use it.

"Tonietto? Hmmm…yes, it suits you. Tonietto," she repeated as she continued to walk around the room. Giggling softly as she came to the shelf on which sat the baron's violin case, "Tonietto, will you play a tune for me?"

"What would you like to hear?" he asked, moving closer to her, reaching past her, as he opened the case.

While he plucked the strings to check the tuning, she answered, "Something sweet, tender. It doesn't matter what."

Tucking the violin under his chin, the baron drew the bow across the strings as he began to play. He had barely played a dozen notes when Abigail clapped her hands together exclaiming, "Wonderful! I know that tune, Vivaldi's concerto number six, A minor," clapping her hands excitedly. "Let's play a duet," she said as she walked to the piano. Smiling, she adjusted her skirts while taking her seat upon the bench.

"A duet would be most delightful, Abby."

The two of them were still playing when Garrett interrupted to announce the arrival of Sir Charles, who followed him into the study. The look on her uncle's face displayed his pleasure at finding Abigail and the baron performing music together. "I don't know much about music," he said, "but that sounded most melodic from what I heard. I'd quite forgotten how well you play, Baron. Much like your father, I understand. I suppose the knack is an inherited one, eh?"

"Yes, I do believe so, Sir Charles, and welcome to my humble home."

"Humble? Not half, I'd say. It quite suits you," replied Sir Charles, graciously.

"Thank you so much for saying so."

Returning the conversation to music, Sir Charles informed the baron, "Abigail's mother was quite the musician, you know."

"No, I didn't," Barlucci answered, smiling at Abigail, "but it certainly shows. Music runs strongly through the blood, Sir Charles, in many families."

"Quite so, quite so," he said, looking contentedly from the baron to his niece. "Well, Abby, did you enjoy the, uh, what did you call it? Phonograph?

"Very much so, Uncle. Would you like to hear?" she

asked then flushed, "I'm sorry, Baron, I didn't mean to presume..."

"Nonsense, my dear, I'd be very happy to crank the box again for another go around."

"I'm afraid I'll have to beg off, Baron. I'm quite anxious to get home this evening. It's beginning to look as though it's going to rain tonight and I'd not like to be caught out in it, if I can help it."

"I quite understand, Sir Charles," the baron said, taking Abigail's wrap from Garrett, who had just appeared with it, slipping it over her shoulders.

"Besides," said Abigail, "we shouldn't leave Aunt Maggie alone for too long when she isn't feeling well."

"Not feeling well?" asked Sir Charles, apparently surprised at the news.

"Oh yes," answered Abigail, "She's been so very tired lately. Even the baron noticed, didn't you, Baron?"

"I'm afraid I did," Barlucci answered, now putting the idea firmly into the mind of Sir Charles. "I hope she's feeling better. Perhaps when she is, you and Lady Margaretta might like to have dinner with me here. In the meantime, old friend, you have an open invitation to stop by at your leisure any evening you wish and I'll crank up the box for your pleasure."

"That's very kind of you, Baron, but I'm afraid I have a bit of a tin ear when it comes to music," replied Sir Charles.

Smiling aside to Abigail, the baron observed, "I'm not quite sure but we should take offense at that, Signorina Abby? Your uncle's flattery was apparently that of a blind man complimenting a painting, wouldn't you say?"

"Hmm? What's that, old boy," Sir Charles looked incredulously at the two of them, who were now laughing out loud. "Oh...dear, I didn't mean..." breaking into laughter himself. "Jolly good, Baron, jolly good."

"I'll be wary of future compliments, Sir Charles," the baron jested.

"Come, Abby, we must be getting along now," Sir Charles persuaded his niece as they moved from the conservatory and down the corridor, toward the door. As they were leaving, the baron heard Sir Charles say to Abigail, "I do believe that is the first time I've ever heard the baron laugh."

Closing the door, the baron reflected on Sir Charles comment. He pondered; could it be he was falling in love with the delightful young Abigail. He didn't think it possible, but there was something quite charmingly familiar in her manner that touched him in a way he had not felt in over a century. In many ways beyond her laughter, Abigail reminded him of his beloved Maria. Smiling to himself, he returned to the conservatory and picked up his violin, continuing with the more melancholy second movement of the piece he and Abigail had shared. As he played, he thought of Maria, and of Abigail.

#

When Dr. Tremaine arrived at Darthmore, the sound of violin music could be heard from behind the large oaken doors to the mansion. He rang the bell at precisely 8:30 p.m. and was greeted by Garrett, who showed the doctor into the drawing room. There he found the baron standing before the fireplace, violin tucked up under his chin, apparently lost in the music he was playing. Seeing the doctor as he turned, Barlucci abruptly stopped playing in order to greet him.

"No, no, please," the doctor urged him, "continue, it is very beautiful and you play it so well."

"Perhaps later, Doctor," the baron protested, "come, sit before the fire and warm yourself, the air is unusually brisk this evening. I've an excellent cognac for you to try."

Accepting the baron's invitation, the doctor inquired, "Where did you study music, Baron?"

As he poured the doctor's drink, he evaded the question with his answer, "It's a mere hobby, I assure you. The piece you heard, the second movement of Vivaldi's concerto in A Minor, is a favorite of mine. It's not technically complex, but has a subtle hypnotic quality I find very relaxing and contemplative. Through years of practice, I've managed a passable performance for my own amusement."

"You are much too modest, Baron, it was lovely."

"Ah, and you are most kind, my dear doctor, but come, I believe our dinner is awaiting us." The baron led Dr. Tremaine into an intimate formal dining room where a sumptuous dinner was being served as Garrett supervised.

The table was set with fine white imported china, glittering silverware and elegant crystal sparkling beneath and complementing the ornate crystal chandelier. The tablecloth and napkins were immaculately white, crisply starched linen. The aroma from the piping hot dinner fare filled the doctor's senses, making his appetite even more sharp. There was pheasant as well as roast beef, two varieties of very rich gravy, fresh vegetables steaming hot in crystal bowls and pate de foie gras.

"Baron, you needn't have gone to so much trouble. This is truly an exquisite looking meal. But I suppose I should have expected as much after the wonderful party you hosted."

"I'm gratified by your appreciation. It's refreshing in one so young and accomplished as yourself." The baron pulled out a chair, "If you will, Doctor, please sit here at the head of the table."

As they were seated, Garrett hustled the hired servants out of the dining room, closing the door to the rear hallway that communicated with the kitchen, ensuring the baron had complete privacy with his guest.

"The food is excellent, Baron, but aren't you going to join me?" the doctor asked as he filled his plate and began to eat.

"I fear, Doctor, that my appetite is a bit, how shall I say it, eccentric, owing to an unusual ailment."

"Ailment?" the doctor inquired politely as he enjoyed the pheasant before him.

"Yes, it's a rather exotic malady and I doubt you'd be very much interested."

"Interested? My dear baron, of course I'd be interested. Exotic diseases are my specialty. Tell me, please," he managed to say around the meat and brown gravy he was hungrily devouring, "what is this infirmity you've mentioned."

"Very well, Doctor, but as I tell it, I beg you to remember it was you who requested me to do so." As he spoke, his gaze grew more intense. Dr. Tremaine found it difficult to look away from the baron's eyes, discovering that his appetite, which had been so ravenous only moments before, had now greatly dissipated.

Baron Barlucci turned toward the doctor, leaning forward so as to close the distance between them. He began to speak in a low, soothing voice that had a strange hypnotic effect, "My condition is of a sanguinary nature, Doctor; one in which I believe you actually will be very much interested. It began many years ago, but the time of its origin is not as important as its manifestation.

"You see before you a feast of exquisite foodstuffs, which I've had prepared especially for you this evening," he said as he passed his hand over the table. "It is obvious, from the way your nostrils flared with expectation as we entered the room, how the saliva began to be generated in your mouth upon seeing the steam rise with the aroma reaching your senses as you actually smelled the food, that it is pleasing to you." He paused, looking intently at the doctor, then continued, "I have not had such a reaction to ordinary food in centuries."

Tremaine uttered, "You speak in hyperbole, Baron. How long has your malediction actually affected your appetite."

"I assure you, Doctor," the baron spoke, placing his hand on the doctor's arm just above the wrist, "it is not hyperbole. I can give you the exact date when this malediction, as you called it, first afflicted me. It was June 29th in the year of our Lord 1243." [2]

---

[2] By 1243, all major Cathar towns and bastions had fallen to the northern invaders, except for a handful of remote, isolated strong points. Chief among these was the majestic mountain citadel of Montsegur, poised like a celestial ark above the surrounding valleys. The fortress was besieged by invaders for ten months. The resistance to the attackers, which numbered upward of ten thousand, was noteworthy. Part of the reason seems to be the alleged existence of a legendary Cathar "treasure".

http://www.halexandria.org/dward221.htm

When he heard the date, the doctor instinctively tried to pull away, but found himself unable to move his left hand, which was pinned at the wrist to the table by the baron in a grip that felt impossibly strong.

The baron continued; as he did, the doctor's instinctive resistance faded away as smoke from a fire, "I was a knight engaged in a crusade against the Cathars in the south of France. I fell in battle when a lance pierced my chest very close to my heart and I was left for dead on the battlefield.

"Fortunately, for me, a Sinti tribe, you would call them gypsies, from a camp nearby was scavenging among the remnants of the battle when they discovered me, still alive, among the throngs of dead Cathars and knights. They carried me back to their camp where they began to treat my wounds. I teetered between life and death for over a week, but I was too close to death by the time they discovered me for their potions and poultices to have the desired effect.

"There was, however, a young girl in the camp who they believed possessed certain powers over death. On the night of the full moon, June 29th, she came to me with her healing herbs and incantations. She continued throughout the night. As dawn approached and my breathing neared its last, she drained the blood of a bat into a cup in which she mixed some herbs. She dipped her finger in the concoction, rubbing it into my wound, then on my lips and into my mouth. She then lifted my head, forcing me to drink what remained, as best I could. She laid me down on the earth, speaking in a tongue incomprehensible to me at the time, as I breathed my last."

Interrupting his story, the baron allowed an amused grin to steal across his face, "Doctor, you appear confused."

"Well, I...," Tremaine began, ignoring the fact he was still unable to move his left arm, "Baron, please, do you really expect me to believe you are over 600 years old? And then to tell me you've died, when I can see for myself you are very much alive? It's too ridiculous! I'm a man of science, Baron. I'm not prone to believe in superstition."

"Ah, yes, my dear doctor, and it is exactly your science

that prompted me to seek you out. The time at which I contracted this particular malady does not matter—six years or six hundred, is inconsequential. But if that fact is unbelievable to you, you will find what more I have to say quite beyond the pale, though I assure you it is all absolutely true." The baron relaxed his grip, removing his hand from the doctor's wrist. "I'm sorry I've failed to convince you of the veracity of my tale, Doctor..." Then, feigning light-headedness, he said, "Please excuse me, I'm feeling a bit faint. Doctor, would you mind taking my pulse?"

"Of course, Baron." Dr. Tremaine reached for the baron's wrist and was immediately taken aback by the complete lack of warmth in his hand, "Baron, have you been diagnosed with any circulatory problems?" The baron leered as Tremaine searched for a pulse, then switched wrists, searching again in vain. "What sort of trickery is this?"

"I assure you, Doctor, there is no trickery involved." Taking the doctor's wrist again, he placed his hand first over his heart, then to his throat, "What do you, in your best medical judgment, Doctor, make of a man with no pulse? What does your science tell you."

"Before tonight," Tremaine said in a plaintive tone, "I would say that man would be dead."

"And in most instances, Doctor, you would be correct, but if not dead, then as in my case, undead."

Stunned, Dr. Tremaine sat back in his chair silently.

"Do you now believe me, Doctor?"

"This is so incredible, I don't know what to believe," the doctor responded in a bewildered voice, recoiling involuntarily.

"Perhaps, Doctor, you should try to suspend your disbelief a bit further, for what I am about to tell you is as unbelievable as it is true."

Instinctively repulsed, the doctor felt much the same as he did during his first autopsy at medical school, sick to his stomach but unable to look away, a peculiar professional curiosity overruled any revulsion or rejection in his mind. "There is more? If you please, Baron, continue."

The baron had arisen from his chair, now standing with

his back to the fire, continuing to glare at Dr. Tremaine. As he did so, a strange hypnotic calmness, which the doctor took for mental fatigue, came over him. At length, after exerting his mental power to sooth the young doctor, the baron continued, "As I've said, that night, the 29th of June, I breathed my last. As I later discovered, the following morning a division of knights arrived at the gypsy camp to inquire as to the site of the battle. When they discovered the weapons and other property of their brethren knights among the Senti, they were incensed. They immediately set about slaughtering every gypsy in the camp. At some point, they discovered my body and despite the ravings of the young girl who'd tended me, they buried me on the spot.

"A fortnight later, during the new moon when the land was black and lifeless, I awakened from my sleep. Slowly and instinctually, I dug myself out of the shallow grave to begin my new life, for lack of a better word. I searched for the gypsy who'd attended me among the dead, but she was nowhere to be found, so I began to make my way back to the last encampment of knights I knew.

"As dawn approached, I found myself becoming suddenly weak. It was not till then I realized how keen my eyesight had been all that previous night. As the sun began to illuminate the eastern sky, my head began to ache, centering just behind my eyes. I sought shelter from the coming light in a small cave in a hillside.

"I remained awake all that day, but I was barely able to move about inside the cave, so weak was I. I believed it to be due to not having eaten anything in I didn't know when, so I decided my first order of business that night would be to find food, although even the thought of food had no enticement for me.

"As day turned to night, my strength returned and, I was surprised to find, so did my appetite. I was voraciously hungry, but at the time I was unaware for what I hungered. Shortly after leaving my cave-sanctuary, I happened upon a shepherd with a small flock of sheep. Being unarmed, looking more dead than alive, I avoided the shepherd, stalking a young lamb instead. Under cover of a moonless night, I was able to separate the lamb from the flock without too much difficulty. When I was at a safe distance from both the flock and the shepherd, I slung it over my neck, carrying it back to my temporary sanctuary. I'd planned to kill it, and make a small fire over which to roast its carcass.

"What followed next both surprised and startled me. I unslung the lamb from my neck and as I was putting it on the ground, I instinctively pounced upon it, turning it on its side as I pierced its neck with canine teeth that had somehow extended themselves from my gums. As the blood gushed forth, I began to drink. I cannot tell you the feeling that overcame me. It was as if I'd never before consumed anything. It was, I assume, akin to a man, who being lost in the desert for some days, suddenly finds himself beside a crystal clear pool of cool, delicious water. I drank until full, still craving more, as if it had only piqued my thirst rather than quenched it.

"Suddenly a powerful feeling came over me; it occurred to me that while the lamb had been somewhat satisfying, how much more so would have been the shepherd. The thought, which came into my mind more as instinct than reflection, simultaneously repulsed and excited me.

"That very night I stole back to the flock, approaching the shepherd's camp. He was asleep beside the fire when I arrived. I felt rather strange, unable to make myself approach nearer. The shepherd's dog suddenly began barking, but never left its master's side. Suddenly awakened, the shepherd saw me and took pains to quiet his dog. He motioned me closer, and bade me to warm myself by his fire.

"I found I was now free of whatever restraint on my movement prevented me from approaching earlier. I came closer. The dog, lying beside his master, continued growling at me. I bent down as if to pet the dog but in fact intentionally provoked it. When it attempted to bite my hand, I caught it by the throat, snapping its neck. Before the shepherd had a chance to react, I pounced, my teeth finding the artery in his throat. Opening it to allow the warm gush of blood, I drank.

"After this I realized the truth of my condition. I no longer required the food of a normal man, only blood—human

87

blood. Although animal blood, such as the lamb, was good, it could not satisfy the hunger. Indeed it only served to increase the need and desire for human blood. I was now a vampire. Thus have I remained, my dear Doctor, from that day to this."

As the baron concluded his story, an unnatural quiet settled over the room. The doctor sat in stunned silence. When at last he spoke, it was as though the words formed his thoughts rather than the other way round, "I am a man of science and that science tells me there is no such thing as a vampire." As he spoke, he avoided looking at the baron, mouthing the words as if speaking to himself. "But it also tells me a man with no pulse, no heart beating in his chest, cannot live. Yet I see before me a man, with whom I have dined, with whom I have spoken and even heard playing the violin," looking now directly at the baron, "who has no pulse, no heartbeat, whose very skin is as cold as the tomb. This shakes the science I believe in to the very core. What more madness would it be to accept his story of having lived, or rather not lived, these past six centuries as a vampire."

Rising from the table, Dr. Tremaine walked slowly toward the fireplace. He placed his hands on the mantle, hanging his head as he gazed into the dying embers, trying to wrap his mind around what he'd witnessed as well as what he'd been told. He tried to fathom what it must have been like to awaken on that cold moonless night only to discover yourself to be a monster. Then, slowly turning back toward his host he said, "Baron, how can I help you?"

"Doctor," said the baron matter-of-factly, "I want you to cure me."

"Cure you? Do you realize, if all you say is true, you are the scientific curiosity of the century…the millennium?!"

The baron's eyes narrowed and Dr. Tremaine again felt the pull of the baron's mind on his own, even as the baron's countenance darkened, "I am not a sideshow freak, Doctor. You would do well to remember that. I am fully capable of draining you and leaving you an empty shell."

The doctor felt an icy chill as the baron said this, for the first time that evening realizing he was in the presence of the most prolific serial killer in the history of the world.

"Please forgive me," the baron said, noting the effect his words had on the doctor. His features softening, he continued, "I assure you I find no pleasure in the taking of a human life. It is an unfortunate necessity due to my condition. I've done what I can to minimize both the number and the worth of my victims."

Although his words were appropriately contrite, there was an air of superiority about them, belying his contrition. A strange contradiction was in evidence as the doctor listened to the baron's profession of regret for the innumerable lives he'd taken, while at the same time noting an unnerving undercurrent of disdain, as if the toll of human lives was of little more consequence than so many slaughtered sheep.

"Baron, your condition is so far beyond anything I have ever seen in my experience, I'm afraid I'm unable to give you any assurances for a cure, but given enough time…"

"Doctor, I've been waiting for over 600 years, if there is one thing I have, it is time. I only ask that you take on this challenge. Money is no object; I've amassed a sizable fortune with which I can furnish you with anything and everything you need." As he was saying this, the baron opened a door leading to the library, which he'd had converted into a small laboratory.

The doctor followed as the baron entered the laboratory. Tremaine walked around looking at the glistening instruments, the latest microscopes and centrifuges, "This is very impressive, baron, but I'm afraid I must return to New York."

"Ah, yes, your upcoming wedding. I assure you, Doctor, I have no intention of interfering with your plans. All this," the baron made a sweeping gesture with his left hand, "is a mere trifle, only something to demonstrate my level of commitment and to allow you to get started in your research, should you agree to delay your return home by a few weeks." As he spoke, he could see the doctor was quite pleased with the quality of the instruments before him. "The shelves here," gesturing toward a set of bookshelves behind a massive mahogany desk, "contain everything ever written, of any significance, concerning vampirism…and, of course," bowing, "I am at your service."

Doctor Tremaine wandered around the room, running his hands over the books and instruments. After some time, during which the baron simply looked on, he said, "Baron, I accept the challenge. I will do whatever I can to find a cure for your ailment."

Chapter 10

CONSCRIPTIVE ASSISTANCE

September 10, 1888

Kissing his wife good-bye as he did every morning before leaving for work, Abberline could not help but wonder how his wife continued to put up with the demands of his job. Normally working six days a week, leaving home at 6 a.m. each day and returning many times late in the evening, left precious little time for the two of them to be together. With the recent murders in Whitechapel, he was now also working weekends, as needed.

During times like this she was left alone for long periods, but Emma was a good and loving wife. She kept his house and stood by him throughout their long life together. It was perhaps because they never had any children of their own she was able to find the strength to put up with the demands of his job. He was all she had and, although he had his job, he knew she was the best part of his life. He took pains to make sure she knew it too.

In order to have more time together, she would often pack a lunch or dinner, bringing it to his office, where they'd take their meal together, if he was able. He'd promised her after he made Inspector First Class, he'd take it a bit easier, but promises, even ones made in good faith, have a way of yielding to reality. Yet she loved him and he her.

As he left today, he took the clean handkerchief she'd given him, placing it inside his jacket pocket. She'd noticed he had a sniffle, he supposed, and just like Emma, she took as good care of him as she was able.

Although he could afford to take a hansom cab to work he rarely did. He preferred the bustle of the trams. He liked staying close to his roots, which were unpretentious and thrifty. Of course, whenever he needed to, he could flash his inspector's badge, commandeering a ride from any cabbie in London. His colleagues chided him for not taking advantage of this perquisite, but he somehow felt it wasn't fair to take a cab for free when the cabbie might otherwise obtain a fare. Besides, the tram was a great place to observe his fellow Londoners, a habit he greatly enjoyed.

Today, as he rode the tram from his home in Kennington down Upper Kennington Lane toward the Vauxhall Bridge, Abberline's mind was preoccupied with what his day might entail. Undoubtedly Sir Charles would want a report on the latest Whitechapel murder. He hoped he would have time to grab a cup of coffee first.

When he arrived at his office, Inspector Abberline found a message awaiting him. Not surprisingly, Sir Charles wished to see him at once. Abberline balled the note up in his fist, tossing it in the rubbish can by the door as he started toward Sir Charles's office, taking the long way round. He was not looking forward to another tongue lashing from the Commissioner.

As he passed his mentor's office, he noticed the door had been propped open and saw Monro inside looking as though he'd been waiting for him. Monro motioned for him to come inside.

"I've been summoned," Abberline told Monro, inclining his head in the direction of Sir Charles office.

"Yes, I know, the matter in Whitechapel…another murder. That's what I wanted to see you about," adding conspiratorially, "please close the door." Abberline removed the ornamental brass spittoon Monro had used as a doorstop, allowing the office door to swing shut. Monro continued, "I expect you've seen the newspapers this morning?"

"Yes, sir, I have. Not very flattering."

"This case is getting a lot of press of late, none of it favorable, I'm afraid. There is a desire in the highest quarters that this matter be resolved quickly. The Home Secretary himself is aware of and very concerned about what we're doing to solve this case. In fact, he wants to know if, perhaps, you could use some assistance with this one," clearing his throat as if hesitant to go on, "from a consultant."

Abberline allowed his disdain of the word to show on his face.

Ignoring Abberline's obvious displeasure, Monro continued, "Sir Charles, as you know, is getting a lot of pressure from the press. As unfortunate as it is typical, when I mentioned to the Secretary about getting an outsider involved, Sir Charles exploded, seeing it as what he calls 'yet another attempt to usurp' his territory. It isn't that way at all, of course. We are all aware of the strain Sir Charles is under and this particular chap comes very highly recommended."

"James…", taking a more familiar tone, "a consultant? The last thing I need is a civilian to muck around with this investigation."

"This is no ordinary civilian. He's a personal friend of Sir Robert, who swears by his talents. His name is Sherlock Holmes."

"Holmes…I've heard the name. It's been mentioned by some of the other inspectors, Lestrade for one, quite favorably as I recall…"

"Ah, then you know of him?" asked Monro.

"Only tangentially, I believe he has a brother. I've heard his name mentioned in connection with a rather odd social club. I believe he works on staff in Parliament, or the Home Office or someplace."

"Yes, something like that. At any rate, Mr. Holmes has been used on some very delicate matters of late… you've perhaps heard of the King of Bohemia affair?"

"Only rumors."

"Potentially a most embarrassing affair that was," he said, musing. Anyway," handing Abberline a slip of paper, "here is the address." Adding in a warmer manner, "Francis, please don't take this as an order, but as a friend, at least stop by and speak with him."

Folding the paper, slipping it into his vest pocket, he reluctantly replied, "I will, James. I promise."

Once outside Monro's office, Abberline retrieved the slip of paper from the pocket of his waist coat reading to himself, "221-B Baker Street," then balled up the paper in his hand, intending to dispose of it in the rubbish can beside Agnes' desk.

At the last minute, he stopped. As he thought about the promise he'd just made to Monro, he unballed the paper and looked at it again. This time he folded it twice, then re-deposited it back into his vest pocket as he continued to the office of Sir Charles.

"Agnes, is Sir Charles in?" Abberline asked as he sniffed the vase of fresh cut flowers on her desk, "I had a message he wished to see me."

"Yes, Inspector, but his mood is as foul this morning as last Friday's kippers, I'd say. Better watch your step," Agnes answered, smiling sweetly at Inspector Abberline.

Abberline plucked one of the carnations from the vase, breaking off the stem as he inserted the flower in his lapel, "Thanks for the tip, Aggie," he said as he knocked firmly on Sir Charles's door.

"Come in!" called Sir Charles gruffly.

"You wished to see me, sir?" Abberline asked as he entered, closing the door behind him.

Sir Charles was sitting behind his desk, with this morning's issue of *The Times* spread out across it, "Ah, Abberline, yes, come in. Do you know what this is, Abberline?"

"It appears to be the newspaper, sir." Abberline said with a serious expression belying the levity in his words.

"What?" asked Sir Charles, a bit piqued by Abberline's apparent lack of perception. "Yes, of course it's a newspaper, Abberline, it's *The Times*. Read what it says here," growled Sir Charles as he pointed to the end of a paragraph in the second column of an account of Annie Chapman's murder.

"It says, 'Nevertheless the police express a strong sentiment that more murders of the kind will be committed before the…'"

"'…before the miscreant is apprehended,'" Sir Charles interrupted, obviously irritated. "Who authorized such a statement to the press, Abberline?"

"I'm sure I don't know, sir, I…"

"You don't know? You don't know!?" Sir Charles repeated, his face becoming redder. "It's you job to know, Abberline! You are in charge of this investigation. No one should

94

be giving press briefings other than you! IS THAT CLEAR?!"

"Perfectly clear, sir," answered Abberline in a calmness, which only seemed to incense Sir Charles all the more. "Is there anything else, sir?"

"Yes!" fumed Sir Charles, "I don't want to see any such statements in the paper again! I'm hearing enough about this case without having my policemen telling the press we expect more of such heinous murders. I don't expect more, Abberline. Do you hear?"

"Yes, Sir Charles, loud and clear, sir."

"This is exactly the sort of thing that will have Henry Matthews on my neck and down around my ears. He has no idea of the problems in running a proper police force. None!" ranted Sir Charles, seemingly talking to himself as much as to Abberline. "That he listens to me at all, with Monro whispering in his ear, is surprising. No, Abberline, I don't expect to read the opinions of every constable in Whitechapel displayed on the pages of *The Times* for Matthews and Monro to chortle over as this case confounds me. What I DO expect," Sir Charles bellowed, rising to his feet, "is that the Inspector in charge of this investigation exercise a little control over his constables. I also expect that same Inspector to leave no stone unturned, no hedgerow unbeaten until this, this...this miscreant is caught and is swinging from the gallows! Do you hear, Abberline?"

"Yes, sir," Abberline answered calmly, his right hand touching the vest pocket in which he'd deposited the address Monro had given him. "I shall use every means at my disposal to find the perpetrator and bring him to justice."

Sitting back down slowly, mopping his brow with a handkerchief, Sir Charles uttered, "Very well, Abberline, very well," closing his eyes, leaning back in his chair, the steam having apparently gone out of him.

"Are you feeling all right, sir?" Abberline asked, genuinely concerned. Though he found Sir Charles a bit difficult to work for at times, Abberline still liked and admired him, despite his blustering.

"What's that? Oh, yes," Sir Charles answered more

95

calmly, "I've a bit of a headache...comes and goes, you know; I'll be all right."

"Here, sir," Abberline said as he poured Sir Charles a glass of water from a pitcher on the side table, "drink this."

Looking up at Abberline, Sir Charles took the glass and said, "Thank you, Inspector," as he drank deeply. After putting the glass down on his desk, he cleared his throat, apparently feeling somewhat more himself, "Now, Abberline, we're to have no more impromptu press briefings from your men, is that quite clear?" Sir Charles asked, in a much calmer voice than before.

"Quite, sir."

"Splendid. That will be all."

Abberline again thought about the address he had in his pocket, "But, sir, I..."

Raising his eyebrows, keeping his voice calm but firm, Sir Charles remonstrated, "I said, that will be all," as he began reading the paper once again.

"Yes, sir," knowing his interview with Sir Charles was over, Abberline departed, closing the door behind him. Walking back to Agnes' desk, he asked, "Agnes?"

"Yes, Inspector?"

"Have you noticed if Sir Charles has been feeling ill at all?"

"Now that you mention it, he has left work twice this week with headaches." Then she added, "And he hasn't been eating his lunch lately, either."

"Yes, I expect the murders in Whitechapel are weighing heavily upon him."

"Oh, to be sure, that and he told me just this morning his wife has suddenly taken ill—out of the blue—and just when they were preparing for a voyage to America."

"I wasn't aware Sir Charles had plans to visit America."

"Oh, no, not Sir Charles, he's too much a work horse to be leaving just now. Lady Margaretta was to escort their niece on a visit to her mother's people in New York." Agnes opined, "A confluence of concerns such as Sir Charles has had lately can weigh heavily on a man his age."

"Yes, I suppose so. I'm afraid we sometimes forget the frailty of the human condition."

"Why, Inspector, I had no idea you were such a philosopher."

"There are a good many things about me you don't know, I would imagine, Agnes."

"I suspect you are right, Inspector," Agnes agreed, then added with a smile, "just as I suspect I'm all the better for it," as she went back to her typing.

#

The following day, Abberline left home a bit later than normal in order to stop by the Baker Street residence of Mr. Sherlock Holmes on his way to work. After kissing his wife goodbye on his way out the door, he begrudgingly picked up the newspaper from the table by his front door to read along the way.

When he'd told his wife about Monro's entreaty for him to see Holmes the previous evening, she remarked what an intelligent man Mr. Holmes appeared to be. He was surprised she'd even heard of him, as she wasn't the least interested in the crimes of the city. She said she'd only recently become acquainted with Holmes's work, through a series of articles she'd been reading by a Dr. John Watson who was chronicling some of Holmes's recent cases. She handed him the paper, which he took, snurling up his nose and turning it over in his hand before tossing it on the table in the entryway. It was this paper he tucked under his arm as he boarded the North Metropolitan Tramway on his way to Baker Street.

Settling into his seat, he reluctantly opened the paper. Frederick Abberline was not used to having his judgment or his professional expertise questioned nor was he in the least bit happy at having to visit a "consulting" detective, but he'd promised James he would and a promise was a promise. Abberline had been on the Metropolitan Police force for twenty-five of his forty-five years. He began his career in Islington, attached to 'N' division, after deciding clock making was not his calling in life. After he was promoted to Inspector, he was moved to Whitechapel where he remained for fourteen years before being transferred on request of James Monro to 'A' Division, which encompasses the very heart of Her Majesty's government. His intelligence, drive and acumen for the job got him transferred to Central Office (CO) Division at Scotland yard within the year as well a promotion to Inspector First Class.

By the time the tram came along Baker Street, Abberline had finished the article. He had to admit that if all Watson had written were true, Holmes was indeed as remarkable as his wife described. But he thought it improbable, feeling this fellow Watson must have embellished on the facts of the matter in order to sell the stories; no one's powers of observation were as keen as Watson described. Dr. Watson, if indeed he were a doctor, was undoubtedly shilling for Holmes and the lengthy, lurid and dramatically written article was no more than a drawn out advertisement meant to drum up business for the "consulting detective".

As Abberline dismounted the tram, he stepped onto the street and into a sizable pothole. Soaking his right foot in the cold water left from an overnight shower increased his already foul mood. Somewhat a loner, Abberline was not enthusiastic about asking anyone for assistance with his cases, particularly not an outsider, regardless how highly they came recommended.

The residence at 221B Baker Street was singularly unimposing. In the middle of the block, the gray stone building stood between two nearly identical buildings. It was distinguished only by the brass number plate and the wrought iron gate, painted Kelly green, enclosing the three steps to the front door, which was topped with an oval transom of opaque glass, also inscribed with the residence number, 221B.

Abberline stepped from the street onto the pavement, stamping his foot in an effort to shake the water from his shoe. Opening the gate, he stepped up to the door and hesitantly twisted the bell ringer. As he stood there believing perhaps no one was at home, he thought to himself that at least he kept his promise to Monro, having made the attempt to contact Holmes. He was about to walk away without ringing again when he was greeted by a well dressed, matronly woman with fashionably styled white hair, save for a single lock, which insisted on floating before her eyes. She looked him over rather disdainfully, brusquely requesting the nature of his business.

"Pardon, madam," tipping his bowler as he spoke, "Would this be the residence of a Mr. Sherlock Holmes?" Abberline could feel Mrs. Hudson sizing him up. He could also feel that in her eyes, at least, he came up wanting.

"Indeed it would, sir, but I'm afraid Mr. Holmes and Dr. Watson are out of town just at the moment. Were they expecting you?"

"I see...no, no, they wouldn't have been expecting me, no...well..." he stammered indecisively, "pardon, but do you know if they will be returning soon or where I might contact them? I'm afraid it's a matter of grave import."

"It generally is, sir, when Mr. Holmes is involved, but I'm afraid I don't know when they're expected back. They don't keep a regular schedule as such and certainly don't keep me informed of their comings and goings. I do know currently they're away in the south of France...Arles, I believe Dr. Watson said—on another matter of grave import, I'm sure," she added somewhat sarcastically. "You might inquire at the local constabulary, thereabouts, they quite possibly may be able to contact them for you."

"Thank you, madam, you've been most helpful," adding a bit of his own sarcasm. Tipping his hat again and turning, Abberline had a sudden thought, "Madam, I don't mean to trouble you further, but if you would be so kind," reaching into his vest pocket, he retrieved his card. "Would you see to it Mr. Holmes gets this card upon his return?", on the back of the card he hurriedly wrote, 'Pls contact upon receipt – Whitechapel murders – Home Secretary requests,' "...it's of the utmost urgency."

Reading the front of his card, Mrs. Hudson's demeanor softened, "Oh dear, Inspector, I do believe I owe you an apology. I'm afraid I mistook you for a common peddler or a banker," looking at his dampened pant leg. "I'm afraid you don't have the look of an Inspector, if you'll pardon my saying," she offered, then immediately felt embarrassed about it.

Shaking his foot, "No apologies necessary, madam, I regret I'm not at my best just now," softening himself, somewhat. "There's a beastly pothole in the street which I had the unfortunate luck to step into," he explained, then asked again, "could you see that Mr. Holmes gets that card? It really is quite urgent."

Chuckling Mrs. Hudson allowed, "Doctor Watson stepped in that very hole less than a week ago. I'll see to it Mr. Holmes gets your card the moment he returns. No trouble at all, sir," then, after hesitating pensively, added, "and again, I apologize if I appeared out of sorts."

"That's quite all right, madam, no harm done, and thank you again, madam," tipping his hat once more, he turned, stepping into the street. This time he carefully avoided the pothole as he hailed a cab to take him back to Whitehall.

Chapter 11

MYSTERY

As they were about to board the train from Dover to London, Watson purchased the most recent copy of *The Times*, while Holmes was replenishing his supply of strong shag from a local tobacconist.

Settling down in their compartment for the long ride back to London, Watson offered Holmes his section of the paper.

"Thank you, Watson," said Holmes as he stretched out to read.

"I say, Holmes, all things considered, this has been a most interesting and delightful trip, eh what?"

"Yes, old friend, but there's no place like England. I was thinking to myself as those shining white cliffs came into view as we were crossing the channel that there's no more welcome sight in all the world."

"True enough," Watson agreed, then motioning toward the painting Holmes had wrapped in brown paper and stowed carefully with their luggage, he continued, "but at least you have that portrait for your trouble."

"Yes, young Vincent was very generous in painting it for me, though I'm not sure it's an entirely accurate rendition."

"Actually, I thought it was quite good in that regard," Watson disagreed, "but it's his use of color I object to. It seems quite primitive to me...I doubt it will ever catch on."

"We shall see, Watson," Holmes replied as his attention became diverted by the newspaper.

A long period of silence followed until it was broken by Watson, who muttered, "Appears to be some dreadful goings on in Whitechapel of late."

"Hmm..? What's that old boy?" Holmes asked distractedly.

"Whitechapel...apparently there's been a series of

murders there."

"Mmm…I don't doubt. London's east end, I'm afraid, is no stranger to violence."

"Says here Scotland Yard has reason to believe these may be related."

"Related? Related to what?"

"Related…er…to each other, I would think."

"Of course. Sorry, old boy, I was only half listening," Holmes apologized, "I was reading about a young Italian immigrant who will be soon tried for murder—unjustly if you believe the detail in this account in the 'agonies'."

"Aren't the accused always such, unjustly?"

"Quite so, Watson," Holmes answered amusedly, "but still, this might be an interesting case to look into once we're back in London."

"Not interested in the Whitechapel murders then?"

"I'm sure Scotland Yard isn't interested in my meddling in their affairs. Besides, merely because the murders occur in a similar manner and place within a short span of time isn't enough to prove they are related. Correlation, as I've mentioned to you many times my dear Watson, does not necessarily indicate causation."

"Yes, I see, still…"

"I'd be much more likely to investigate this poor boy's case," said Holmes pointing at the newspaper with his unlit pipe. "A young Italian chap comes to our shores seeking work and before he even arrives, he's locked up in chains to await the gallows."

"I say, who was the victim?"

"The article does not say," lighting his pipe. "What it does say," blue smoke swirling round his head, "is that the boy is wrongly accused and his friend, who placed the article, is hoping someone can come to his aid." Holmes paused to see if Watson's interest was raised. Satisfied that it had been, he continued, "The article reads:

'Seeking assistance to friend unjustly accused of murder Newgate Prison. While journeying to England

102

from Italy in search of a journeyman printer position, Carlino Gaetano stands most wrongly accused of murder by the parents of the deceased. No witness accuses, only circumstance. Seeking legal and/or financial aid to save my friend.'

"Murder at sea, then," observed Watson. "No witnesses. Hard case to prove, wouldn't you say?"

"Harder to disprove I'd say, old boy," drawing deeply on his pipe. "Think of it, Watson. A ship sails into one of our English ports on which a murder has occurred, or rather, there has been a disappearance, for we must take nothing for granted."

"Quite so, I was readying to point that out myself."

"I was sure you would, old boy. Nevertheless, the maritime authorities have the well-placed parents insisting it is a murder and two young, penniless immigrants saying it isn't so. Who would you believe, Watson?"

"Well, I'd have to…wait a minute, Holmes, how do you know the parents are well placed?"

"Elementary. If they were on an equal or lower station with the accused, there would be an inquiry rather than a trial. Their superior station gives their version of events greater weight with the authorities. Hence, disproving the charge, in this particular case, is the more difficult task rather than proving, do you see?"

"Why yes, but I say when you explain it in those terms, it appears somewhat unfair."

"Unfair, indeed, Watson, which is precisely why I've decided to have a chat with this young man and see for myself."

#

September 17, 1888

Watson and Holmes were seated at a plain wooden table with three chairs when Carlino was led into the interrogation room the following morning, his wrists in manacles. The only light in the room came from the one small window, reinforced with iron bars, high in the center of the wall opposite the door. The gas lamps on the adjacent walls were extinguished.

103

Holmes motioned for Carlino to sit as he dismissed the attending guard, "You may wait outside."

"I've orders to guard the prisoner."

"Where do you suspect he can go," Holmes motioned to the barred window, "wait outside, I'll take full responsibility." Reluctantly, the guard stepped outside of the questioning room, closing the door behind him.

"Would you like a cigarette?" Holmes asked Carlino, reaching inside the breast pocket of his jacket and removing a small silver cigarette case.

"No, thank you," Carlino looked at him suspiciously.

"Very well," said Holmes glancing quickly at Dr. Watson, "this is Dr. Watson, and I am Sherlock Holmes. We are here to try and help you."

"Help me? Why…are you a barrister?"

Holmes and Watson looked at each other and shared a smile, "No, I'm not a barrister. I'm what you might call a 'consulting detective'. I take on cases in which my clients can find no other recourse to aid them."

"You will take my case?" Carlino asked hopefully.

"Not just yet," Holmes said quietly, noting the look of desperation in Carlino's eyes. "You apparently have a friend in the city who has advertised on your behalf in the paper," pointing to the article in the agonies column, "do you know who may have placed this?"

"Vittorio," he said as he read the ad, "we traveled here together. We were going to work for a newspaper."

"Vittorio," Holmes repeated, glancing back to Watson to see if he was taking notes, "does he have a last name?"

"Yes, Vittorio Martini."

"And where might we find Vittorio."

"I'm afraid I do not know. He visits me almost every evening, but I am unfamiliar with the city and do not know where it is he is staying."

"I see," reaching into his vest pocket, "when he comes this evening, give him this" handing Carlino a card with his Baker Street address. "Tell him to come round and see us at this address." As Carlino looked at the card, putting it into his pocket, Holmes continued, "Now, tell us what you know of the murder of Gianetta Rossini."

At the mention of her name, Carlino's eyes began to tear, "Murder? Who could wish to murder my Gianetta?" Carlino asked, looking from Holmes to Watson, "No...I refuse to believe it. It must have been a terrible accident."

"Come, Carlino, you are accused of her murder. Your case comes before the Magistrate of the High Court of the Admiralty in less than a fortnight. There is no time; you must tell us what you know. For example, how did you come to have her comb in your trunk?" Holmes probed.

"The comb..." stumbling for the words, "they took it from me. It is all I have of my Gianetta's," Carlino again began to weep.

"Come, man, pull yourself together," said Watson.

"Yes, if we are to help you, you cannot keep going to pieces," Holmes said as he again offered Carlino a cigarette. This time Carlino accepted. He lighted the cigarette from the match in Holmes's hand and after a short coughing jag began to speak, "I fell in love with her the moment I saw her from the dock in Genoa. We were both boarding the ship—her with her parents and me with Vittorio. I could see right away that her parents did not like the looks of me or Vito.

"Gianetta and I began to steal moments together from that first day. She told me she was going to England to marry a man she barely knew and did not love, that her parents had arranged it. The man was quite wealthy, she said, and her parents own fortunes had recently taken a turn for the worse."

"I understand," interrupted Holmes, "You and Gianetta fell in love, but we must know how you came to have her comb if we are to assist you in any way."

"Yes, the comb," Carlino inhaled deeply on the cigarette, this time coughing only slightly. "The night before...before Gianetta disappeared, we met on deck, after her parents were asleep. We had been doing so every night of the voyage from the first night, but this night we pledged our love. I gave Gianetta a ring with my family's crest, and she gave me one of her combs to keep until we could be together forever."

"Ah...I see," said Holmes, apparently satisfied with the answer, "and do you have the ring?"

"No, it is with Gianetta."

"Yes, of course. Can you describe it...size, color, the crest...?"

"It is fine gold with a ruby stone set into it onto which is etched the crest of my family—a shield with three stars, on top of which sits an eagle with spreaded wings."

Watson repeated the description as he wrote it down, word for word, "Fine gold...ruby stone...crest...three stars...eagle".

"Now, Carlino, what happened on the night Gianetta disappeared?" Holmes asked as he leaned closer.

"That night, as I was leaving our room, Vito stopped me. He told me I should be careful, he had heard Gianetta's father tell her mother that if he caught Gianetta and I together, he would toss me over the side of the ship, that I was not going to disturb their plans for Gianetta's marriage."

"And what did you reply?"

"I told Vito not to worry, that Gianetta and I were in love, but we knew we would have to be careful. Gianetta had told me her parents were both very heavy sleepers and there was nothing to worry about once they were asleep. I promised to be careful."

"And you did not find Gianetta that night?"

"No, Signore. When I went on deck, I was just a few minutes later than normal and Gianetta was nowhere in sight. I searched the ship and finally decided that perhaps her parents had discovered her leaving their room and prevented her from doing so. After a while, I gave up my search and went to bed."

"Where was Vittorio when you returned to your room."

"He was asleep, Signore, why?"

"Never mind," Holmes said dismissively, "now, tell us about the other passengers, and the crew. If you didn't murder Gianetta, we must determine who might have done so."

106

"No one could have a reason to murder an angel such as my Gianetta," said Carlino earnestly.

"Perhaps, but please describe everyone onboard, and we shall see."

"Aside from myself and Vito, there was Signore and Signora Rossini, Signore Magdalena, he is a retired banker and Signora Anna, his wife. I do not know the name of the other passenger. He stayed in the Captain's cabin and did not take his meals with the rest of us, but instead dined alone in his cabin. In fact, during the entire passage, I only saw him once, briefly, when Gianetta and I met on deck early in the voyage."

"Did any of the other guests know this man?"

"No, I do not believe so. The ship's captain told us that he was mourning his father's death and did not wish to be disturbed."

"And you say he stayed with the Captain in his cabin?" asked Watson, as he continued writing.

"No, Signore, he did not stay with the Captain. The Captain shared the First Mate's quarters."

"Interesting…" said Holmes as he tapped his cheek with his unlighted pipe, "and you say you do not know his name?" Not waiting for an answer, Holmes continued, "No matter. We shall have a look at the ship's manifest."

"Then you believe me, Signore Holmes? You will help me?"

"Let us say that thus far I do not *disbelieve* you, Carlino, and if what you've told us bears fruit, I will do what I can to help you. Take heart, you are a long way from the gallows yet," he said rising. "Come, Watson, we've work to do."

#

September 18, 1888

The following morning, as Watson came into the sitting room Holmes was already dressed and stood bent over his desk. "Interesting…" Holmes noted as he studied the document under the glaring light of his desk lamp.

"What is it?" asked Watson, who was just pouring

himself a cup of strong tea.

"Ahh…good morning, old boy, I was beginning to think you would sleep the day away."

"Sleep the day away? It can't be later than 9 o'clock.

"Precisely, and already I've set out my net for the *Lira's* elusive passenger in addition to acquiring what might prove to be a vital piece of evidence in our young Italian's case."

"Is that what you have there?"

"Yes, the ship's manifest."

"And what, may I ask, is so vital?"

"It appears the manifest has been altered. Look here." As he offered the glass to Watson, he pointed to the passenger list on the manifest, "Clearly, the number has been changed. What was originally a numeral 7 has been changed to the word 'six' crammed into the space. See how the spacing between the rest of the words is uniform and here it runs together. It lists only six passengers on the *Lira*, not seven as our young Carlino has told us."

"What about the names, and other information, that would be difficult to alter, would it not?"

"Yes, but fortunately for the person falsifying the record, the official stamp is affixed only on the top sheet of the manifest, and the names begin on the top sheet, but continue on the second sheet. Thus it would be a small matter to rewrite the rest of the document omitting the name of the mystery guest."

"Hmm…I see. So, what do you make of it, Holmes?"

"I feel it's too early to know for sure why, but if I were to conjecture, I would say the guest in the Captain's cabin did not wish to be involved in any official inquiries. The fact that none of the other passengers mentioned him to the authorities would indicate he was above suspicion."

"Yes, I suppose that would explain it, if indeed there actually was a guest in the Captain's cabin. What makes you so sure there was?"

"Precisely because a lie would be too easily seen through. Why would Carlino make up a fictitious stranger when his assertion could so easily be proven false? No, it would be much easier to hide a passenger from the authorities than from the other passengers."

"But why wouldn't the authorities question this once Carlino had mentioned him. Wouldn't it come to light that the manifest was falsified during the investigation?"

"Ah, you are now assuming Carlino would think to mention him, but I'm afraid he wouldn't have told us, had we not ask for an accounting of the passengers, so why would he bother the authorities with what they and he assumed to be superfluous data. The authorities had the manifest, which officially lists all passengers, so there would be no need for them to elicit that information. All onboard, with the exception of Vittorio, believed Carlino to be guilty and so no mention was made of this mystery passenger."

"I see, of course you're right. But I doubt it's enough to get the charges dismissed.

"Undoubtedly it is not; however, it may be enough to gain us some time to investigate the whereabouts of the absent passenger, if I can get the Chief Magistrate to give Carlino's case a postponement."

"Then you've decided to take up the case?"

"I have. I believe young Carlino has told us the truth and the manifest appears to corroborate that belief."

"Still, there's no guarantee you can locate the missing passenger, if he exists. Even if you do, he may have nothing to do with the murder. In that case, perhaps your manifest is of no consequence, after all."

"Perhaps, old boy, but quite often it's the overlooked clue that proves most conclusive, as well as, in this case, most elusive."

"Quite so."

Just then, their page knocked on the door. Holmes called out, "Yes, William, what is it?"

"Mr. Holmes, sir," came the reply through the door, "a gentleman is her to see you. He says his name is Vittorio." The page added in a loud whisper, "He's foreign, sir."

Smiling at Watson, "Show him in, William."

109

As the door opened, Holmes rose from his desk and crossed the sitting room, "Ah, Mr. Martini, please come in."

A young, auburn-haired man, holding his worn, black felt, hat in front of him, hesitantly entered the sitting room. "You are Signore Sherlock Holmes?" he asked haltingly.

"Yes, and this is my associate, Dr. Watson. Please have a seat, won't you?" Holmes invited him as he directed Vittorio to the chair by the fire. "So it was you who placed the advertisement in the agonies, was it not?"

"Yes. Carlino is innocent. You must help him."

"And we intend to, Mr. Martini, but I wanted to ask you a few questions, if you don't mind."

"Of course I do not mind, Signore, if it will help Carlino."

"You and Carlino are very close, aren't you Mr. Martini?"

"He is like a brother to me."

"Did you approve of Carlino's relationship with Gianetta Rossini?"

"Approve? I do not understand. Carlino loved Gianetta. What was there to approve?"

"But nonetheless, you tried to keep him from seeing her on the night she went missing, did you not?

"No, Signore, I only asked that he be careful. I had overheard the parents of Gianetta speaking about Carlino. I was afraid they would make trouble for him. They did not like Carlino or me."

"What time did Carlino return that evening?"

"I am not sure, Signore, I must have been asleep when he returned." He looked down at the hat on his lap as he asked, plaintively, "Do you think you can help him, Signore?"

"I have every reason to believe I may be of some help, Mr. Martini."

"Your friend couldn't be in better hands, Mr. Martini, I assure you," Watson added.

"One last thing, Mr. Martini...I understand there was a passenger staying in the Captain's cabin. Do you recall his

110

name?"

"That one? No, Signore, I do not. He did not speak to the other passengers. The First Mate told us he wished to remain anonymous. He was in mourning and we never saw him about the ship."

"I see…" Holmes said, a little disappointedly, "well, you've been very helpful," he continued as he stood up, signaling to Vittorio that the interview was over. "I hope to see you again very soon. Perhaps we will have some good news."

"Thank you, Signore Holmes, Signore Doctor," he said as he rose, bowing slightly to Holmes and Watson.

After Vittorio left, Holmes turned to Watson, "Their stories appear to agree in every detail."

"Yes, indeed, down to neither of them being able to tell you anything helpful about the mystery passenger."

"Which," said Holmes with a wry smile, "may in itself tell me something useful." Striking a match on the underside of the fireplace mantle and lighting his pipe, Holmes returned to his desk and again examined the manifest from the ill-fated ship, *Lira*.

Chapter 12

PLANS

"Baron," cried Sir Charles as he arose from his chair near the fire in the study to greet Barlucci, "to what do I owe this honor?" Focusing on the baron with eyes somewhat affected by the cognac he'd been sipping Sir Charles exclaimed, "My God, old boy, are you quite all right? You look ghastly!"

Looking a bit puzzled, "Did not Signorina Abigail tell you? I am taking her to a concert this evening at Covent Garden. The orchestra is performing an entire evening of works by Vivaldi," trying to ignore Sir Charles second question.

"Vivaldi, you say, ah, yes…yes, she did mention it," noting the relief show on the baron's face. Then he added with a renewed look of concern, "But are you sure you are all right?"

"Quite so, Sir Charles. I suppose perhaps I've been working a bit too hard," he answered as he guided Sir Charles to bring the observation back on himself. "Did you forget Abigail and I were going out this evening?"

"Yes, I'm afraid I quite forgot," he confessed with a mirthless chuckle. "You must forgive me, old boy, I try not to bring my work home with me, but we've had a recent spate of nasty business in the East End and I'm afraid we have no clue, as yet, on how to solve it."

"I'm very sorry to hear that, Sir Charles."

"Not to worry, old boy, not to worry, we'll get the bugger." shaking the baron's hand, "Abby will be down in a minute I'm sure, in the meantime," he said drawing closer, "we'll have a glass of brandy, eh?" he said as he closed the door to the study.

As Sir Charles poured the brandy, the baron began to reach out with his mind, attempting to probe Sir Charles, "I understand from what you said at dinner last week that Signorina Abigail is planning a journey to America, Sir Charles."

112

"Charley, you're to call me Charley, remember?"

"Charley."

"Yes, she is…" Sir Charles's face slowly darkened as the baron's mind found the opening it sought. "I suppose you know Abby is going to visit her mother's people in America."

"Yes, both you and she have mentioned it to me," answered the baron as he concentrated on guiding Sir Charles thoughts.

"What? Yes, of course," clearing his throat, "well, I'm not a stickler for protocol and that sort of thing, you understand," he lied, "but I am not at all sure Abby will be safe traveling alone. My wife was going to accompany her, but as you know, her health has not been good of late and I'm afraid she will be unable to do so."

"I'm sorry to hear Lady Margaretta is not feeling well."

"Oh, I'm quite sure she'll come around, but just now is not the time for her to be traipsing off to America."

"I quite agree," the baron smiled to himself. Sir Charles was quite easily manipulated once entry to his thoughts were gained, much like his father before him, the baron thought.

"Which brings me to a question."

"Yes, Sir Char…," the baron corrected himself, "I mean Charley?"

"Well then, I believe you said you too are planning a peregrination to America and that in fact your destination is the same as Abby's, New York."

"Yes, yes that is correct, I've spoken of it to Signorina Abigail," silently thinking, 'and planted the idea that she remind you of the fact'.

"Yes, quite. Well, it occurred to me, insomuch as you are planning a sojourn of your own, and being so close to our family, as it were—as I've said many times, I think of you as family. Ahem, I was wondering, hoping really, that you might take it upon yourself to escort my niece on her journey. She would be so disappointed to have to postpone it until her aunt can accompany her."

"Sir Charles, I…"

Holding up his hand to cut off the baron's response, "Tut, tut, you needn't say more, I realize it is an imposition and I apologize for attempting to play upon our friendship. I should never have…"

"But Sir Charles, Charley," the baron laughed charmingly, "I would be delighted to act as Signorina Abigail's escort to America. It would be no imposition at all, but I have not yet completed my affairs in London and have not confirmed my travel plans."

"Certainly. That's understood, Baron, and I assure you Abby's plans can be made to accommodate your own. You have no idea how much it relieves me to know she will be under your care. Since my brother and his wife passed, Abby has been like a daughter to me, to us. I'm afraid Maggie and I fret a bit too much over her well being."

"Not at all, it's most admirable of you to care for your brother's daughter as your own. You are to be commended."

Clapping the baron on the shoulder, "You cannot imagine what a relief this brings me, my dear boy."

Just at that moment, Abigail entered the room, "Uncle have you…oh," smiling as she saw the baron, "I was just going to ask if Uncle had heard from you. I was afraid you'd had to cancel our evening at the concert."

"I wouldn't dream of it, Signorina," the baron said rising. "Your uncle and I were just having a chat."

"How nice, but if we don't hurry, we'll miss the opening number," pausing and looking closely at the baron, she added, "are you sure you're feeling well? You look tired."

"Yes," agreed Sir Charles, "that's exactly what I told him. You do appear a bit peaked, old boy."

"Nonsense," the baron replied, "I'm sure it's nothing more than a bit of fatigue. I've been overworking a bit, perhaps, but I'm fine…not to worry," the baron prevaricated, knowing the abstinence he'd engaged in for the sakes of Dr. Tremaine and the lovely Abigail was beginning to tell in his countenance. Soon it would tell in other ways, if he did not soon slake the thirst growing within him.

114

"I'm glad to hear it, sir. Now, if you aren't going to be late, you two had better run along. Enjoy yourselves."

Offering Abigail his arm, "Signorina Abigail," the two of them left the study and proceeded into the baron's brougham, which Garrett was tending in the front of the house.

As he helped her into the coach, the baron squeezed Abigail's gloved hand gently, eliciting a smile as she found her seat. Climbing in beside her, he called up to Garrett, "Covent Garden."

Sitting side by side in the privacy of the coach, Abigail shifted her weight toward the baron, "I'm so excited. An entire evening of Vivaldi…" shyly smiling, her eyes rising to meet his, "…with you. You are sure you are all right."

Taking her hand in his, he squeezed it briefly and gently, "I'm fine, my dear, and I feel the same, Abby," smiling back at her, "I'm looking forward to an evening with you…", then he added smiling, "and Vivaldi."

As they rode along, Abigail noticed a slight smirk on the baron's face. Looking at him smiling, she asked, "What is it? You look as though you were the proverbial cat who's swallowed the canary."

"I have some news, Abby, that I hope you will find pleasing."

"News? What is it, Tonietto?" she asked, flushing slightly as she said his name.

"Your uncle and I were just conversing about your upcoming voyage to America…"

"Yes?" she asked expectantly.

"…and the coincidence of my own plans to journey to New York. He has asked me to act as your escort and to check in on you occasionally after we arrive in New York."

"Truly?" beaming her brightest smile.

"Yes, truly. Then you approve?"

"Oh Tonietto, I prayed it might be so, but I never dreamed Uncle would…"

"Your uncle is a wise man who has only your best interest and safety at heart, Abby."

"Oh, I know, he is a dear man. I must give him a kiss when I return home."

"A dear man, and a lucky man, too," teasing her.

"Why, Baron," she said in a most proper tone, "whatever do you mean? You aren't suggesting that I might give you a kiss too? I'm not sure that would be proper."

"I'm sure it would not," he said, his eyes burning into hers, resisting the temptation to *influence* her.

Tenderly, she leaned over and their lips met. She closed her eyes for just a second, then withdrew, with a slight giggle, "Why, Baron, the weather doesn't appear to agree with you. Your lips are a bit chilly."

"Ah, I'm told I have a slight circulatory problem," he explained. "I hope it doesn't displease you too much."

Fearing she may have wounded his feelings, she caressed his cheek with her hand, "Oh no, Tonietto, no, no," and she leaned close to kiss him again.

Chapter 13

COTERIE

As he gazed out at the long shadows of a late afternoon on Baker Street, his pipe clinched between his teeth, Holmes remarked, "Interesting, isn't it, Watson? Eight passengers on that ship, two being our clients, and we can find no who is able to assist us in young Carlino's defense. One is deceased and two more related to the deceased, leaving three supposedly objective observers: an elderly couple and a mysteriously anonymous passenger. The victim's parents, quite naturally, won't even speak with me and the old banker and his wife were quite unsuitable as witnesses. They didn't remember our mysterious passenger and they were a bit confused even about the uncontested facts in the case."

"Yes, if one were a suspicious sort, one would think the entire passenger list had been arranged to allow the murder to go unsolved, eh what?"

"Not unsolved, old boy, but resolved in an errant manner, leaving the true murderer to escape without suspicion. I detect an intellect at work here, which is far beyond a common murderer. A seemingly senseless murder, but one orchestrated in such a manner as to afford the perpetrator complete anonymity. It's as if he never existed at all and were it not for the altered manifest, I would have my doubts."

"I see what you mean, old boy," Watson replied, "very strange indeed...but quite fortunate for young Gaetano."

"Oh?" Holmes injected quizzically, "How so?"

"Well, old boy, had you not happened upon the case in the papers and not seen fit to speak with the boy, no one would be the least interested in finding this mysterious passenger at all. Hence it is fortunate for the young lad in question that you happen to read the agonies."

"You have a point, old friend, but consider..."

117

A knock on the door announcing supper interrupted the two, and Mrs. Hudson brought in a large tray of meat and vegetables with two plates, and a pitcher of water, "You two haven't been eating properly in my absence, I see. You look thin and wan."

"Ah, Mrs. Hudson, you spoil us," Holmes joked, rising from his desk. "Watson and I were just saying yesterday we couldn't wait for you to return. We were hoping perhaps you'd make your famous kidney pie."

"Yes, that's true, Mrs. Hudson, we've missed your cooking dreadfully. First, with us off in the south of France, then with you visiting your sister," pausing, "I say, how rude of me, how is your sister, Mrs. Hudson."

"Oh my, she's fine…fine. We had a grand visit, we did. How nice of you to ask. I suppose you and Mr. Holmes have been helping that nice young detective, then, while I've been gone."

"Detective?" asked Holmes, tapping his pipe out in the fireplace. "What detective would that be?"

"Why, the one whose card I laid on your entry table the day before I left on holiday."

Holmes and Watson looked at one another in confusion. "We saw no card, Mrs. Hudson. Are you sure…"

"Of course I'm sure, Doctor, I laid it there myself."

All three moved to the small slant top secretary, which stood by the door of the sitting room. The only thing on it was Watson's hat.

"I'm sure I left it there for you two to find…" said Mrs. Hudson, a bit indignantly.

"I'm sure you did just that, Mrs. Hudson. Here's a clue," picking up Watson's hat. "Dr. Watson is clearly in the habit of removing his hat upon entering our sitting room and flopping it down on the secretary while he removes his overcoat and scarf. I remember him doing exactly that on the evening we returned from France."

"I'm not sure what you're getting at, old boy," said Watson, a bit irritated.

"Bear with me, I'm on the scent. Now, if the card were on the secretary, as you say and I've no doubt it was, when Watson flopped down his hat in the darkened room, the disturbed air on the top of the secretary must have swept up the card and," pausing as he slid the secretary away from the wall, "voila, pushed the card behind the secretary where it was caught between it and the wall," extracting a small card.

"There, just as I said," Mrs. Hudson expressed her satisfaction as she exited, leaving Holmes and Watson to their own devices.

"I dare say any such breeze could have done the same," defended Watson.

Holmes's attention was now on the card as he read aloud, "'Inspector Francis Abberline, Criminal Investigations Division, Scotland Yard,'" then flipping it over, continued, "'Pls contact upon receipt – Whitechapel murders – Home Secretary requests,' hmmm...perhaps I should contact Home Secretary Matthews."

"It appears they would like you to 'meddle' after all, Holmes."

"Yes, but why…"

"I'd say they are feeling a bit of heat from the Home Secretary."

"Yes, yes, Watson, and with Henry Matthews calling the shots, I doubt he will want our involvement known. But why…murder isn't unknown in Whitechapel. A man discovers his wife is unfaithful, loses his temper and grabs the first thing at hand he finds, a stick, a club, a knife, and the poor woman ends up in various stages of ill-repair as a result. No, this must be something quite different."

"The newspapers have been saying these last murders were perpetrated by a single hand or group of hands, some fiend or fiends, who is killing for the pleasure of killing."

"Yes, Watson, I know, but the newspapers are always seeing a fiend behind every unsolved case. And why not? It sells copy."

"But in this case, it would appear, there may be

something to their lurid stories."

"Perhaps so," replied Holmes, walking back toward the table of food, "I shall send a post at once to Henry entreating his desires as to our involvement. At any rate, we must contact the inspector and see what is about." Holmes serious look melted away as he drew closer to the dining table, "But now, I'm going to enjoy the wonderful meal our dear Mrs. Hudson has prepared, sitting down and spreading the napkin on his lap. "Tell me, Watson, did you suspend our delivery of *The Times* while we've been gone? A review of the stories concerning these murders may be invaluable in familiarizing ourselves with the murders."

Watson, settling himself in replied, "Knowing, as I do, your methods, I took the precaution of having our page pack them away in the lumber room. I shall bring down the past few months' worth after supper."

"Splendid, Watson, I could hardly get on without you," obviously pleased with his associate's foresight. "Very well, then, I'll spend the rest of the evening accumulating such facts as are available and tomorrow we shall go to see Inspector Abberline."

"Aren't you forgetting the trial of the young Gaetano boy?"

"You're quite right, Watson. I must be in court to get a delay in the trial in order to investigate; but there is nothing preventing you from meeting with the good inspector, discovering the true nature of these murders in Whitechapel and inviting him back to Baker Street for a more thorough debrief."

"Very well, Holmes old boy, though I'm not sure I like being the second team called in, as it were."

"Nonsense, Watson. You are first rate—as a doctor. But even a matador sends out his picador to soften the bull, does he not?" Holmes said smiling, as he stuck his fork into the brisket before him, and they both began to laugh.

#

September 26, 1888

Two weeks had passed since Abberline left his card at

Baker Street. He'd begun to wonder if he would hear from Sherlock Holmes at all—however it wasn't Holmes who contacted him at his office at Scotland Yard, but Dr. Watson.

Watson found Inspector Abberline examining a knife discovered in the vicinity of Buck's Row when he arrived. "Inspector Abberline, may I presume?" asked Watson as he stood in the doorway to the inspector's office.

"Yes, and you are…?" eyeing the stranger over the top of the knife he'd been examining.

Extending his hand as he stepped into the office he introduced himself, "Dr. John Watson, regimental retired, friend and confidante to Mr. Sherlock Holmes, at your service, sir."

"Dr. Watson," standing and accepting the handshake, "a pleasure, Doctor."

Watson, eyeing the knife now lying on Abberline's desk, asked, "Is this perhaps a weapon used in the murders, Inspector?"

"It was found in Buck's Row the day after the murder there; however, it doesn't match the wounds found on the Nichols woman. The blade is much too short." Placing the knife down on his desk, "I take it you understood the meaning of my note, then, Doctor?"

"Yes, of course, it was rather straightforward, actually, and with all the hubbub in the papers, don't you know. Well, as a result Mr. Holmes thought it better I initiate contact, as he is rather well known by some of your compatriots and he normally tries to maintain some discretion when consulting on sensitive matters such as this. Besides, he has another engagement this morning."

"I appreciate yours and Mr. Holmes's concern, but we have the Secretary's approval."

Inclining his head in a confidential manner, "It is at the Secretary's request we are exercising this degree of discretion. We're quite aware Commissioner Warren is not amenable to the idea of an 'interloper', as I believe the Secretary put it. Can't say I blame him with the amount of criticism the papers are dishing out to him."

"Yes, they've been rather brutal."

"Indeed. As a result, officially speaking, Mr. Holmes and myself shall have no connection to this matter. No record of Mr. Holmes's involvement must be made. I've even promised the Secretary not to chronicle this case, at least not for some time. What with the uproar over this spate of murders in the newspapers, the Home office doesn't want to give them more fodder, as it were."

"Yes, of course…very reasonable."

"Mr. Holmes and I have been following accounts of the case in the newspapers, as much as possible, since we've returned from France. But I'm afraid Mr. Holmes has not been able to formulate a hypothesis based on those sensational stories." Leaning forward, "He's very keen on having all the data before he commits himself, you know. He's asked me to collect any pertinent hard facts – means of death, time of death, who discovered the bodies and when, etc. – as well as to ascertain when you might be available to come by Baker Street to give him any impressions you may have directly."

"I'm at Mr. Holmes's disposal, of course."

"One thing more," Watson said most seriously, "should another victim be discovered, Mr. Holmes is to be contacted immediately." Leaning forward once again, he added, "And no one is to touch the body until Mr. Holmes has had an opportunity to examine it – that is of utmost importance. The victim is the best witness in a murder, you know."

"Yes, of course," Abberline nodded, then drew out his notebook. For the better part of an hour, he relayed the information he'd collected, separating hard fact from the impressions of people interviewed as well as his own theories and impressions. Watson was impressed by the meticulous and orderly detail Inspector Abberline had recorded.

As Dr. Watson rose to leave, the two men shook hands and Abberline walked him to the door, "Tell Mr. Holmes I shall be at Baker Street at 10:00 a.m. on the morrow."

"Very well, Inspector, we shall be expecting you."

#

"I see the Inspector is very punctual," Holmes drily observed from the window, checking his watch as he tamped tobacco into his pipe.

"Doesn't surprise me in the least," Watson replied. "He appeared to me to be very well organized, unlike some at Scotland Yard."

Upon hearing their landlady answering the door, Holmes called down the stairs, "Ask the good Inspector to come right up, Mrs. Hudson, we've been expecting him."

Abberline had removed his coat while ascending the seventeen stairs to Watson and Holmes's apartments. Upon entering, he nodded to Dr. Watson, "Doctor," he said, then, turning, "Mr. Holmes, I presume." Abberline extended his right hand, holding his bowler in his left. He was quite satisfied with Holmes's appearance, which was nearly as he expected in all respects, lean, taller than himself, sharp features with an intelligent brow.

"My dear Inspector Abberline," accepting his hand, "I congratulate you for successfully navigating the potholed street and not soaking your right foot again."

"Mrs. Hudson told you of my first visit, then?" asked Abberline.

"On the contrary, Mrs. Hudson, beyond telling us you left your card, hasn't said a word about your visit."

"Mr. Holmes, I'm acquainted with your reported powers of observation, but there is nothing here for you to observe in order to know that I stepped into a puddle on a previous visit here. Therefore, you must have been told about it."

"Quite to the contrary, Inspector. The fact of your stepping into that pothole on a previous visit is as obvious to one who makes a study of observation as is the toast and Marmite you had for breakfast and are now wearing a bit of on your vest."

Checking his vest, Abberline descried a small brown speck. Unconvinced Holmes could identify it as Marmite from such a small morsel, he scraped if off with his finger and tasted it.

"Well, done, Mr. Holmes, but in this case there was something to observe…" noted Abberline.

"As there usually is if one knows where to look," interrupted Holmes. "I was watching the street out of this window when you alighted from the tram only minutes ago. I watched as you deftly averted a pothole that Dr. Watson, who has lived at this address and is well acquainted with the street, has stepped into no fewer than three times this past month. I deduced that since you'd been here before, you must have had reason to remember that particular pothole."

"Yes, but that…"

"Further," Holmes continued, "the sole of your right shoe, even though you have apparently applied polish to the upper, shows signs of having been soaked in water. Note how the layers of leather have begun to separate."

Looking down at his shoe, as he turned his foot to the side, Abberline had to admit it did show signs of water damage. "I'm impressed, Mr. Holmes, your powers of observation and deduction would appear to be well founded."

"Thank you, Inspector, I pride myself on taking notice of the important details others ignore."

Quite pleased with the effect his little show had on the inspector, Holmes took his arm. "Please, come, sit down," guiding him to a chair, which he had situated directly across from his own velvet-cushioned arm chair with a small coffee table between. "I've discussed the case with Dr. Watson and am most eager to hear your impressions."

For the next hour and a half Inspector Abberline went over in great detail both murders, in a nearly identical manner as he had with Watson. The difference in timing is accounted for by the numerous questions interjected by Holmes. Each time Holmes interrupted Abberline's narrative with a query, it caused the inspector to pause. In many cases he was able to recall some small detail he had not written in his notes.

By the end of his discussion of the case, Inspector

Abberline was thoroughly impressed by Holmes and his ability to grasp each fact and wring out of it the last drop of germaneness.

Holmes, hands together, fingertips on his chin, looked at Abberline, "I wonder, Inspector, if you've omitted any matters of fact in your retelling of your observations?"

"Why no, Mr. Holmes, that is everything."

"Come now, Inspector, if we are to be of use in this case, we must be in possession of all the facts. It is an axiom of mine that to theorize before you have all the data is generally a lethal mistake in investigations of this sort."

"What's that, Holmes," interrupted Watson, "it's exactly as he related the facts to me yesterday. What is it you're getting at, old boy?"

Abberline objected, "I'm afraid I don't know what you mean."

"Don't you," insisted Holmes, "you've made no mention, in either accounting apparently, of the puncture wounds."

Surprised by the question, Abberline stammered, "Puncture wounds?"

"Come now, Inspector, did you think I wouldn't notice the notations you'd made on several pages of your notes, along with the diagrams?" Holmes fixed Abberline in his gaze, "I've trained myself to read upside down. It's actually quite easy with a little practice. It's second nature to me and comes in quite handy."

"I'm sorry, I don't see how they…the puncture wounds, could possibly…" Abberline's voice trailed off.

"I doubt you'd have been so meticulous in your notations had you not believed they had some relevance." Leaning forward Holmes entreated, "I implore you, Inspector, you must take us into your confidence, tell me your thoughts."

"Mr. Holmes, you'll only think me foolish," Abberline said, reluctantly, "or worse."

"Not at all, Inspector, but if we are to unravel the mystery and stop these fiendish murders, we must have all of the data."

"Well, sir, let me start by explaining that my grandmother on my mother's side was from the old country in the Carpathian Mountains of east Europe."

Holmes glanced at Watson for an instant, to ensure the doctor was taking notes, "Please continue."

"When I was a child, my grandmother would tell us the most chilling stories of when she was a young girl and her village in Romania was terrorized by a vampire."

"Surely, sir," Watson interrupted, "you don't mean to tell us you believe…"

"Nonsense, Watson," Holmes interjected, "I'm sure the inspector is merely pointing out some similarity, isn't that right, Inspector."

"Oh, I never believed the stories, sir, though she swore them to be true. But she said the vampire had been killed by her own father, who had found it latched onto my grandmother, draining the blood from her neck."

"Poppycock!" Watson said under his breath, continuing his note taking.

"Quite so, sir, at least I've always thought so," Abberline responded having turned toward Watson. "My grandmother, as long as I can remember, wore a scarf about her neck. On one occasion, being somewhat vexed that we didn't believe her, she showed us the marks on her throat she claimed were left from her encounter with the vampire, two round scars spaced about two inches apart."

Holmes, having watched the inspector intently as he related his story, asked, "And what has changed your mind, Inspector?"

"Mr. Holmes, I know it cannot be possible that a vampire has done these terrible deeds, but…" Abberline's voice trailed off again.

"But what, Inspector?" Holmes, suddenly piquish, scolded him, "Your obfuscation is growing quite tiresome!"

"The marks," Abberline looked from Watson to Holmes, "both Mary Ann Nichols and Annie Chapman had identical

126

marks on their throats."

"That may be, but their throats were cut," reminded Holmes.

Abberline looked directly into Holmes eyes and firmly replied, "And the slashes on both victims were driven through the puncture wounds."

"Are you suggesting," asked Holmes, "the slashes to the throat were meant to obscure the puncture wounds?"

"I'm not sure, sir, but it is a possibility, is it not?"

"What about the abdominal mutilations?" interrupted Watson, "surely the work of a madman!"

"If I follow the inspector's train of thought," ventured Holmes, "the abdominal mutilations are merely window dressing meant to further divert attention. Isn't that so, Inspector?"

"Again, sir, a possibility."

"Intriguing." Holmes sat back, eyes darkening into an introspective trance-like state of concentration all too familiar to Dr. Watson.

"May I get you some tea, Inspector?" Watson offered, as he arose and poured himself a cup. "It's best not to disturb Mr. Holmes when he's like this. He'll come out of it eventually. Often as not he emerges with the key to solving the case."

Watson and Abberline retired to the other side of the sitting room while Holmes, a swirl of blue smoke growing round his head, mulled over the facts of the case and the suppositions before him, turning them over in his mind to examine them from every possible angle.

As they sipped tea, Abberline and Watson chatted like long lost friends reacquainting themselves. They discussed Watson's time in Afghanistan, including the wound to his leg and his long recovery as well as his first meeting with Holmes. They also discussed Abberline's career back to the time he walked a beat in Whitechapel.

At last Holmes stood up, walked to the fireplace silently, refilled his pipe and after lighting it, a fresh cloud of thick blue smoke circling his head, turned to Watson and Abberline.

"These facts are irrefutable. From what you've told me,

Inspector, both women died where they were found, not transported from elsewhere. That is the conclusion of your investigation and all the facts you've related support it, with the exception of the small amount of blood at the scene in both instances. This is doubly strange in that from the attending physicians' reports both women appeared to have been drained of most of their blood."

Holmes began to pace in front of the fire. "Also, we know both women had their throats cut in a manner so vicious as to nearly decapitate them, and yet the blood at the scenes were of a considerably lesser amount than would be expected of such wounds. These circumstances, as thus far related, are very similar to a series of murders occurring this past summer in Paris." Turning to face Dr. Watson, Holmes asked, "You remember Inspector Renard's description, don't you, Watson?"

"Indeed I do, Holmes, but those women were pulled from the Seine and there was no mention of puncture wounds."

"Yes, that is where the similarities diverge," agreed Holmes. "That and the fact those women did not suffer the further indignities evident in this case." Continuing, "As noted, in addition to the slash wounds on the throat, there were also puncture wounds of uniform size and distance from one another. Further, on both women the slash in the throat cut through the puncture wounds, as if the slash began at, or very near, the punctures." The words were coming more quickly, "Also, both victims were mutilated by having their abdomens cut open and in the case of Annie Chapman, there was the further degradation of having her intestines pulled from her body and draped over her shoulder with at least two organs removed from the scene."

Holmes paused, looking from Abberline to Watson then back to Abberline, and in a calm voice asked, much as a teacher would prompt a student, "What does this tell us?" But before they had a chance to respond, Holmes continued, "Your instincts are very keen, Inspector. I believe the slashes to be a red herring, camouflage if you will, as are the mutilations."

"Holmes! You can't mean you believe this vampire business?" Watson objected.

"One does not necessarily lead to the other, my dear Watson. On the contrary, I am a man of science. These silly superstitions are no more than old wives' tales told to frighten small children." Seeing the effect his words had on Abberline, as the inspector's face slackened and he looked downward, "Tut, tut, Inspector. You aren't far off the mark, I believe, but you've allowed your childhood memories of a beloved grandmother to prevent you from reaching the logical deduction that our quarry is a madman who only thinks he's a vampire."

Unconvinced, Watson interjects, "You're assuming the puncture wounds are, in themselves, significant. There's the possibility, don't you think, that they are mere coincidence?"

"Coincidence, my dear Watson, is the residue of design."

"Mr. Holmes," ventured Abberline, "if that's the case, what's our next move? How do we find him?"

"Elementary, Inspector," Holmes said, looking from Watson directly into Inspector Abberline's eyes with a wry smile, "we become vampire hunters."

Chapter 14

FIRST WATCH

September 28, 1888

The Metropolitan Police force, in order to maintain the peace and be available should the occasion arise when they are needed, is organized into neighborhood police stations, one for each of the division in the metropolitan area, resulting in twenty-one neighborhood stations and an additional six dockyard stations. In addition, there are numerable patrols throughout the districts as well as Fixed Points at various conspicuous locations and intersections, each of which is manned by a constable between the hours of 9 a.m. and 1 a.m.

Due to the unusual amount of attention drawn to Whitechapel by the series of murders, Inspector Abberline had extended the hours for manning the forty-three Fixed Points in Divisions 'H' and 'J' from sixteen to twenty-four hours per day. In addition, Holmes had requested a supplement to those assigned as Fixed Point duty to allow the constables to rotate from one fixed point to the next creating, as it were, a second or auxiliary patrol.

Inspector Abberline was briefing the reasons for this increased manning to the chief inspectors, sergeants and constables in Divisions H & J, which cover most of the Whitechapel district, as Holmes and Watson arrived to join him on their first night of "vampire" hunting.

Although there was no guarantee the Whitechapel murderer, or 'Jack the Ripper', as the newspapers were now calling him, would strike again in these districts, Holmes believed past behavior to be the best indicator of future events. He explained the criminal mind, and indeed any mind, will almost invariably return to a pattern that has proven successful, terming it "causal pattern fixation". He asserted it was a characteristic of human nature.

After concluding his briefing, Abberline introduced

Holmes and Watson to the constables, directing them to follow Holmes instructions to the letter.

"Now then, gentlemen," Holmes directed, "as unpredictability is of the essence, I want you to vary your nightly routines, taking different routes as you cover your beats." While he spoke, he surveyed the constables, looking at each one directly. He concluded his remarks imploring them "And remember, keep your whistles always at the ready. If you come upon anything suspicious or, God forbid, a body, lay upon the whistle as though the devil himself were after you until assistance arrives."

After the briefing, Holmes took Watson and Abberline aside. "Gentlemen, we shall roam the various districts in shifts throughout the night. I believe we should use Aldgate East station as our starting point and meeting place. If there are no objections, I shall take the first shift this evening, from 9 p.m. to midnight. I'm anxious to get the lay of the land by night. Inspector, if you don't mind, I'd like you to stand from midnight to 3 a.m. That leaves Watson to take the 3 a.m. to 6 a.m. watch to finish up the evening's festivities."

"I don't mind at all, Mr. Holmes," agreed Abberline.

"Well, then, if I'm to be up at 3 a.m., I think I shall be getting back to Baker Street for a nap," grumbled Watson, as he put on his overcoat and shuffled out the door.

"I'm afraid the good doctor may be feeling sorely used, Inspector. He's not terribly fond of late hours," Holmes remarked amusedly.

"Perhaps I can take the late watch tomorrow, then," offered Abberline.

"Actually, Inspector, I would prefer you take the first watch tomorrow, provided we come up empty-handed tonight. My good friend, Dr. Watson can take the midwatch and I shall stand from 3 a.m. to 6 a.m.. The watch can continue to rotate thusly and none shall be too terribly inconvenienced."

"As you wish, Mr. Holmes, I couldn't have set it up better myself" Abberline agreed, "and now I think I shall follow Dr. Watson's lead and get some rest."

"Very well, Inspector, I shall see you at midnight."

Holmes buttoned up his overcoat and fastened his scarf around his neck, following Inspector Abberline out into the cold autumn evening.

The fog was thick on most nights this time of year and this evening was no exception. The air was calm and still as Holmes made his way through the streets of Whitechapel, but the streets bustled with activity as men and women congregated in public houses, on street corners and in alleyways. As the night drew on, their numbers dwindled.

Holmes had worked out a pattern allowing him to make contact with each constable patrolling Whitechapel at least twice during his three hour watch period. He planned to pass along the method to Abberline and Watson.

Holmes decided to take the first watch, 9 p.m. to midnight in order to get a firsthand look at Whitechapel by night. Earlier, he had inspected the sites where Mary Ann Nichols and Annie Chapman were found. He was not under any illusion of finding fresh clues, as both sites had been left open to the public and were objects of much curiosity, making them bereft of useful forensic evidence in the usual sense.

Instead, he was looking for similarities in the murder sites themselves. The most obvious similarity between the two locations was that each was out of the way of foot traffic and there were no street lamps in direct line of sight. This made each of the sites completely engulfed in shadow. It also suggested cunning on the part of the murderer. As he walked the beat, Holmes made copious notes of areas most similar in character with the murder sites in order to pass the information on to Abberline and Watson.

Abberline took the second watch and, having walked a beat in Whitechapel for a few years, was very familiar with the turf. He took Holmes's notes and he knew most of the areas Holmes had detailed. Many of the similarities he had himself noted. As he covered the area throughout his watch, he queried each constable he encountered to ensure they'd been varying their routes per Holmes's instructions.

When the end of his watch came around at 3 a.m., Abberline found Watson waiting for him at the pre-arranged location by the Aldgate East Underground station. The Aldgate and Aldgate East stations had separate entrances and served different lines of the Underground but were actually one large station beneath the street, with Aldgate being the easternmost excursion of the Metropolitan Line and Aldgate East connecting two branches of the Underground that travel east, the Colchester Line and south, the Blackwall Line.

Holmes had deduced that since the Nichols and Chapman murders occurred in close proximity with a nexus of Underground stations, these areas, it could be surmised, were pre-selected as they provided an easy avenue of escape, should the act be discovered, with the pursuer being left to decide from a number of possible choices which way to pursue. The Aldgate nexus provided another such escape option. Therefore, Holmes concluded this intersection to be a prime area of concern.

As Watson and Abberline were exchanging pleasantries, a shabbily dressed, obviously intoxicated, older gentleman suddenly roused himself from his stupor on the steps to the Underground. He rose slowly, then tipped his hat saying, "Beg pardon, gov'nor, could you spare tuppence for the Underground? I'm a bit down on me luck."

Watson tried to ignore him, but as he turned away, the old man moved with surprising agility to stay directly in front of him. At last, Watson reached under his greatcoat and pulled a change purse from his trouser pocket, "Here, take this," handing the man two pence. "Now, on your way and don't let me see you begging here again."

The old man backed away, bowing and tipping his hat, "Thank you," and disappeared down the steps of the tube.

"You really shouldn't encourage them, Doctor," Abberline cautioned.

"Yes, yes, I know, but I can't help feeling some bit of pity for some of these wretched beggars, particularly those who are on in years."

"All the same, he'll be using that two pence for a pint not

a passage, I'd wager." Then Abberline clapped Watson on the arm, "I beg your pardon, Doctor. Years on the beat have hardened my heart, I'm afraid. Still, I'd not be pulling out your purse again, else a hidden compatriot might relieve you of more than two pence."

"Right you are, sir," Watson chortled, "right you are."

"Take care, Doctor, and I'll see you in the morning."

"Goodnight, Inspector," Watson said as he secured his purse beneath his great coat, "I believe that's your ride now." A police landau pulled up at the station and Abberline climbed in, waving goodnight to Watson. Shuddering against the cold, Watson, his hand on his pistol in the pocket of his greatcoat, walked north on Goulston Street to start his watch.

He had gone less than two hundred yards when he heard the sound of a woman's voice in some distress. The sound was coming from a doorway, which was recessed in an empty union meeting hall. Watson approached cautiously. He grasped the pistol in the pocket of his greatcoat. The police whistle he clenched in his teeth at the ready. When he reached the doorway, he could only see the back of a rather large man and heard the woman make a gurgling sound. Believing the worst, Watson pulled his pistol out of his greatcoat as he blew on the whistle for all he was worth.

"What 'ell!" the man, whose back was still to Watson, exclaimed loudly as he turned around. Watson could see in the dim light the man's trousers were around his knees and, mercifully, little else.

"'Ere now," cried the woman seeing Watson's pistol, "no need for that, he's done...we're leavin'," she said while pulling her skirts down and straightening her bodice and hat.

Two constables came running up on the scene from two different directions.

"Blimey!" the woman cried again, "getting so a woman can't make a decent livin' anymore."

The man, who'd busied himself hitching his trousers and buttoning his coat, said nothing.

"'Ere now," one of the constables said, "what goes on

134

here? Who blew the alarm?"

"I'm afraid that was me, constable," Watson admitted.

The two out of breath constables looked from Watson to the couple in the doorway, then at each other. A grin broke out on both their faces, "Good work, Doctor," one constable said, stifling a laugh.

"Yes," chuckled the other, "looks like the 'Ripper', here, was stickin' it to her good," and the two constables guffawed, much to Watson's chagrin.

"'Ey, was we under arrest?" asked the "Ripper".

"Well, now, that'd be up to Dr. Watson, 'ere," answered Constable Dew, "you *are* his cuff," laughing, "what say ye, Doctor?"

Red-faced, Watson waved them away, "Go on, get on with you," then to the constables, "very well could have been the, uh, what did you call him, the 'Ripper'?"

"Right, Doctor, it could, but you must admit it was a bloody-well funny sight to come upon," Constable Dew chuckled.

Watson, feeling somewhat redeemed, replied, "Well, yes, indeed I 'spose it was at that," chortling. "All right, boys, back at it, then," and the three of them departed in separate directions.

The remainder of the watch passed uneventfully and when Watson returned to Baker Street shortly after 7 a.m., he found Holmes fast asleep, as Watson was soon to be himself.

#

September 29, 1888

Rising at about noon, Watson found Holmes still in his dressing gown, pouring over a map of London's East End, smoke from his pipe swirling over his head. "What have we here?" Watson questioned, interrupting Holmes train of thought.

"Hmm?" Holmes looked up, "Ah, Watson, splendid…come, look here," pointing to the map with his pipe, "what do you think?

Watson, still rubbing the sleep from his eyes noted, "East

135

End…very nice."

Impatient, Holmes explained, "I've annotated the map with the location of the murders, the red 'X's'. I've also noted the beats of the local constabulary with these dashed lines as well as the neighborhood fixed points, here and here, and the locations of the tube stations, blue circles, police station houses, blue squares, etc., etc."

"I see, but," Watson pointed to two locations on the map labeled Smith and Tabram, "Smith wasn't killed and Tabram, although she was stabbed to death, didn't have her throat cut. Nasty attacks, to be sure, but far less heinous than either Nichols or Chapman."

"Precisely, Watson, as usual you've seized on an important distinction. Those two attacks, which might appear to be the first two in a series were, I believe, totally unconnected and random acts of violence, which are more or less the normal course in Whitechapel. I've included them here to show the contrast of those attacks with the cunning and utter savagery of the Nichols and Chapman attacks."

Holmes started to become quite animated as he often did when he was hot on the trail. Giving voice to his thoughts served the purpose of cementing them in his mind if they held up to this scrutiny. If they did not, it exposed them as false, allowing him to expunge them from the catalog of facts in his mind. "Notice how the Nichols and Chapman murders both occurred near a nexus of Underground stations and other public conveyances," drawing a circle around the stations indicated on the map with his pipe stem. "I'm convinced our murderer selected these locations to allow himself easy escape should his foul deeds be discovered."

"I see," looking back to the Smith and Tabram locations, Watson ventured, "and these occurred nowhere near a, what did you call it, a nexus?"

"Bravo, Watson, and the negative on the one hand lends credence to the positive on the other. Excellent!"

"And these areas," pointing to four large red circles drawn on the map, "these would be what?"

136

"Why, projected murder sites, of course, old boy, areas of concentration owing to the aforementioned nexuses and the characteristics of the known murder sites."

"This one," pointing to a circle drawn around Mitre Square, "is very near where Inspector Abberline and I met up this morning."

"Ah, yes, thanks for reminding me," said Holmes as he reached into his dressing gown pocket, "as it turns out, I didn't need this after all," handing Watson two pence.

Turning the coins over in his hand, "You didn't need...what's this?" Watson's eyes flashed as he remembered the old beggar. Darting a glance at Holmes, he met the amused gaze of his colleague, "It was you..."

"Yes, old boy, and you nearly caused me to come clean last night. Luckily the constables were closer than I when you sounded the alarm."

Embarrassed, Watson shrugged, "Yes, lucky indeed."

"There now, old chap, it was an honest mistake."

The bell interrupted Holmes playful jabbing at Watson, "Mr. Holmes," Mrs. Hudson called from outside the door, "Inspector Abberline is here to see you, sir; he says he's expected."

"Very well, Mrs. Hudson, please show him in."

Abberline entered, "Good day, Mr. Holmes, Dr. Watson. I had a message you wished me to come by today." Seeing both Holmes and Watson still in their dressing gowns, he continued, "I hope the hour is not inconvenient."

"Not at all, Inspector, I've something to show you, which I believe you will find most interesting." Holmes tapped out the ashes of his pipe into the fireplace, then refilled it with tobacco retrieved from the Persian slipper on the mantle, "There," pointing to the map, "on the table."

Abberline walked over to the table and looked down at the map. After a few seconds he bent over the table to gain a better look, fingers tracing over all the notations Holmes had made, "Remarkable!"

"Thank you, Inspector," a pleased Holmes replied as he

137

lit his pipe.

"You have everything here but the timing of the constable patrols," Abberline said admiringly.

"Yes, but my hope is your men will eliminate that as a factor by varying their routines as they patrol. If we are fortunate, this variance in routine coupled with the additional constables roving randomly between the fixed points randomly should result in a tightening of the web of law enforcement. The end result, I should hope, will be to close the noose around our murderer."

Pointing at Miter Square, "If this means what I think it means," Abberline continued, "you believe these areas to be likely future murder spots…"

"Precisely," interrupted Holmes.

"Then we will need to get the City of London Police engaged to cooperate with this investigation. This is in their jurisdiction."

"Quite," replied Holmes. "Major Henry Smith is the Chief Superintendent of the City police, and a longstanding acquaintance of mine. I'm certain there won't be a problem. Leave that to me."

Chapter 15

GUILT and COMPLICITY

September 29, 1888
My dearest darling, Julia,

It has been four months since I left you standing at the dock in New York harbor and my heart yearns to be with you again. Please know that if I could, I would leave this minute and fly to your arms, but fate has lain before me a most challenging, and if I'm successful, a most rewarding task.

In my last letter to you, I mentioned meeting Baron Barlucci, who was kind enough to throw a celebration in my honor. Since that time, I have moved from my hotel and am now living in his residence, Darthmore Hall, in order to treat him for a most unusual ailment. I sha'n't explain it to you now, but it should suffice to tell you that if I am able to find a cure for his ailment, one which to date has never been documented, it will secure my fame and reputation for all time.

Baron Barlucci is an unusual, and charming man for whom I have a great deal of sympathy due to his ailment. I say ailment because his condition, the cause of which I'm only beginning to understand, isn't a disease in the classical sense, but I do believe it to be curable, or at the very least, treatable.

As I've said, the baron is charming, but he is also somewhat intimidating, although I do not believe him to be dangerous, at least, not to me. I shouldn't say too much more, except to say my letters have been sparse this past month because I am close, very close I feel, to having an initial treatment that will mitigate many of the baron's outward symptoms. I've been working night and day on a formula and believe within the week it will be ready for trial.

139

I ask your indulgence, my sweet, for a while longer. Once I have a treatment for the baron, I will feel better about leaving him alone until he can meet me in New York. I trust you will forgive me for delaying our reunion these few weeks. Please know my love for you only grows stronger and our plans to marry upon my arrival are, as always, utmost in my mind and heart.

Until we are together once more, I remain, yours truly,

Alan

"Ah, Garrett," cried Dr. Tremaine. Garrett entered the laboratory just as he sealed the envelope of the letter he'd written, "please see to it this is in the first post tomorrow, won't you?"

"Of course, Doctor," Garrett responded, taking the envelope from Tremaine knowing the baron would wish to read it before it was posted. "Baron Barlucci would like to see you in the drawing room, sir."

"Very well, thank you, Garrett," said the doctor as he left his laboratory and walked down the corridor to the drawing room. When he arrived, the baron was just removing the needle from the cylinder of his phonograph.

"A remarkable device, don't you think, Doctor?"

"Yes, quite remarkable, Baron."

"But even as remarkable as it is, my dear Doctor, it is infinitely inferior to the real thing, do you agree?"

"Why, yes, I would imagine it is," replied the doctor wondering where it was the baron was heading with this.

"I've acquired two tickets for this evening's performance of Rigoletto at the Palace Theatre. Have you ever seen it performed, Doctor?"

"No, Baron, I'm afraid I'm not much for the opera. It's always seemed...," pausing, searching for the right word to convey his feeling without offending the baron, "...so unnecessary."

"Ahhh, yesss...unnecessary. And so it is, my friend, and

140

so it is. But what would life be without a few unnecessary things. I would like you to join me this evening, Doctor, I think you will enjoy it."

"But Baron, my work, I…"

"Your work will wait for you, Doctor. I've noticed you have been working too hard of late. I'm sure you would advise your own patients to take a break from the stress of work once in a while, would you not?"

"Yes, I suppose I would, but…"

"Nonsense. It's settled, then," the baron said as he turned away from Tremaine. "I've taken the liberty of purchasing suitable clothing for you. Garrett has put it in your wardrobe. We leave in one hour."

"But Baron…"

"Oh, please, Doctor, I don't mean to order you about, but I'm concerned you don't overwork yourself," the baron entreated, adding, "I need you to stay healthy, to keep your mind alert. Besides, what will your bride think of me if I allow you to work yourself to exhaustion."

The baron's mention of the doctor's future wedding brought a smile to the doctor's face. "Of course, Baron, I know you're right. I'd be happy to accompany you tonight."

"Excellent, Doctor," the baron replied. After the doctor returned to his laboratory, the baron picked up his violin and plucked at the strings. Of course he was genuinely concerned about the doctor working himself to exhaustion, although the concern was not the least bit altruistic, being less distressed about the doctor's health than how the doctor's health might affect his work. But there was another reason the baron wished to go to the opera this evening.

As the days since Tremaine had come to stay at the baron's estate had turned to weeks, the baron felt the hunger slowly rise within him. Out of deference to the doctor, the baron had stretched his abstinence to the limit. He would have to feed tonight or risk the dire consequences that he knew could and probably would follow.

During the opera, Tremaine noticed the baron, rather

141

than watching the opera itself, was gazing out over the audience from his vantage point in their box seats with a strange and vaguely predatory look on his face. The baron's eyes as he observed the crowd of humanity left the doctor cold inside and he pointedly avoided looking at him for the rest of the evening.

After the performance, which Tremaine enthusiastically enjoyed despite his initial reluctance and his discomfort with his host, the baron secured a hansom cab to take the doctor home.

"Aren't you going back to Darthmore, Baron?" asked Tremaine, noting the intense expression on the baron's face.

"I'm afraid I have another engagement this evening, Doctor. I may be quite late." He added with a grave tone, "Please forgive me," and, bowing graciously, he held open the door to the cab.

Dr. Tremaine felt uneasy as he climbed into the cab, noting a strangeness in the baron's eyes and sensing the baron was hiding his true intentions. Garrett stood by the baron's coach, door open. It wasn't until the hansom was on its way toward Darthmore that the doctor realized the meaning and intent of the baron's "engagement" and shuddered.

As the baron climbed into his coach, Garrett turned the dapple in the direction of Whitechapel.

#

September 29, 1888

There was nothing holy about the Three Nuns Hotel in London's East End. The building itself was old and run down, in dire need of paint. The windows on the east side of the ground floor were painted black to keep inquisitive eyes from seeing into the pub. Rooms at the hotel could be had for three and a half shillings per night or by the hour for a shilling. Most of the rooms were hired by the hour.

While the baron sat in the coach, Garrett went into the public house of the hotel to inquire about a tryst. Ordering a pint of ale, he looked from the innkeeper's glass eye to his good one, then back again, as if trying to determine which was seeing him, and asked, "How does a gentleman arrange for a dolly hereabouts?"

"Blimey, mate, take your pick, rooms upstairs are a bob an hour," replied the innkeeper as he wiped the bar with a dirty rag.

"Listen, keep, it ain't for me. My gov'nor has a taste for women of the lower order but doesn't like being seen about, although he isn't particular as to where he gets his 'faction, if you understands. He's like as not to satisfy his needs in the cover of a doorway or other satisfactory location, so long as he doesn't need to be seen publicly addressing the tart."

"'Ere," the innkeeper sat down the bottle of rye and pointed to the corner table, "see that greasy looking little *broadsman* taking those two jack tars for a penny a play? That there's Albert. 'E's been known to arrange such services for other gentlemen, for a price. Go talk to 'im."

Walking through the crowded, smoke filled pub, Garrett put his massive hand down on the table between Albert and one of the sailors.

"'Ere now, what do you want?" the sailor asked.

Reaching behind the young boy, Garrett grasped the back of his chair, "Your seat, swab," and jerked it out from under him cleanly in a show of bravado as well as strength. The sailor fell to the floor. Clamoring to his feet, he made a move toward Garrett. His friend, having observed both the size of Garrett and the ease with which he'd pulled the chair from under his friend, grabbed his shipmate's arm and convinced him they could find a better class of company in the pub down the street.

"Now why'd you go and do that for, mate?" asked Albert, wary of his guest's size and intent.

"I've some business you may be interested in."

"Is that so. What sort of business?"

"My gov'nor is in need of a lady friend, but he don't want to soil his shoes in a joint like this."

"Oh? Gentleman, eh? What's 'is likes?"

"He has a taste for common dollies and he'd as soon

meet 'em in the street, in some dark corner. Quick and easy, if you knows what I mean," winking in Albert's direction.

"Tell 'im to be walkin' down Berner from Commercial in twenty minutes. I think I got just wot 'e's lookin' for. I know an unfortunate in need of doss money, goes by the name 'Long Liz'. I'll have 'er waitin' for 'im."

"Good enough," Garrett said, rising.

Albert grabbed Garrett's forearm, "Ain't you forgettin' somthin', friend?"

Garrett reached into his pocket and then dropped two shillings on the table.

Albert, leering up at Garrett, rubbed his thumb against his index and middle fingers and Garrett dropped a third shilling as Albert let his arm go.

After reporting back to the baron concerning the arrangements, Garrett drove the coach to the corner of Commercial and Berner streets. Once the baron departed, he turned the coach around to make his way slowly back to Darthmore Hall, by an indirect route. Before driving off, Garrett watched as the baron disappeared down Berner and into the fog. He listened as the baron's walking stick struck the cobblestones. A small tear drifted down the large man's stubbled cheek.

The first time Garrett drove the baron into Whitechapel, he figured the baron had the same need for sport he'd seen other gentlemen of his class take in the East End of London. Even when he learned of the Nichols murder, not a hundred paces from where he'd let the baron out of the carriage that night, he didn't think, or wouldn't allow himself to think, the baron had been the hideous murderer that was the talk of all the tabloids.

It was only through his many conversations with Dr. Tremaine that Garrett came to realize the baron was anything but typical of the gentlemen who took their pleasure in Whitechapel. Those conversations had sparked his curiosity.

Although taken to be simple-minded, due to his size and his slow manner, Garrett was not as simple as he appeared. It would surprise the doctor, for example, to know Garrett could read at all. But read he could, and did. Each afternoon, when he was cleaning up the laboratory, while the doctor was eating dinner and briefing the baron on the latest developments or disappointments, Garrett read the doctor's journals.

Although he didn't understand much of the technical medical terminology, he understood enough to know what the baron was and to realize the Whitechapel murders of Mary Ann Nichols and Annie Chapman were due to the baron's "hunger", as it was termed in the doctor's journals. He also realized he had unwittingly been party to both those murders. That knowledge began to eat away at the large man's conscience.

So, on this last Friday night in September, he was all too aware of what was about to occur down that poorly lit side street; aware, yes, but powerless to stop it.

Chapter 16

BLIND PURSUIT

September 29-30, 1888

Abberline took the first watch on this Saturday, as had been prearranged. His watch passed quickly and uneventfully. There were, of course, a number of small incidents involving petty theft and drunkenness, but not so much as a nosebleed's worth of violence on his rounds. As he was passing on his observations to Watson, standing outside the Underground station at Aldgate, he noticed a well-appointed London coach coming down Aldgate High Street from Whitechapel. Although it certainly wasn't unusual to see fine livery in Whitechapel— gentlemen mostly, looking for "sport" at this time of night— something about this coach caught his eye and he made particular note of its style and detail.

Watson and Abberline stamped their feet against the cold in front of the station waiting for the police landau that would pick up Abberline. At the appointed time it came and after bidding Watson a safe night, he climbed in and was gone.

As Watson was leaving the station, a pathetic drunk sat on the steps, begging for pennies. Watson bent down to get a better glimpse of the man, "Here now, begging for pennies tonight, then?"

"Beg pardon, sir, but I'm in need of some food and coffee, as it were. I've a game leg which makes it difficult to find work. If you have a penny or two to spare, sir," he beseeched as he held his hand up to Watson.

Leaning down to whisper, "I say, old boy, this get up isn't nearly as good as the last, what?" Then more loudly, "Here you go, sir, here's half a crown. Get yourself a meal and make better of yourself." Once again leaning down and whispering, "I'll expect that back in the morning, then," Watson said with a wink.

The bewildered drunk took the half crown from Watson

and smiled, winking back, "Bless you, sir...thank you," and toddled off, laughing to himself as he disappeared into the night.

#

It had been three weeks since he had last taken a victim and the hunger welled up in the baron like a primitive beast. He'd been sensitive, perhaps too sensitive, to Dr. Tremaine's presence in his house and displayed for him a restraint in his appetite that belied his need for succor. This need was heightened by the physical closeness of the company he'd been keeping with Abigail. He'd restrained his baser instincts while being with her largely because he'd begun to have feelings for her, but the closeness they'd enjoyed was difficult for a predatory creature like the baron, causing him to forego seeing her these past few days, lest he allow the beast its head. All this made it imperative the baron feed—and soon.

Normally, he would have patrolled his hunting ground like a wolf on the prowl or a bird of prey, attacking at random. This evening, however, in order to ensure a kill he had used Garrett to arrange a suitable subject in just the right setting.

The London fog was a friend and ally in the baron's quest this night as it had been on his last outing. The baron could not help feeling confident as he strolled down Berner Street. London was an ideal habitat for a creature such as he, heavily populated with the affluent upper class in close contact with the impecunious lower class and a climate that frequently produced a fog so thick one had difficulty seeing a hand in front of one's face. The baron felt, and was beginning to treat it like, the East End of London was his own personal preserve, well stocked and private.

As he walked down Berner, the baron slowed his pace, now carrying his walking stick rather than allowing it to strike the cobblestones, ensuring his approach would be unheard as well as unseen in the thick fog. He was still several yards from her when he saw her standing in a doorway. His extraordinarily keen eyesight was only one attribute his unusual condition provided. He was certain she would not be able to see him until he was almost upon her. Silently, he came within three feet of her and asked in a low voice, "Pardon me, may I presume you to be Long Liz?"

"Blimey," she said, turning toward his voice, "you like to scared me silly. Yes, Long Liz is what they calls me. Are you the gentleman, then? My, ain't you a fancy one," she said as she began to pull up her skirt.

"Not here," the baron caught her by the arm and said in the same low voice, "down the road just a trifle."

"Awright, gov'nor, awright," she replied following him, her arm still in his grip. The baron led her a little ways into the entrance of a yard situated beside a socialist meeting hall. He pulled her through an open gate and to one side of the walkway. Slipping his arm around her waist, he pulled her close.

Amused at first at what she considered to be a rather clumsy attempt at passion, she looked up at him with the intent of telling him to calm down, Lizzie would take care of him. But when looked up at his face, into his eyes, her jaw went slack. Terror paralyzed her, preventing her from screaming. His eyes showed her no life, no feeling. As his lips descended upon her neck, there was a sudden noise close by.

A wagon, pulled by a single dray, delivering wool to the textiles factories nearby, stopped within ten feet of them as the driver got down to relieve himself. The fog concealed the baron, but the interruption had momentarily broken his hold on the woman's mind. Before she'd recovered enough to register a complaint, however, the baron unsheathed his blade and in one swift move cut her throat from ear to ear.

As he lowered her noiselessly to the ground, the fresh smell of blood on the air, he cleaned the knife on her dress, returned it to his walking stick and with a casualness belying the raging beast within, or perhaps because of a cavalier attitude the hunger brought on, an almost reckless bravado, the baron walked further down Berner Street, brazenly striking his stick on the cobblestones as he disappeared into the fog.

#

Watson chuckled to himself as he left the Underground, thinking about how cleverly he saw through Holmes's disguise this time. Reveling in his own cleverness, Watson headed down Aldgate making his way to Bishopsgate Police Station, there to make contact with the City of London Inspector in charge of that station, as had been pre-arranged by Holmes. The fog was especially thick tonight, thought Watson. As he walked, he pulled his great coat closer round his neck against the cold.

The Police Station at Bishopsgate was a great gray stone edifice with two gaslights on either side of the entry. Two sets of double doors stood at the top tier of three wide steps. Watson entered and asked the sergeant tending the desk for the office of Inspector Waters. After being shown in, Watson introduced himself, "Good evening, Inspector. Dr. John Watson, at your service," giving a courteous nod and bow.

"Yes, I was told you'd be here. Word came down from Major Henry himself." The Inspector looked up at Watson, "You're rather a V.I.P., I take it," but he remained seated.

"Hardly me, sir, but my associate, Mr. Sherlock Holmes, I believe gave the Major some little assistance a while back, with a rather prickly matter and they've been on the best of terms since, I understand."

"A prickly matter, you say? Hmm, yes, well perhaps you might tell me about it sometime," smiling. "So, what can I do for you this evening, Doctor?"

"I'm here just to touch wickets with you and to ensure your men have been assigned as agreed to at the briefing earlier today."

"You needn't have troubled yourself. All is as was agreed, I assure you." The Inspector appeared cold and distant, and Watson thought perhaps he was a bit out of sorts at having to follow the advice and instructions of a total stranger and someone he would consider a "civilian". It wasn't the normal course for the Chief Superintendent to become involved in day to day affairs, Watson supposed, and this might add a bit to his reticence.

Just as Watson was turning to leave, the inspector

remarked, "You must forgive me for not getting up, Doctor. I took a jezail bullet in the hip at Peiwar Kotal and on these cold, damp nights, it tends to give me a bit of trouble, you see."

Brightening up, Watson responded, "Aha, I know only too well, having been wounded twice myself."

"I thought I detected a military man," now rising with a wince.

"Please, don't bother, Inspector, I must be going," Watson said, turning to leave. At the door he hesitated, "Perhaps we could get together over tea sometime, compare notes, so to speak."

"Splendid! I believe I'd like that," smiling, as Watson nodded and departed.

As he walked from the Inspector's office back to the desk of the charge officer, Watson ran into Detective Sergeant Mulberry checking on a woman who had apparently passed out in her cell.

"What's wrong with this one?" asked Watson, more out of idle curiosity than professional interest, "can't say I care for her choice in footwear," he chuckled, looking at the pair of men's boots on the unconscious woman's feet.

"'Er? Public drunkenness. Just keepin' 'er 'ere till she's sober enough to get 'erself 'ome."

"Probably better off here than on the streets as long as that monster is about," remarked Watson as he buttoned his coat on the way out of the station.

"Aye, indeed, but we ain't runnin' no boardin' house," said the sergeant. "She'll be given the road as soon as she's up and about."

"Yes, I suppose," replied Watson, shaking his head as he adjusted his scarf against the cold. He remarked, "Pitiful creature," under his breath out of genuine sympathy for the poor destitute woman in the cell as he walked out the door of the station.

Watson checked his watch as he stood on the stoop outside of Bishopsgate station, "12:40 a.m.," he muttered to himself, "better get on over toward Buck's Row," as he got his bearings and began to walk.

#

During the long nights he'd spent in London, the baron had explored and committed to memory not only the sewer system in the East End, but also the locations of every police and underground station, public house and inn, the beats walked by the local constabulary and the schedules of the public transportation systems as well as every dark, secluded area in Whitechapel. The baron was a predator of astounding cunning and as such, he knew his territory well. Over centuries he had worked at perfecting his craft.

He made his way to Aldgate East through the sewer channel from Fairclough street. He entered the station through a grating in a secluded end, near the platform. Making his way past the few inattentive passengers awaiting their trains, he hesitated. It was only through a great force of will the baron succeeded in passing them by without making an attempt to quench his thirst then and there.

Finally, he ascended the stairs to the street. Emerging from the station, the baron was aware just how much more exaggerated his hunger had become. The encounter on Berner Street served to heighten both the need and his determination to slake his thirst. He knew he must find a victim, and quickly, or like in Budapest, the need would spiral beyond his control.

The baron's thoughts were on that small Hungarian village outside Budapest as he walked down Aldgate street. With the scent of fresh blood still in his nostrils, he knew he was frightfully close to the point of utter frenzy. Unless he soon found a victim, the city of London would suffer in a manner that would be most unpleasant.

Fortunately, not long after turning onto Houndsditch, fortunately, the baron spied his quarry. A woman, obviously in her drink, was leaning against the gaslight post at Duke Street.

When he drew close to her, he intoned, "My dear, you look as though you might need a drink."

151

"Wot's that to you?" she asked, too bleary-eyed to see that death was glowering at her in the baron's gaze.

"I too am in need of something," he said cryptically, the words dripping like honey from his lips, "perhaps we could come to some, ahem, agreement," producing a bottle of spirits from beneath his cloak and wagging it in front of her face.

Catherine Eddowes eyes followed the bottle's movements as she licked her lips and began to smile, "We might at that."

"Come," taking her by the wrist, "let us find a suitable spot for our transaction."

"'ere now, wot's your hurry, gov'nor?" Catherine trailed behind him as he quickly led her down Duke Street and into St. James Place Square. Early morning traffic along King Street into the square made it unsuitable to the baron's purpose, so he continued into a narrow alleyway emerging into a second, smaller, darker square. Mitre Square was deserted at this hour of the morning and after walking a few paces from the alley, the baron swung Catherine around, giving her the bottle and bidding her to drink.

"Ahhh...there's the stuff," she said. As she took the bottle in her right hand, her practiced left fished in the pocket of the baron's greatcoat. In search of a bit of change or perhaps a purse, she found nothing but a handkerchief for her trouble.

When she tilted back her head to drink, pausing to give the baron a wink, he lowered his lips to her throat. With his hand on the back of her neck, he bit, causing her to jolt forward with a muddled gasp, then, as the feeling of ecstasy engulfed her, she fell limp in his grip. The baron drained her as completely as he could, then as he drew back from her throat, he lowered her to the ground and with his now unconcealed blade, sliced open her throat, driving the blade through the bite marks.

Quickly now, and with the precision of a practiced hand, the baron lifted her skirts to expose her abdomen and with the bloody knife, opened her up, then pulled out her intestines draping them over her body. With these aside, he deftly removed a kidney and her uterus, gorged in rich blood. After draining

152

these too of the last drop of precious blood, he tossed what remained toward a nearby garbage can where two large alley cats were foraging. He watched delighted as the felines fought over the morsels.

Having completed his work, the baron rose to leave, casually cutting a square from Catherine's apron as he did and wiping the knife, which he once again secreted in his walking stick. As he calmly walked away from the scene of decimation he'd just wrought, he wiped the remaining blood from his hands.

Exiting the square, the baron paused as he stepped back onto Duke Street. A cold and mirthless smile formed on his lips as the faint squeal of a police whistle floated through the fog and touched his ears. Then, making his way to Shoreditch Station, he disappeared into that fog.

#

He'd been walking for about twenty-five minutes when Watson heard the first faint tweet of a policeman's whistle as it carried dully on the foggy night air. Instinctively, he turned towards the direction of the sound, which appeared to come from the general direction of Whitechapel Street. As he reached the thoroughfare, he heard the clattering of horse hooves as a police wagon passed by him at a gallop. He watched as it made a wide turn onto Commercial Street and then hurried down to follow, favoring his right leg, concerned he might lose sight of the wagon.

As Watson turned off Whitechapel Road onto Commercial, a street urchin of about ten years nearly knocked him down, "Here, here, young man, where to in such a hurry. You nearly ran me over."

"Sorry, gov'nor, I'm off to get the doctor. There's a bad one down Berner Street way. The copper set me on to the hospital."

"Down Berner, you say…very well, off you go, then." With this new information, Watson made his way down Commercial toward Berner Street."

Turning onto Berner, Watson pulled his greatcoat tighter about him as the chill in the air seemed palpably more intense in the dark gray confines of the narrow thoroughfare. When he arrived at the scene, he saw someone bent over the body with a torch in his hand. Approaching closer, Watson could see by the light of the torch the ghastly scene. He could also see it was Holmes who was giving the body a close examination with his torch in one hand and his glass in the other.

"Ah, Watson," Holmes said, looking up, "you're here."

"I say, Holmes, I see you've doffed your disguise from earlier. Not one of your most convincing, if I may say."

"Disguise? Nonsense, Watson," Holmes brushed off Watson's inconsequential chatter, explaining "it appears our nemesis may have been interrupted this time, possibly by the driver of that delivery cart there," pointing to the dog cart by the gate. "This woman's throat has been cut, but there are no puncture marks, no abdominal mutilation and there's a good deal more blood here than at the other scenes." Holmes walked down the street, away from the cart, examining the ground with his torch. Watson followed close behind him.

"Hallo!" Holmes exclaimed and dropped to one knee to get a closer look at this area of ground. Watson could see nothing out of the ordinary. "Look here," said Holmes, and Watson dutifully bent over to examine the spot Holmes indicated with his torch.

"I don't see anything unusual," Watson finally admitted.

"Perhaps not," Holmes said, producing a pen knife from his pocket along with a small envelope. He scraped a small amount of earth and rock from the spot he'd been examining, and deposited it into the envelope, "but unless I miss my guess, our murderer passed this way and left a trail." Before rising and moving on, Holmes took a small piece of chalk from his other pocket, marking the spot from whence he'd taken his sample.

In a partial crouch, Holmes, torch before him and Watson following, examined the street, stopping at regular intervals to mark with the chalk. Shortly after turning the corner at Fairclough Street, he paused, looking all around.

"What is it, Holmes?" Watson asked anxiously.

"They've stopped," Holmes replied, then, "Aha!"

Holmes was looking down at a sewer grate saying, "Watson, bear a hand, here," as he bent down to grasp the grating.

Together, with some great effort, they moved the grating aside. Looking down into the sewer, Holmes said, "It appears to lead in the direction of Aldgate Station. Watson, I'm going to follow it to see where it winds up. Meet me at Aldgate."

"Be careful, old boy," but Holmes had already disappeared into the sewer.

Holmes followed the sewer in a westerly direction he believed would bring him to Aldgate East Station. The stench and filth were staggering as he made his way along. Using the lapel of his greatcoat as a makeshift filter against the putrid air, Holmes continued. He was making good time even though he was selective about where he made his footfalls. Using the lantern to determine the least offensive trail, he picked his way through debris, keeping mainly to the sides of the sewer.

He was amazed by the size of some of the sewer rats, which appeared oblivious to both his presence and the light from his torch. Once he'd nearly drawn his pistol when one of the more aggressive ones appeared to be charging him. Rather than risk alerting his quarry he was on his trail, Holmes instead managed to use the toe of his shoe to dislodge a brick and send it skittering toward the oversized rodent making it rethink its course.

Finally, through another grate above, he heard the sounds of an Underground station. He was able to move the grate enough to squeeze through it and into Aldgate East Station.

Holmes made his way past the small knot of passengers awaiting the next train and through the station to the entrance. As he emerged onto the street from the stairs, he immediately saw Watson. "Just as I suspected, Watson, our murderer is as cunning as he is deadly."

Before Watson had a chance to respond, the sound of a police whistle could be heard, and not too far away. "Come, Watson, the game's afoot."

Both Holmes and Watson began to run in the direction of the whistle, down Aldgate. At the corner of Aldgate and Duke

Streets, Watson called to his friend, "This way!" continuing down Aldgate.

Holmes responded, "No, this way." His words were immediately followed by another blast on the whistle confirming Holmes was correct as they turned and headed up Duke Street, in the direction Holmes indicated.

On the left side of the street, a constable, clearly shaken by what he'd seen, paused as he exited an alleyway opening onto Duke Street, hands on the brickwork of the Jewish chandlery building, and promptly expelled the roast beef and kippers that had been lovingly prepared by his wife before he went on shift. Avoiding the constable, Holmes and Watson turned down the alley leading to Miter Square and continued to the southwest corner, where a second constable was kneeling beside a body.

"Touch nothing!" called Holmes as he approached and brushed the constable aside.

"'Ere now..." the constable began, then, "Oh, Mr. 'Olmes, it's you."

Ignoring him in that way he had of pushing aside anything that would interfere with his concentration on the task at hand, Holmes began a careful examination of the body as well as the area around the body with the aid of his torch and glass. When he'd finished, he stood and said to Watson, "Just as I suspected."

"What's that, old boy?" asked Watson.

"Our murderer," Holmes began, "interrupted by the cart driver on Berner and unable to achieve the full depravity of his act with his first victim, went in search of a second. Note the characteristic lack of blood at the scene and the evisceration of the body."

Watson took Holmes torch and swept it over and around the victim lying at their feet, "Yes, it does appear his aim was to fully degrade his victim," Watson replied.

"I'm afraid we must not jump to a conclusion as to the murderer's motives, Watson."

"What's that?" returned Watson.

"In your surmisal of the murderer's motive, you've

fallen into the trap of your own emotion."

"How's that, old boy?" asked Watson, a bit annoyed.

"Don't be cross, friend, it's only because you are a genuinely caring man that you allow your own emotional reaction to the scene before you to, quite naturally, steer your conclusion that the intent of the perpetrator was to evoke just such a reaction."

"And you don't believe that to be the case?"

"It might very well be, old boy, but the danger is in concluding that to be the case over all other possibilities. We must be dispassionate and allow the facts to uncover the truth."

As they were about to leave, Watson looked back at the body of the woman lying dead in the square, "Dear God, Holmes, I saw that woman earlier tonight at the Bishopsgate Police Station."

"Are you sure?"

"Positively, I recognize her shoes."

"Hmmm...yes," Holmes answered without looking back, "men's boots. I thought that was highly unusual, yet not terribly important. Tell me, Watson, what is the most obvious difference between these two attacks tonight?"

Watson thought about this for a moment, then ventured, "The first victim's abdomen was unmolested."

"Exactly," agreed Holmes, "and yet the volume of blood here is a mere fraction of that found beneath the first."

"Yes, of course, you're right!" Thinking about the story Abberline told them of his grandmother, he added, "You don't think..."

"There appears to be some missing data, here, Watson, and as you are well aware, it's an axiom of mine that to theorize without all the data is counter-productive." Turning to the constable, Holmes said, "You may call the doctor now and remove the body for autopsy. I wish to be informed if any organs are discovered missing."

"Aye, sir, Mr. 'Olmes, right away, sir."

As Holmes and Watson walked away, Holmes remarked, "Yes, Watson, we appear to lack all of the data. For instance, there's been a small bit of the woman's dress cut away which is nowhere to be found in this vicinity. I'm not certain what to make of it. It may or may not be of import." Then, giving Watson a sideways glance, "But we do have this," producing a fine, linen handkerchief stained with blood he had concealed in the sleeve of his greatcoat. He handed it to Watson, who unfolded it, noting the letter "B" in the corner. "It was clutched in the victim's hand, behind her back."

"Do you think it belongs to her?"

"I think not, Watson. This is fine Italian linen, of fairly new origin, the price of which would be quite dear. I doubt this unfortunate woman has had the wherewithal in recent times to have purchased such a thing. No, I believe this and the markings on Berner Street are the first hard physical clues we've had in this case."

September 30, 1888

"Good evening, Doctor," the baron said as he noiselessly entered Tremaine's laboratory, "I trust you enjoyed the performance last evening?"

At the sound of the baron's voice, Dr. Tremaine dropped the empty vial into which he was about to pour a dense liquid, "Baron, I wish you wouldn't just appear like that."

"I apologize, Doctor. Stealth is a habit, I'm afraid. But I must know, did you enjoy the opera?"

"I did, very much so, thank you for insisting I attend." Looking at the baron, Tremaine smiled as he thought to himself how well the baron looked today, more healthful and vibrant. Then, as the realization of the reason for the baron's healthful glaze dawned on him, the smile faded and he turned away from the baron. He hoped he wasn't too obvious in his display of aversion.

"Ah, my dear doctor, I see concern in your eyes. Let me try to dissuade you from mourning too much," the baron walked slowly round the bench covered with test tubes, beakers and vials until he was standing in front of Dr. Tremaine. "It's true I fed the hunger that consumes me last night and in so doing, successfully drove the beast back into its cave, so to speak. But let me assure you that had I not quieted it, at some point I would be unable to control the impulse and no one, not even you, my dear doctor, would be safe until it was sated."

Again Tremaine felt the icy finger on his spine and the clinging nausea in the pit of his stomach.

"The victim was of no consequence, a common dolly, a street prostitute," he sneered with characteristic disdain. "No doubt she'd be dead from drink and disease in short order, had I not come along."

"Baron, I must ask…" hesitating, Tremaine looked away.

"Please, Doctor, you have nothing to fear from me. I've been more open and honest with you than with any man in the past three centuries. I want you to feel free to be equally honest with me."

"Very well, Baron," Dr. Tremaine said, screwing up his courage, "I'd like to ask you how long I can expect…how long can you go before you need to…to feed again?"

The baron did not answer, but slowly circled Tremaine instead, not unlike a predatory beast, taking his measure of the doctor as he contemplated the question.

"Please, Baron, don't think this is a trivial or idle question. I am working on a serum for you, a serum that will, I believe, greatly relieve the symptoms of your malady, making it possible for you to find sustenance without taking another human life."

"Doctor," the baron said, stopping in his tracks, "if you could do that…" The baron's thoughts went first to the letter he'd read from the doctor to his fiancée, then to Abigail and what the serum would or could mean regarding his relationship with her.

"I believe I am very close, perhaps days."

"I see, and you want to know if I shall need to feed again before you finish," coming out of his reverie.

"Yes," looking directly into the baron's eyes, "even a

prostitute is of consequence to someone."

"Of course, Doctor. You are right, and please believe me when I tell you I don't mean to trivialize human life. I truly grieve for every victim. I do not wish to appear cavalier," looking suddenly very tired and even sad, "I've lost so many loved ones through the centuries I am afraid I've developed a hard exterior, somewhat like a callus, but it is not what's truly in my heart. It is merely a protective mechanism. I'm sure you can well imagine that I can ill afford to be as sympathetic as you regarding my, how shall I say, habits."

"Forgive me, Baron, I do not mean to stand in judgment of you," suddenly feeling moved to pity for the baron, "I'm sure I can never understand how much suffering your malady has caused you."

"Not at all, Doctor, I know I must seem a monster to you, as I do, at times, to myself. But to answer your question, three weeks is the approximate limit to my strong control over the impulse, from there it begins to control me. If it gains the upper hand, it can lead to a frenzy of the worst kind of carnage, which can go on far longer than is required to sate the hunger itself."

"Then I shall work day and night, Baron, to finish the serum. Once it's finished, you must accompany me to New York that we may seek a true cure for your condition."

"I don't understand, Doctor. The serum is not the cure?"

"I wish it were that easy, Baron. I'm afraid the effects of the serum may wear off after some months. Because of this, you must tell me of any changes you notice, no matter how small or insignificant they may appear to you."

"Of course, Doctor, I understand and will join you in New York as planned, but I cannot leave immediately. I'm sure you can understand I have a good many details to attend to before I can absent myself for any length of time."

"If the serum works as I believe it will, you can follow me at your convenience, Baron, but I must return as soon as possible. I've promised my fiancée that I will return before the last leaves have fallen. I shouldn't wish her to think her future husband regards her so little as to make idle promises," he said, smiling. "With this serum, I will be able to leave you with complete confidence that your condition will be in check until you can travel to New York."

"Of course, Doctor, I understand. I am awaiting a shipment of my belongings in anticipation of moving indefinitely to America. I expect to have matters here concluded by the time it arrives, at which time I shall travel, with the shipment, to America, to meet you in New York."

"Excellent, Baron. Now if you'll excuse me, I must get back to work."

Chapter 17

THE STRAWMAN

October 1, 1888

The Monday morning after the double murder in Whitechapel, Holmes invited Inspector Abberline to Baker Street to share his findings and announce his hypothesis. When he arrived, Watson ushered him into the sitting room. "Thank goodness, you're here," said Watson, "I've been unable to get anything out of him."

Holmes, who'd been sitting in his overstuffed chair, fingers templed before his eyes as he contemplated the trail of events, clues and possible conclusions suddenly rose and spoke, directing his words to Abberline, "Inspector, we are looking for a man of about 6 feet, 2 inches in height, slim with dark hair, of some means and most likely of Italian origin. If not Italian, he has at least travelled there recently." He fixed Abberline in his gaze waiting for his reaction.

Dumbfounded, Abberline paused, then thinking Holmes must be joking, he smiled he said, "Remarkable…and how have you come to this amazingly specific set of conclusions, Mr. Holmes."

"That's not all, Inspector, I believe I also may know how our man came to be in London."

"Really, Mr. Holmes?" Now believing both Holmes and Watson must be pulling his leg, "Please, do tell."

"At this very moment, in Newgate Prison, there is a young Italian boy awaiting trial and, by all accounts, a short trip to the gallows."

"What has this boy to do with the murders in Whitechapel?"

"Why, nothing at all, Inspector," smiled Holmes who, detecting the inspector's skepticism, was now toying with him, "nothing at all." As Abberline stood silent, his mouth slightly agape, Holmes suddenly became serious again, "Nothing except there is a good chance this boy is awaiting trial for a crime committed by our murderer. He is accused of murdering a young girl and disposing of her body on the high seas."

"Then you know who our murderer is?"

Holmes mood turned decidedly darker, "No. Unfortunately, the young man in question doesn't know the name of his fellow passenger and the ship's manifest was altered to eliminate any trace of our quarry's presence. Since the ship is currently out to sea, we cannot question the captain and, also unfortunately, we've been unable to gain any useful intelligence from any of the other passengers to date, with the exception of the boy's friend and traveling companion."

"Then all of this is conjecture?"

"Conjecture, yes, but I prefer to think of it as an informed conjecture, Inspector, rather than a blind one. A working theory that fits the facts as we now know them and which will, I believe, lead us to solving this case."

"If you don't know who the murderer is, I must go back to my original question of how you came to your remarkable conclusions on his description? Are you basing it on the word of your accused murderer and his friend?"

"Not at all, although their rather sketchy description corroborates what I've deduced." At this, Holmes handed him the monogrammed handkerchief, "I took that from the hand of the second victim, just last night."

"Mr. Holmes!" the inspector said with an air of official indignity, "I must protest. You should not have removed evidence from the scene."

"It was necessary, I assure you, Inspector. I could little risk having your men, you'll pardon the expression, misplace such a valuable piece of evidence before I'd had a chance to examine it thoroughly."

"And you deduced your description of the murderer from this handkerchief?"

"Not entirely and not exclusively, Inspector." Holmes went on to elaborate, "There were three strands of dark brown hair in the folds of this handkerchief. The victim's hair was light brown to red. As to the handkerchief itself, you may be aware the weave and materials used in linen can be quite distinct; possibly you're familiar with a monograph I've written on the subject." Continuing, "This particular handkerchief, I've discovered, is made from a variety of the *linum usitatissimum*, or flax plant, which is grown and used almost exclusively in northern Italy. This, along with a heel print left at the scene of the first murder last night, points to our murderer being of Italian origin. The heel of the Italian shoemakers has a very distinctive shape and slant, and our murderer was kind enough to step into some soft clay where some of the cobblestones on Berner Street were dislodged. The rather shallow depth of the imprint indicates a slim build."

"And his height, Mr. Holmes?"

"I'm sorry, Inspector, I assumed you were aware of the measurements I had your men take for me of the distances between the chalk marks I left on the road last night."

"Yes, Mr. Holmes, I was aware of the measurements, but not their purpose."

"Quite elementary, Inspector; I'm sure you are familiar with the method of extrapolating a man's height from a measure of his stride."

"Yes, of course."

"Very good. I merely applied this same methodology to the distance between the chalk marks, which indicate the distance between where our murderer's walking stick struck the cobblestones, dividing the average of the measures by two, as the stick would only strike the street at every other step."

"...and you know these strike marks are from our murderer because...?"

"Ah. I took a sample from the area where the stick first struck and found it to be positive for human blood. The re-agent I used is one of my own formula and reacts only to human blood. The walking stick, therefore, must have inadvertently been dipped into the pool of blood by the body and as its owner walked away, left a trail of bread crumbs, if you will, for us to follow."

"But couldn't an innocent passerby have done the same

thing?"

"Hardly, inspector. Our deliveryman told us last night that just before he found the body of Elizabeth Stride, he heard the sound of a man walking away down Berner, with what sounded like a walking stick striking the cobblestones. The only possible person who could have been walking in that direction at that exact time was the murderer himself, else the deliveryman would have heard the fellow approach. The fleeing murderer would have had to nearly step over the body of the unfortunate Stride woman to make his escape, as the deliveryman's cart was blocking his egress."

"That's quite remarkable, Mr. Holmes."

"Not at all, Inspector, it's actually a very simple example of the scientific method."

"Well now, Mr. Holmes, I've brought you two other bits of evidence to ponder and apply your 'scientific method'."

"Indeed, Inspector," said Holmes, eyes becoming instantly more attentive.

Holding a bit of cloth he'd produced from his pocket, "This piece of cloth was discovered this morning. As you can see, it's stained with blood."

"Ah, the missing corner of the victim's apron. Good work, Inspector," Holmes remarked as he took the bit of material and examined it.

Surprised, Abberline continued, "I suppose I should have guessed you would have noticed it missing."

"A square of that size missing from the victim's apron would be difficult to miss."

"I'm afraid I missed it," admitted Watson.

"But then, it was I and not you, Watson, who examined the body," disculpating his colleague. "I must say I wasn't sure it had bearing on the murder though. Bravo on your men finding it, Inspector. Where was it discovered?"

"On Goulston Street, near Wentworth. It was taken, cut, actually, from the second victim's apron. It matches exactly."

"I see," Holmes said, continuing his examination of the cloth, "but you mentioned two pieces of evidence, Inspector."

"Yes, the other was a message scrawled on the brickwork where the cloth was found," taking a piece of paper from his waistcoat. "It read, *'The Juwes are the men that will not be blamed for nothing'*. It is believed it may have been written by the murderer."

"I assume by the tone of your voice when you say, 'it is believed', you mean this is the official Metropolitan Police position, but that you may have reservations," Holmes observed.

"Quite correct, Mr. Holmes. Personally, I believe this merely to be an example of anti-Semitic sentiment that is quite typical in this part of the East End. I've seen the like before.

The area surrounding Mitre Square is populated by a great many Jewish establishments. We've had many instances of graffiti, broken glass in shop windows and worse in this area and those surrounding from time to time. Goulston Street fronts no fewer than five shops as well as a bank, all Jewish owned, and there is a synagogue within three blocks of the doorway where the graffiti was found. The fact the cloth was discovered beneath the writing is, I think, mere happenstance."

"Perhaps, Inspector, or it could be a clever attempt at providing yet another red herring for the police to chase," said Holmes as he packed tobacco into his pipe. "If one looks closely enough, there might appear to be any number of 'meanings' one could surmise from this 'clue'."

Holmes paused as he struck a match and lighted his pipe, "For example, the last murder took place in Mitre Square. Consider that along with the message on the wall and two divergent meanings could be inferred," puffing as he paced back and forth.

"On the one hand, a mitre is a form of headgear worn by bishops and abbots of both the Anglican and Catholic churches, which when taken with the word 'Juwes' might give a rather biblical tone to the clue." Looking from Watson to Abberline, he continued, "Whereas on the other hand, a mitre and square plays into a Masonic connection, as does the same word 'Juwes' from the message." Again pausing as he thoughtfully puffed on his pipe, "Yes, I'd be very interested in seeing the message for myself."

"I'm afraid that's not possible, Mr. Holmes, it was washed away not long after it was discovered."

"Erased? What on earth for?" said Holmes, "On whose order?"

"On the order of Sir Charles himself. He was called to the scene shortly after it was discovered and was concerned that with all the attention being paid to it by the police, and knowing the street would soon be full of Jewish vendors and Christian buyers, that there would likely be violence visited upon the Jewish merchants."

"Fool. Now we may never know," Holmes said remorsefully. Then, he thoughtfully concluded, "Of course, if it is indeed a red herring as I suspect, Sir Charles's effacement of the message may have done us a great service in removing it from the equation, ensuring we don't chase down that particular rabbit hole."

"Like Alice, eh Holmes?" remarked Watson with a smile.

"What's that, Watson? Alice? Alice who?" asked Holmes, somewhat annoyed.

"Never mind, old boy, I'd quite forgotten..." Watson's voice trailed off.

Changing the topic, Abberline asked, "May I see the handkerchief again, Mr. Holmes?"

"Of course, Inspector," handing it to Abberline.

"This monogram; it's familiar to me...I've seen it somewhere..."

Excited, Holmes pressed him, "You have? Think, man, where!?"

Turning the cloth over in his hand, rubbing the embroidered letter between thumb and forefinger thoughtfully, at last he looked up at Holmes, "There was a coach, last night on Aldgate, near the station where I met up with Watson."

"Yes," said Watson, "now that you mention it, I do remember a coach...black, I believe it was, pulled by two dapples, or was it one. I must say I don't recall the monogram."

"I remember clearly, a single dapple...and this monogram painted on the doors of the coach. I remember wondering what sport the gentleman who owned that coach might be seeking at this hour, but it appeared to be quite empty as it passed."

"Inspector, you may have solved the case," Holmes said in a congratulatory tone, "we've only to track down that coach and we'll have our man!"

#

October 2, 1888

The sun had risen well above St. Paul's Cathedral to the east, in central London when Holmes, Watson and Vittorio Rossini arrived at Newgate Prison. As Holmes tended to the necessary paperwork to see the accused, Vittorio and Watson waited in the corridor, outside the office of the Chief Gaoler.

"You must try and encourage your friend that all is not lost. Mr. Holmes and I are lately confirmed in our opinion that your friend has not committed the horrible deed of which he is accused."

"I know he did not do it, Signore Doctor. He was in love with Gianetta, he could never have hurt her."

"Yes, so both you and he have said, but we have firmer proof than...ah, here comes Mr. Holmes."

"They are bringing him to the interrogation room now," said Holmes as he exited the gaoler's office. They made their way to the small room behind the stairway leading to the cellar interrogation room in which they had first met Carlino. When they arrived, Carlino was already inside. His face was badly bruised and his lip was cut.

"My God, what has happened to this man?" Dr. Watson demanded of the guard.

"Carlino, are you all right?" asked Vittorio.

"It is nothing, Signore Doctor, please," Carlino said, and Holmes quickly understood Carlino was fearful of retaliation,

168

should Watson be too forceful in his protestations.

He gripped Watson's arm tightly, "Never mind, old boy, we have other business here," he said in an off-handed way that disarmed the more combative Watson.

"Very well," replied Watson, in a gruff manner as he looked at the guard sternly.

The guard smirked, "I suspect you'll want me to wait outside, eh?"

"If you please," answered Holmes in an almost deferential manner.

"All right, then, you've got thirty minutes and not a minute more, mind you," and he closed the door behind him, smiling all the while.

"That fellow has some cheek," remarked Watson.

"Never mind that now, Watson, we shall see about the gaoler's conduct presently. Prison is a difficult place...particularly for the innocent."

At Holmes's words, Carlino looked up, "Innocent? Then you believe me, Signore Holmes?"

"That it wasn't you who murdered Gianetta Rossini? Yes, which is why I interceded to get a postponement of your trial, in order to make inquiries on your behalf, but I need your help and that of Vittorio if we are to find the man who did it."

"Of course, Signore," said Vittorio.

"How can Vito and I help?" asked Carlino.

Watson had already taken out his pencil and pad to take notes. "We have until the first of November to find the real murderer of Gianetta Rossini. To that end, I need to know more about the mysterious passenger in the Captain's cabin," said Holmes, "anything you can remember, no matter how small a detail, could prove vital in our finding him and bringing him to justice."

"Signore Holmes, as I told you before, I only saw him one time and only briefly. I'm not sure I can be of help."

"Think back to when you saw him," prodded Holmes, "close your eyes and picture it in your mind," turning from Carlino to Vittorio, "both of you."

"Carlino, I remember he was quite tall, over six feet," began Vittorio.

"Yes, I remember that, and he was dressed in black. I remember his shoes were of the most expensive style, and his cloak was seamless and perfect," offered Carlino.

Vittorio added, "And he carried a walking stick, with a silver handle." At this Holmes and Watson exchanged a knowing look, as Vittorio continued, "His hands were very pale."

"Excellent," said Holmes, "excellent. Now, try to remember the name he travelled under."

The two sat silent, then Carlino looked up at Holmes, "Signore, he was of the noble class, perhaps a count or marquess or something. Gianetta heard her parents speak of it."

"Unfortunately," said Holmes, "the Rossinis have told me in no uncertain terms they have nothing to say—especially if it is to aid in your defense. I would have thought they'd want to see the real murderer of their daughter brought to justice and hanged."

"They are probably just as satisfied knowing he shall be," blurted out Watson, who was immediately sorry when he saw Carlino's crestfallen look.

"Buck up, Carlino, you are not hanged yet. Watson and I will do our best to see to it the hangman finds another neck to fit his noose. Now on another topic, your friend Vito, here, has told us your father cabled the Bank of London to make available a sum of money for your defense and also to make your stay at Newgate more tolerable. Is that so?"

"I have heard nothing of this except from Vito, Mr. Holmes."

"Then you've received no accounting of it here?"

"No, Mr. Holmes."

"No upgrade in your meals or bedding? No other allowances? Cigarettes?"

"No, Signore, nothing."

"Hmmm…that's odd. When did you receive that cut on your lip and the bruises? What were the circumstances?"

"When Vito visited me a few days ago, he told me what

170

you just told me, that my father had sent money for my care. I didn't believe it. My father was very angry with me when I told him I was coming to England. He said he would disown me."

"A father's love is a persistent yet peculiar thing. Undoubtedly he regrets the circumstances of your departure," remarked Watson.

"Perhaps, Signore Doctor, but when I asked the gaoler about additional rations, he had the guards beat me, then he told me the only additional rations I would receive would be of a like nature, and if I were to ask, he would be only too happy to oblige me."

"I take it, you've learned not to ask?" suggested Holmes.

"Yes, Signore Holmes" answered Carlino resignedly. "Perhaps Vito's father, from whom Vito received the message, misunderstood my father."

"Perhaps, Carlino, perhaps," said Holmes, "Dr. Watson and I shall make a few discreet inquiries on your behalf, then, if you do not object."

"Of course not, Signore Holmes, only…"

"Very well, then. Don't worry, we have avenues that will keep your name completely out of it." Holmes added, smiling, "So you shall not receive any increased, um, rations," Holmes added smiling as he patted Carlino's arm.

Calling the gaoler, Holmes, Watson and Vittorio said their good-bye's to Carlino, encouraging him not to lose hope and left the prison. Once outside, Holmes hailed a cab and put Vittorio into it telling the driver to take him back to his place of employment. Vittorio reached out of the cab to shake Holmes's hand, "You will see to it Carlino is not hanged?"

"We shall do our very best," promised Holmes.

"Your friend's life could not be in more capable hands than Mr. Holmes's, Vittorio, I assure you," added Watson.

The look on Vittorio's face as the cab pulled away was dire, but hopeful. When he'd gone, Holmes turned to Watson, "We have our work cut out for us, old boy."

"Yes, and a mere month in which to do it," agreed Watson.

"Come," said Holmes, clapping his friend on the shoulder, "I believe we should make a visit to the Bank of England before we return to Baker Street."

Hailing a cab, Holmes asked Watson, "Have you a ten pound note on you, old boy?" as he fished inside his overcoat for a notebook and an envelope containing a fine white powder. After climbing into the hansom, Holmes took the note from Watson and put on a pair of leather gloves.

"I say, Holmes, what is this about?" asked Watson.

"I've heard from various sources recently that there is a conspiracy to fleece the unsuspecting benefactors of people unfortunate enough to find themselves under the care of Her Majesty's justice system," Holmes explained as he carefully spread the ten pound note on his lap. "Unfortunately, until now, I've not had the opportunity to investigate it."

"I see, and what do you intend to do with my ten pounds?" asked a concerned Watson.

"In order to set a proper trap, you need a proper bait. This powder," he explained as he put a small amount on the note, then folded it over rubbing the powder between the two halves, then doing the same with two five pound notes from his own purse, "will become embedded in the fibers of the paper of these notes."

"I'm afraid I don't follow. What does that have to do with setting a trap?"

"You don't follow because you don't yet know that this powder is a reactant. When the powder is exposed to the correct reagent, it turns a bright blue color."

"I see, then you can track the note by exposing it to the reagent. But why not simply copy the serial number of the note and track it that way."

"Because, my dear Watson, we are not simply tracking the note, but who has actually touched it. Anyone who has handled the note will retain a small bit of residue from the powder on their fingers for a few days, which can be detected by the application of the aforementioned reagent."

"Yes, of course, I see," said Watson, "you mean to say

the powder, when exposed or immersed in a liquid containing a high acid or base content will react with it, turning the fingers either blue or red. Is that it?"

"Precisely! The powder is so fine that even with vigorous washing, there will remain, for several weeks, a residue indicating who has handled the notes. In fact, washing with soap will only cause the reactant to persist in a blue color. We have only to put the money into the bank system, marking it for Carlino in Newgate Prison from his father, and if there is mischief involved, it will soon become clear who has had a hand in it, if you will."

"But Holmes, what if they merely substitute other notes for these."

"I've thought of that, Watson. Each time the tellers go into the vault, they must tally their transactions with amounts, received from whom and charged to whom, etc. No, if our perpetrator is in the bank, as I suspect he must be, he will not want to have any mention whatever of the money on bank records. This means whoever is receiving the money is the most likely perpetrator, splitting the money with an accomplice in the prison to silence any protests from the inmates."

"Very good, old boy," admired Watson.

"Ah," exclaimed Holmes, "here we are."

Having carefully deposited the "seeded" notes into a clean envelope and placing it inside his jacket pocket, Holmes, along with Dr. Watson, strode into the Bank of London.

Situated on Threadneedle Street in the heart of London, The Bank of England was an enormous stone and concrete edifice in three distinct sections with twenty-two massive classic Roman columns running along the front, six in front of each wing and ten in front of the main central lobby.

After entering through the large glass and steel doors, Holmes walked up to the teller, explaining that he was delivering a sum of money meant for the care of an inmate at Newgate Prison and was told the bank handles such transactions. He was directed to the Public Services Teller at the distant end of the bank. As they walked to this window, Holmes said to Watson in a low voice, "I expected as much. It would be too strange if the money was handled through the regular teller windows, too hit and miss."

"Rather," agreed Watson.

Stepping up to the window, Holmes addressed the teller, "I say, the teller at window number two directed me to your window. I have a sum of money that has just arrived from Italy for a prisoner's care at Newgate Prison. Do you take care of such business?"

"Yes, indeed, sir, among a good many other public services, I do," the bespectacled young man said, smiling.

Holmes handed him the envelope, "Here is twenty pounds. It is for a prisoner by the name of Carlino Gaetano, newly from Italy, currently incarcerated in Newgate," watching as the teller took down the information onto a receipt note. "The money comes from his Aunt and his Mother, who wish to remain anonymous."

"You can be quite sure, sir," the teller said as he looked up and smiled, "no one shall know of the transaction."

"Thank you," Holmes said as he watched the teller pin the receipt note onto the envelope.

"No problem at all, sir. Is there anything else?"

Holmes looked at him and smiled, "Shouldn't I receive a receipt?"

"Of course, sir, beg pardon," he said, smiling again, although it now appeared just a bit strained.

"Thank you," Holmes said again, and he and Watson walked out of the bank.

"Now what, old boy?" Watson expectantly asked Holmes.

"Now, we go to Baker Street," Holmes replied before hailing a cab to take the two back to their flat.

"Baker Street? What about our twenty pounds?"

"Think of it as an investment, Watson," Holmes said wryly.

"An investment?" Watson repeated questioningly, "An investment in what?"

"Why, an investment in bait, bait which will catch men rather than fish, I should think, if all goes according to plan," answered Holmes as they climbed into the hansom. "I've a few arrangements to make with some officials in both the Bank of England and at Newgate, but I should say in a month's time, we should be able to haul in a sizable catch."

Chapter 18

REDEMPTION REALIZED

October 4, 1888

"Baron!" Dr. Tremaine burst into the conservatory, interrupting a contemplative baron as he performed the *Grosso Mogul* concerto, said to have been written by Vivaldi to evoke the emotion of the Albigensian Crusade. The baron flashed a look in the direction of the doctor displaying his annoyance at the interruption, "Forgive me, Baron, but I have what I believe is wonderful news."

"Forgive me, Doctor, my mind was in, shall we say, another place" explained the baron immediately regaining his composure, "what is your news?"

"The serum...I believe it's ready," exuded the doctor, barely able to contain his excitement. "I didn't wish to say anything until I was sure, but my latest tests confirm that it is stable enough for injection."

"Are you sure, Doctor?"

"Yes, Baron, I'm very sure. I've triple checked all the tests. I can inject the serum tonight, if you like."

The baron turned away from Tremaine and walked behind his desk, placing his violin down gingerly upon it, then looked at Tremaine, "No. I think it might be better if we await the dawn to inject your serum, Doctor."

"I don't understand." Tremaine was perplexed. "I thought you would be as excited as I, even more so," he said with a look of astonishment.

"I am, Doctor. Believe me, I am. But I'm concerned for you."

Tremaine continued to look bewildered, "I'm afraid I still don't understand, Baron. You're afraid for me?"

Smiling, the baron continued, "Yes, Doctor, for you. This serum has, obviously, never before been tried. What do you suppose would happen if I were to have a violent reaction to it?"

"We would, of course, take the normal precautions of binding your arms and legs in such a manner as you would be unable to harm yourself or anyone else," explained Tremaine.

As Tremaine described the safeguards, the baron picked up a poker from the fireplace and with the effort one would make snapping a twig, he bent it back upon itself, "Do you think your bindings are strong enough?" he asked. "My affliction has certain, shall we say, advantages of which you are unaware, Doctor. Preternatural strength is one of them," he explained as he straightened the poker, with equal ease. "No. I think it would be better for us to await the dawn, when I am considerably weaker. Don't you agree, Doctor?"

Tremaine was nearly speechless as he watched the baron's display of brute force. Regaining his voice, "Yes…yes, Baron, perhaps that would be better. Are you certain it will be safe even then?"

"With the proper precautions, as you have described, and with Garrett standing by, I'm confident I can be sufficiently subdued as to assure your safety, Doctor," the baron persuaded.

"Then I shall make the necessary preparations. If you will excuse me, Baron," requested the doctor.

"Of course, Doctor," allowed the baron as he again picked up his violin and began playing. This time, the tune was much less melancholy than when the doctor arrived.

Tremaine set about preparing the table on which the baron would recline as he received his injection. He had Garrett affix strong leather straps with which to secure the baron's arms and legs. As a precaution, more straps were added to secure the shoulder and torso area.

Not until all the preparations were complete and Garrett had been instructed to return just before dawn did Tremaine lie down on a makeshift cot he'd had installed in the lab to rest until the appointed time.

The doctor was soon awakened by the baron who was standing before him. Garrett was also in the lab and took the baron's shirt as he removed it. Addressing the doctor, "I believe it is time, Doctor, the dawn approaches."

"But baron, it's still quite dark" said the doctor cautiously.

"I've had Garrett secure all the shutters in the house and crepe all the windows for my comfort. I hope you don't mind, Doctor."

"Not at all, Baron, I should have thought of that myself."

"I'm sure you've had other things on your mind," the baron smiled and as he did, Tremaine, who had never seen the baron during the daylight hours, noticed the sallowness of the baron's skin as well as the yellow tinge to his eyes. He noticed too that the baron didn't appear as robust as usual and in fact gave the impression of a much older man.

"You look surprised, Doctor," the baron said with an amused look. "I'm sure now you can see for yourself why I thought it more prudent to wait until dawn," offered the baron as he sat on the edge of the table prepared by the doctor.

"Yes, I see, baron" accorded Tremaine as he arose and accumulated the necessary implements. "Please, baron, lie down and try to get comfortable. Garrett will secure the straps, if you don't mind."

"Of course, Doctor," the baron agreed as he reclined onto the table, Garrett tending the straps.

The doctor placed two hypodermic syringes and two bottles on the small table at the head of the one on which the baron reclined—one bottle contained the serum, the other a solution of carbolic acid, "Two syringes, doctor? Is there more than one serum?"

"No, baron, only one. The second syringe is to extract a sample of your blood once the serum has had time to assimilate into your bloodstream. The other bottle is to disinfect the area of the injection."

"Ah, yes, of course," he said as he relaxed his head and closed his eyes, "whenever you are ready, doctor."

Taking a gauze bandage, Tremaine dampened it with the carbolic acid solution and swabbed the area of the baron's inner elbow. Carefully, he filled the first hypodermic with the serum. Pausing, he asked, "Baron, are the bindings quite secure?"

The baron tested the straps and was unable to budge them, "I believe you are quite safe, Doctor."

"Perhaps this would be a good time to discuss my fee," Tremaine joked.

"Why, Doctor, I wasn't aware you had such a droll sense of humor," remarked the baron, "perhaps you'd like to discuss it with Garrett?" nodding toward his stalwart guardian.

"Touché, Baron. Now, this may stick a bit as the needle goes in."

"You've little notion how this turns the tables, Doctor."

As the needle slid into the vein, the doctor cautioned, "Try not to talk, Baron," and he began to administer the serum. After he'd fully depressed the syringe, he withdrew the needle, placing the dampened bandage over the puncture mark, "There. Now, Baron, let me know if you feel any…"

Before Tremaine had finished his sentence, the baron's entire body convulsed on the table. He clenched his teeth groaning as the veins on his forehead and neck stood out alarmingly. The straps restraining his wrists began to give way, causing both Garrett and Tremaine to take a step backward. His eyes bulged in his head as he gasped in a great volume of air, then collapsed on the table completely still.

"You've killed him!" cried an unnerved Garrett.

"Nonsense!" shouted Tremaine as he feverishly attempted to revive the collapsed baron. With Garrett eagerly looking on, the doctor gently slapped the baron to no effect. He tried again, harder. He made three more attempts, each with more force than the last. He was about to slap him a fourth time when the baron's hand, which apparently had escaped the restraint, stayed his attack.

"That won't be necessary, Doctor."

"Baron, you're all right!" Tremaine exclaimed, noticing Garrett relax.

"Yes, Doctor, it appears you haven't yet disposed of me."

"How do you feel, Baron?"

Breathing deeply, the baron replied, "Not appreciably

different than before, aside from a slight ringing in my ears, thanks to your right hand."

"I apologize, Baron."

"Not at all, Doctor, it was a strange sensation. I was fully conscious of what was occurring, but I was unable to assert myself. A most unusual circumstance," looking up at Tremaine's face, "now, if you'll remove the remaining restraints, I think I should like to retire."

"Of course, Baron," replied Tremaine, "Garrett, please remove the straps." Garrett obediently loosened and removed the heavy leather straps. "Before you go, Baron, I'd like to take a sample of your blood now and again this evening."

"Naturally, Doctor," with an amused look on his face.

"What is it, Baron?" asked Tremaine, noticing the wry smile wash over Barlucci's face.

"Forgive the dark humor, Doctor, but you must appreciate the irony of the situation."

"Irony? I'm not sure…oh, I see," Tremaine agreed, but was unable to join in the baron's apparent amusement. Without looking back at the baron, he took the second syringe and after disinfecting both it and the baron's arm, he drew a sample from Barlucci's vein. "There, Baron, now I agree with you that you should retire. I'll see you this evening. Garrett, the baron may be somewhat uneasy on his feet. Please assist him to his quarters."

The baron stood by the table declaring, "That won't be necessary. I am perfectly capable of making my own way."

"As you wish, Baron, but at least allow Garrett to accompany you in the event there are any lingering effects of the serum."

"Very well…I shall see you this evening, Doctor," giving a short bow, he and Garrett left the doctor alone.

Once Tremaine was sure they were gone, he sat down to write his fiancée.

October 5, 1888

Julia, my love,

Today is a momentous day. I've just injected Baron Barlucci with the serum that I am sure will arrest his condition making it possible for me to return to you without concern. You've no idea how exhilarated I feel. But even that exhilaration pales beside what I will feel when I can again hold you in my arms, my dear, sweet Julia.

Barring any difficulties, I shall be leaving London in two weeks. I've already booked tentative passage and am counting the hours until I can again kiss your lips and smell your hair. I cannot wait until we are man and wife, my Julia, though I know I must – we must.

I shall close now, as I am quite exhausted from the day's endeavors. I shall see you in my dreams, as always, my love, and until we are together, I remain only yours, truly,

Alan

#

October 14, 1888

He'd nearly forgotten how the late afternoon sun elongated shadows and how the birds songs played on the airy breeze. These small, seemingly insignificant things the baron took great note of as he rode in his coach to see Abigail. He was genuinely surprised by the things he'd forgotten about life in the light of day and it caused him to notice and appreciate such small things in a way he never had before. His awareness of his newfound appreciation made him realize, in the darkest corner of his mind that he would never become again the man he was before, no matter how much he tried or how fondly he wished for it.

He began life as part of the privileged aristocracy of northern Italy. When he was a small boy he was tutored in Latin, Greek and French by the Cistercian monks in the mountain monastery, Certosa di Pavia, that bordered a hunting park owned by the Barlucci family. When he turned fourteen, he received his father's blessing to study to become a monk himself. After eleven years inside the monastery, he made a fateful pilgrimage to Rome, which set him on this path, a journey that took him through what he considered no less than hell on earth.

It was while he was in Rome he saw his first Poor Fellow-Soldiers of Christ, in their distinctive white robes emblazoned with a red cross. They were in Rome to receive Pope Innocent IV's blessing before they departed on the final stage of a crusade against the Cathars in southern France and northern Italy. He was impressed by the manner and obvious stature of the Templar Knights as they were shown deference by the local populace and the bishops in Rome as well.

Brother Barlucci sought out the Templar Master, Armand of Perigord, expressing his desire to become a Templar. At the time it was not unusual for the Templars to recruit members from other orders and after a suitable period of trial, during which his obedience and loyalty were tested, Barlucci became a Templar. His faith was strong and with great conviction in the righteousness of his cause, he marched with his brother Templars to cleanse Europe of the heretical Cathars and to capture their stronghold of Montsegur, where it was rumored they held fantastic treasures.

In the intervening centuries since that crusade, Baron Barlucci's view of worldly matters became transformed. At first he was involved in other righteous conflicts, bringing his unique talents to bear, but as these conflicts came and went he began to step back, to observe how the petty squabbles of one day, which to those involved seemed paramount, rose and fell as the tides. Indeed, he watched as nations too were, for a time, mighty, then fell into ruin. He began to question the meaning of righteousness itself and, moreover, his role. Eventually, he came to realize that righteousness as a concept was as fleeting and transitory as the people who proclaimed it. Now it might rest with this king, pope or country while in a blink of an eye, as he came to view a lifetime, it would come to rest with another.

No, the very stars in heaven had shifted too far for him to step back into his former naïve skin again, even if a cure for his malady was at hand. He was too wise to now play the fool, too wary to be deceived.

And yet, perhaps with Abigail he might shed his cynicism and callousness like the skin of a snake to reveal a fresh, new skin. But even if he were so able, isn't a snake is still a snake after all?

The baron's coach pulled up to Commissioner Warren's house in the late afternoon, before the sun had set. Abigail was in the garden, picking some late autumn blossoms and was surprised when the baron stepped out of the coach. He was dressed in black, as usual, and wore tinted glasses to shield his eyes.

"Baron," she said when he'd drawn near enough to hear. "This is a most pleasant surprise."

"Have you forgotten our engagement this evening?"

"Of course not," she replied, "but I must say that I didn't expect you for some time, per your usual habits."

"Ah, then perhaps I should come back later," he said as he began to turn around.

"No, wait, I didn't mean..." fearing she'd offended him. Then she saw the smile he was trying to hide on his face, "You are teasing me," she laughed.

"Ahhh...your laughter is sweet music, my Abby," he spoke softly, ensuring no one but she could hear, "my love."

At his words she flushed, then looked about her to see if anyone was close by who might hear, "Baron...Tonietto, you speak so familiarly..."

"Are you offended, then."

"No...not offended," smiling sweetly, "surprised. You've never...I mean, you..." giggling quietly, she looked down and away.

In a low tone, "I've never spoken my heart, is this what you mean?"

Looking up with just her eyes, she answered "Yes."

"Am I too presumptuous? Do I assume too much?"

Again, Abigail looked down at the blossoms she had just cut, "No, Tonietto, you do not assume too much," she said almost in a whisper.

"Then, you feel the same?"

Turning her face toward him and gazing lovingly into his eyes, "I do. Yes, my Tonietto, I do," with cheeks flushing once more.

She turned and began to walk deeper into the garden, away from the house and any curious ears that might be nearby. The baron followed her.

As they neared an old well with a stone bench beside it, the baron took Abigail's hand and bade her sit beside him. He was reminded of another garden in which he'd had a conversation similar to the one he was about to have with Abigail.

He'd been walking in the garden of Maria's home, just after midnight, when he bade her to sit on a large rock while he summoned the courage to confront her with the truth that tormented him, much as he would soon confront Abigail. He knew too well what he had to say could make him abhorrent in her eyes, but he loved her too much not to be totally honest with her. He loved Abigail, he realized, as much as he'd love Maria a century before. His fear was that his revelation might cause him to lose Abigail, just as he lost Maria.

Maria told him, in her gentle way, that she could not marry him, but would never stop loving him and they must not see each other again. She promised him she would keep his dark secret and pray for him always. The realization that they would not be together stabbed him like a dagger in the heart. He left the garden that night, seeing Maria only once more before she died.

The pain of that parting was much on his mind as he took Abigail's hand in his, "Abby, my Abby, there is much I must tell you, things you do not know."

"What is it, Tonietto?" she asked, concern in her eyes.

"What I have to say you may find repulsive. You may find me repulsive after you hear…"

Touching her finger to his lips, "No, Tonietto, there can

184

be nothing about you that could ever repulse me. You have given my heart reason to laugh. I have never felt this way before."

Taking a firmer tone, "No, Abigail. You must hear what I have to say before we speak of our feelings further."

For the better part of an hour they sat deep in the garden, far from any prying eyes or ears, as the baron explained to Abigail of his strange and horrible malady, much as he had explained it to Maria a century before. Abigail found it difficult, at first, to take him seriously, but perforce of his words and the power of his mind to direct her thoughts not to avoid what he was saying, he persuaded her of the truth of his condition.

Her natural instinct to be repulsed by one such as he was easily overcome by the intense feelings she had developed for him. So easily, in fact, the baron was surprised her reaction to the truth was so mild. She did not hesitate when he asked her if she could love someone such as he.

"I could love no one else, my Tonietto," she said calmly. In truth, she felt a guilty exhilaration at knowing his secret. It served to heighten her passions toward him in a way that both excited and frightened her.

Upon hearing her words, the baron took Abigail into his arms and kissed her passionately for the first time. She met his kiss with equal ardor. As they parted, she spoke, "But, Tonietto, if all you say is true, and I don't doubt it is, how is it you've come to me at this early hour. Isn't the sunlight harmful to you?"

"Ah, but this is the most exciting and remarkable part of what I have to tell you, my dear, sweet Abby." She could see the excitement in his eyes as he continued, "I am undergoing treatment for my condition. Do you remember the young doctor whom you met at the party where we were first introduced?

"I remember every detail of the night I met you, Tonietto, yes."

"He is a great American doctor. A hematologist…a doctor of blood disorders, and he has taken my case. In fact, it is he who I am going to see in New York."

"How does this allow you to come here tonight."

"I'm sorry, I get ahead of myself," the baron said,

realizing he'd left out part of the story. "Before Dr. Tremaine returns to America, he has agreed and has been living with me at Darthmore while working on finding a cure for my condition. In so doing he's developed a serum that, while it is not a complete cure, has ameliorated the symptoms of my condition to such a degree I am steadily increasing the amount of sunlight I can withstand."

"My darling, that's wonderful," she smiled, then thoughtfully she asked, "and the other symptoms? Are they also, ameliorated?"

"Yes, my sweet, over the last two weeks my cravings have steadily decreased. It is a very liberating feeling." Once again he kissed her deeply, then said, "very liberating."

Playfully, she pushed him away, "perhaps a bit too liberating," then laughed. Then he joined her and they laughed together.

#

October 18, 1888

Even though the day was overcast, the baron's coach was outfitted with thick black curtains covering the windows. The baron himself was sitting well back in the coach, his greatcoat drawn up to his face, on which he wore a pair of dark tinted glasses. "Baron, there was no need for you to see me off like this. I know how averse you are to the light of day."

"Nonsense, Doctor. Your marvelous serum has made a world of difference in my constitution. I may not yet be able to remain in full sunlight for long without ill effect, but I am certainly not as incapacitated by it as I am accustomed. With each passing day I feel more at ease with the sunlight. These past two weeks have been extraordinarily exciting."

"Regardless, Baron, please do not overdo it. Remember, two injections per day and record anything out of the ordinary in your journal. I will need that upon your arrival in New York."

"I understand perfectly, Doctor. Two injections per day,

entries in the journal and don't overdo. You worry far too much," emitting a rare laugh, "besides, you've given me so much to hope for I could not allow you to leave without seeing you off myself. Now, hurry aboard, they are making ready to bring in the gangplank."

Standing outside the coach, Dr. Tremaine looked down the dock toward the ship, "You're right, baron, I'd better be going. Reaching into the coach and taking the baron's hand, "I shall see you in New York, then."

"By year's end at the latest. Perhaps even in time for your wedding," he smiled. "Now, bon voyage."

"I shall be expecting it!" he replied, tipping his hat and giving a curt bow as he'd seen the baron do so often.

Reaching up to shake Garrett's hand, the doctor said a heartfelt goodbye. Garrett grasped his hand tightly and with tears welling up in his eyes said, "Thank you, Doctor."

A moment of silent recognition passed between the two men. In that moment, Dr. Tremaine realized Garrett had understood all along what the baron was and what Tremaine had done to help him. When Garrett released his hand, Tremaine turned slowly and walked down toward the ship.

Barlucci observed as Dr. Tremaine made his way along the pier through the throngs of well wishers seeing their loved ones off to America. Sitting quietly in his cocoon, the baron watched as Dr. Tremaine made his way up the gangplank, disappearing behind the crowds standing along the rail of the ship. He continued watching as the lines were cast off, and the crowd began to dissipate. As the ship made its way to the middle of the channel, the baron's coach began making its way back to Darthmore Hall.

The baron worked steadily through the nights preparing his papers for an extended stay in America. Working through the auspices of Perry, Dingle & Guild, he transferred large sums of money to be available, on call, with several large banking interests in New York and arranged for a complicated trust to be put into effect for most of his European holdings. He decided to maintain ownership of Darthmore Hall. He'd become quite enamored of its charm and style. Besides, he thought he might have occasion to return to London, perhaps permanently, once he'd been cured.

The baron found himself, in the days since Dr. Tremaine's departure, becoming uncharacteristically optimistic about the future. Faithfully, he injected the serum into his arm twice daily. He entered into his journal that he'd begun to extend his active daily routine into the late afternoon and early morning, without ill effect.

The hunger with which he'd lived as a constantly gnawing, odious companion, began slowly to dissipate with each passing day, instead of steadily increasing. For the first time in many long centuries, the baron began to feel enthusiastic about his future, a future he hoped would be without the malady that had so long plagued him.

Chapter 19

IDENTITY REVEALED

October 31, 1888

There were 316 sign-painters, livery stables and coach-makers in metropolitan London. Holmes, Watson and Abberline divided the number between them and one by one visited their shops and places of business, making inquiries, to find the one that had provided the emblem on the coach door of the suspected Whitechapel murderer.

It was not until October 31st, when they'd already been to 243 places of business that Inspector Abberline walked into the shop of Wellington & Son, Sign Painters. Coincidentally, it was not far from Sherlock Holmes's Baker Street apartments.

The inspector entered the shop after noting that its rear entrance opened into a large yard, accessible through an alley, making it convenient for a business that serviced wagons and coaches. At this time of day, just after noon, there was only one person in the shop and, as it happened, it was the owner, Walter Wellington, Sr. After introducing himself as an inspector from the Central Investigations Division, he asked whether the shop had recently filled an order, in the last several months, for a monogram of the letter "B" on the doors of a black coach.

"Well now, let's see what we've got in the books," Wellington responded, while thumbing through a ledger of accounts, "a black coach, you say…hmmm…" opening a second ledger, "…the letter 'B'…ah, here it is, sir… July 23rd, for a Mr. Becker."

"Do you have an address?"

"Only a business address, I'm afraid, sir, Perry, Dingle & Guild, Barristers, #13, Bedford Row, Camden."

Abberline, writing the information in his notebook, gave a quick, "Thank you," and turned to leave.

"What's the caper, sir, what have they done?"

"Routine investigation," then, as an afterthought, "but

tell no one I was inquiring, it's a confidential matter."

"Very well, sir, mum's the word, then," he called after him, but Abberline was already out the door.

Excited by this latest piece of news, and being close to Baker Street, Abberline made his way across Regent's Park to share the news with Holmes and Watson. When he arrived, Watson was out, but he found Holmes examining some documents at his desk by the window.

"Ah, Inspector, come in."

"Good afternoon, Mr. Holmes, I see Dr. Watson is out."

"Yes, he's running down some more of the sign-makers."

Looking over Holmes shoulder, "Are those the 'Ripper' letters?"

"A messenger brought them over this morning. I've just this minute sat down to analyze them. I'm afraid a cursory examination doesn't indicate much, perhaps a closer scrutiny will prove fruitful."

"I have a bit of news, Mr. Holmes."

Sitting upright, Holmes asked, "Another murder?"

"No, thank goodness," noting what he thought might be disappointment registering on Holmes's face. "I've found the sign-painter, his shop is just a bit off the other side of Regent's Park."

Turning to face the inspector, "And the customer who ordered the monogram? You have his name?"

"Yes, sir, a Mr. Becker," pulling out his notebook, "of Perry, Dingle & Guild barristers. Their office is situated in Camden. I have the address."

"Yes, I've heard of them. A very reputable firm, as I recall, not the sort to get mixed up in something like this, I would think."

Watson entered the room, returning from his latest efforts to find the sign shop and appearing quite foot weary. He flopped down in his overstuffed chair exclaiming, "I've ten more shops to go on my list. I'm beginning to think perhaps the coach was purchased somewhere outside London."

Before Watson had time to get comfortable, Holmes was up putting on his coat, "Come along, Watson, You're finished searching sign shops, we've more important work to do."

"What's that? You've found it, then?"

"Yes," answered Holmes, "now come along, old boy, we're about to meet the prime suspect."

The trio bounded down the stairs and onto the street hailing a four-wheeler. During the coach ride to Perry, Dingle and Guild, Barristers, Abberline was clearly excited and pleased with himself that he had found the sign shop for which they'd been searching. He was equally pleased that the name of the man whose initial was on the coach was, apparently, an English barrister, possibly of German descent, and not an Italian. It wasn't that he held any malice toward Holmes, quite the contrary. He admired Holmes and respected his insight and powers of observation and concentration. But still, he thought it was nice to know he was eminently fallible all the same.

"Well, Mr. Holmes," Abberline said, "it appears we are chasing a domestic brand of murderer rather than an Italian import."

"Holmes, recognizing the good-humored challenge to his deduction returned, "Perhaps, Inspector, but I'm of the opinion one cannot be sure of a rooster's pedigree until all the chicks have hatched."

As they entered the offices of Perry, Dingle & Guild, Abberline identified himself as an inspector from CID and asked the receptionist for Mr. Becker.

Checking the calendar of appointments on her desk, she asked, "Is he expecting you?"

"No," Inspector Abberline displayed his identification for her, "but the matter is urgent."

"Please wait here a minute, gentlemen, and I'll see if Mr. Becker is available," she said and disappeared through one of several interior doors in the rich, mahogany paneled office. In a minute, the receptionist returned and showed them into the office of John B. Becker, Esquire.

"Come in, gentlemen," rising from behind his desk and

extending his hand, "how may I help you?"

The size of the desk only served to make Mr. Becker appear even more diminutive than his barely five-foot frame. He was the antithesis to Holmes's description of the murderer, causing a confused look to pass between Watson and Abberline.

"Mr. Becker," Holmes, smiling, broke the momentary awkward silence, "we are here to inquire about one of your clients."

"I see. I have a great many clients. Can you tell me the name of the particular one in whom you are interested?"

"We are rather hoping you can tell us his name," responded Holmes.

"I'm afraid I don't understand," a quizzical look coming over Becker's face.

"It's rather simple, really," Holmes explained. "I believe you have a client for whom you secured a coach onto which you had a rather ornate monogram of the letter 'B' painted by Wellington & Son, sign painters. Do you recall?"

"Yes, of course, you are speaking of the Baron Barlucci, Baron Antonio Barlucci, the Italian financier."

Holmes exchanged a satisfied glance with Inspector Abberline, "He's Italian, then?"

"Why yes, yes indeed, a very old and distinguished family, I'm told."

"Mr. Becker," Abberline interjected, "do you know where the baron resides?"

"I should, I secured the estate for him. A very handsome buy, too, I don't mind saying. A bargain. Apparently, the baron, who I understand is most wealthy, has a habit of purchasing estates wherever he is inclined to visit for any length of time. It's quite an elegant place and private. As I recall, a seven foot wall surrounds it on all sides, with an iron gate securing the drive. And as I said, an excellent bargain. Of course there were some modifications necessary to make it suitable. For instance, the baron is a connoisseur of fine wines and..."

"Where, Mr. Becker?" Holmes interrupted impatiently, "It's of vital importance that we speak to him."

"Why, Darthmore Hall, on Westbourne Grove Place, just off Hyde Park."

"Thank you, Mr. Becker, you've been most helpful," said Holmes as they departed.

Abblerline added, "You'll keep our inquiries confidential, I trust."

"Of course, sir, is there any trouble?"

"Purely routine, sir, I assure you," hurrying out the door to catch up with Holmes and Watson. "Good day."

"Mr. Holmes," said Abberline as they emerged from the office and onto the street, "now that we have an address and a name, I will need to secure a warrant before we proceed."

"Capital idea, Inspector, but I suggest we act quickly. Our murderer has been dormant these past four weeks. My fear is that he's bound to strike again, and very soon."

"Don't forget young Gaetano," interjected Watson, "his trial is set to start tomorrow. Catching this villain before it concludes is paramount I would say."

"Don't worry, Watson, the Chief Magistrate owes me a small favor. I'm sure if I were to explain our plans and that the arrest of the real murderer of Miss Rossini is imminent, he will accommodate a further postponement."

"I shall do my best to complete the necessary paperwork today. If all goes well, I'll meet you at Baker Street by 6:00 p.m. tonight."

"I say, that sounds very reasonable, eh Holmes?" asked Watson.

"Yes, well it will have to do. Done then." Holmes extended his hand, "We shall expect you this evening, Inspector."

Tipping his hat, Abberline bade them good-bye, "Mr. Holmes...Dr. Watson." They parted company with Holmes and Watson hailing a cab to take them back to Baker Street and Abberline hiring a hansom to take him to Whitehall.

On the way back to Baker Street, Holmes remarked, "I think it's time we wired Inspector Renard."

"Renard? Of the Parisian Prefect of Police? Whatever

for?"

"Don't you see the parallels, old boy? Women of ill repute having their throats cut?"

"Yes, I see that, but the differences...don't you think differences are a bit, er, different?"

"Are you referring to the victims being disposed of in the river in Paris, and the abdominal mutilations here in London?"

"Well, yes, those would be the main differences, don't you agree?"

"I'm now convinced those differences can be easily explained, old boy. Regarding the disposal of the victims in the Seine, it would be much more difficult for the murderer to similarly use the Thames. It is, after all, London's lifeblood of commerce, much more so than the Seine. This makes it less accessible as means of disposal."

"Yes, I suppose that's true, but what about the mutilations?"

"It follows, my dear Watson, as does the night follow the day, that since he no longer had the deleterious effects of the river acting on the body to disguise his handiwork, he required additional...how did Abberline say it? Camouflage; the mutilations are meant to divert attention from the throat."

"My word, Holmes. You never cease to amaze me," commented Watson. "This time, though, I think you may be off the mark."

"We shall see, Watson, we shall see," answered Holmes pensively. "Nonetheless, a cable indicating the possibility of the Seine slasher being actively at work here in London, I think, is not out of order. Besides, I have some questions for which he may be able to supply the answers."

"Very well, old boy, we *shall* see."

#

"This is preposterous, Inspector!" Sir Charles was livid with the news Inspector Abberline brought him, "Baron Barlucci is from one of the finest and oldest families in Italy and a close personal friend. I've known him for years. How have you come to this ridiculous conclusion?"

194

"Sir Charles, the evidence is very clear. Mr. Holmes and I are convinced..."

"And that's another thing," Sir Charles interrupted, "since when does the Metropolitan Police Force, the most modern law enforcement agency in the world, resort to using a...a...civilian," the word dripping with venom, "to solve their cases?!"

"I'm sorry, Sir Charles, but Mr. Monro suggested..."

"MONRO!? I should have known! Abberline, you are hereby directed to drop this line of inquiry at once. Monro has no jurisdiction with this case."

"But, Sir Charles, I..."

"And Abberline," Sir Charles added as the vein in his forehead throbbed, "Mr. Holmes is off the case. That's an order, Abberline, or you can clear out your desk at once. Is that clear?"

"Sir Charles, I implore you to reconsider. I'm afraid your close ties with the suspect may be clouding your judgment."

"Clouding my judgment?" he puffed, standing to his full height, "See here, Abberline, if you continue down this path, I'll see to it you are sacked before the day is out! Now get out of my office before I lose my temper!"

Reluctantly, Abberline responded, "Yes, sir, Sir Charles, but I..." backing toward the door.

Sir Charles strode quickly across his office, opening the door for Abberline to exit, "This meeting is over!" As Abberline walked out, Sir Charles slammed the door shut.

"Yes, Sir Charles," Abberline said to himself as he departed.

Upon leaving Sir Charles's office, and contrary to Sir Charles instructions, Abberline went directly to the office of James Monro.

"Yes, Inspector?" Monro asked from behind a stack of newspapers, "What can I do for you?"

"Sir," said Abberline, "I'm this close to chucking it all in," holding his thumb and forefinger before his face to illustrate the point.

"I see," striking a match to re-light his pipe as he settled

195

back in his chair, "What has you in such a stir, Francis?" taking on a more conciliatory tone.

"Sir Charles!"

"And what has old Charley been up to now?"

"I've been working the Whitechapel murders, with Mr. Holmes, per your suggestion," Abberline began.

"Yes, yes, go on."

"It's been over a month now and we have just now uncovered evidence that brings us very close to an arrest. In fact, I only came in this afternoon to secure the warrant. Unfortunately, Sir Charles got wind of it and called me into his office." Agitatedly, Abberline paced in front of Monro's desk, hands waving as he spoke, slicing the air, "We were so very close, James...so very close!"

"What did Sir Charles say?"

"He has as much as ordered me, at the risk of losing my job, to drop this entire line of the investigation!"

"Has he given you a reason?"

"Apparently the object of the warrant, Antonio Barlucci, an Italian baron, is of too important a family, and as it so happens, he's also a friend of Sir Charles."

"A friend of Sir Charles, you say...interesting."

"Yes, a close friend, apparently; although I take Sir Charles putting us off to be as much a slap at you as consideration for his friend."

"I don't follow."

"I mentioned that you suggested using Mr. Holmes in the investigation and..."

"Oh dear, I'll wager that didn't sit well."

"No, sir. Sir Charles became quite livid. He's ordered Holmes off the case and allowed as you do not have jurisdiction."

"Well, he's correct there, for the time being at any rate. But as for Mr. Holmes, he is a civilian and I don't think Sir Charles's orders will hold much sway."

"True enough, sir, but I'm afraid my hands are tied, if I fancy keeping my job. I cannot continue this line of inquiry –

officially, that is. And if I wish to keep my position I cannot risk aiding Mr. Holmes in his continuance of the investigation"

"Francis, I know what you are thinking. Exercise caution, my boy. I wouldn't want to lose you from the force. Your best course of action is to stay in communication with Mr. Holmes, but steer clear of any official contact. Is that clear?"

"Yes, sir, I understand, sir."

After leaving Monro, Abberline hurried to his own office where he wrote Holmes a quick message to be delivered by the afternoon post. In it he explained the situation regarding Sir Charles and that until further notice, he could have no official contact with Holmes and he'd been ordered to drop his investigation of Baron Barlucci in connection with the Whitechapel murders. He further cautioned Holmes that should he and Dr. Watson continue their inquiries on their own, he, Abberline, would be unable to lend any assistance—officially. He closed by saying he fervently hoped this would be a temporary condition soon remedied, but he did not say how.

Holmes received the post from Abberline as he and Watson were enjoying their afternoon tea. Holmes read the message quietly, with the only expression given being a slight furrowing of his brow above his long, slender nose as he tapped his pipe stem against his cheek.

"What is it, Holmes, bad news?" asked Watson as he cooled his tea in his saucer.

"No, not at all, old boy, but I'm afraid our inspector has been detained. We sha'n't be calling upon the baron tonight after all, I'm afraid."

"Oh? Why's that?" Watson inquired.

"It appears the Home Secretary has requested we suspend our investigation for a few days pending the resolution of some difficulties on the diplomatic front. It should be only a few days and apparently the baron is out of town on business at any rate. I'm sure we'll be back on the case in no time."

"Well, I can't say I'm disappointed. I was afraid I'd miss the pinch, having another engagement and all that."

"There, there, Watson, you needn't worry, then. You can

keep your appointment with your lady friend without concern of missing 'the pinch', as you say," said Holmes as he folded the letter and slipped it into his jacket pocket.

Holmes, of course, had no intention of leaving things lie until the officialities within the Metropolitan Police were straightened out, but he saw no reason to cause Watson to miss his engagement, as he knew Watson would insist on accompanying him had he known the true situation.

Holmes waited patiently until Watson had departed, then threw on his greatcoat, placing a freshly tamped pipe in the breast pocket. When he'd reached the door, he hesitated, then, as an added precaution, doubled back across the apartment to retrieve the Webley revolver from his desk, which he slipped into the pocket of his coat.

Chapter 20

ENCOUNTER

October 31, 1888

Abigail and the baron were nearly giddy as they returned to Darthmore after an afternoon visit to the London zoo.

"It's amazing to me how much I've missed the daytime. One doesn't realize it at the time, but when your existence is confined to darkness, it has a dampening effect on everything you do."

"You certainly seem happier, my Tonietto, but the nighttime can be lovely as well" Abigail remarked with a sly grin.

"Who wouldn't be happy who was with you, my dear—day or night. Your very presence makes the day more radiant and the night more enticing."

"I think my love is a bit capricious today," teased Abigail.

"Capricious? I'd say dizzy—dizzy with love, my Abby, with love for you. I cannot wait until we are off to America."

"Nor can I, my love," smiled Abigail.

"My ship should be here soon. When it arrives, we shall sail together to America."

"Oh Tonietto, I feel so happy…I feel like dancing," and she began to twirl around the room as the baron watched, smiling. "Let us play a duet together, as we did on the night I first called you Tonietto."

"Of course, my love," taking her hand and leading her to the piano. Retrieving his violin from the shelf, he started to play. Abigail joined him. Moving behind her, he stopped playing and bent down to kiss the nape of her neck.

"Tonietto, please," she giggled, "I'm playing."

"Don't stop, my love," he said as he slid his arm around her waist, the scent of her perfume arousing his ardor as he nibbled at her ear.

"Tonietto!" she said, feigning shock, then stopped playing as she turned to kiss him. As they embraced, the clock struck 5 o'clock.

Pushing him away, gently, Abby said, "Tonietto, I promised Uncle I would return early tonight. Aunt Maggie isn't feeling well and I need to look in on her before she goes to bed."

"Of course, my love, my apologies," he said as he stood and offered her his hand, allowing her to rise, "I'm afraid I let myself get carried away with your beauty."

Flushing, "We'll have plenty of time once we are at sea, my love," looking away, embarrassed by her own boldness.

"Aha! Methinks the lady finds me attractive…"

"She does…but I must be going, my love. I must say adieu."

Taking her hand gently and kissing it as he bowed from the waist, "Of course, my love, I understand. Please give my best to your uncle and aunt and tell them I hope Lady Margaretta is feeling better." Opening the door to the study, he called to Garrett to have her carriage brought around.

As she turned to go, he caught her hand and pulled her back, "You cannot know how much your love means to me, my dear, sweet Abby," drawing her hand up to his lips, kissing her fingers.

"Nor yours to me, Tonietto," she drew his hand to her and kissed it in return. "Goodnight, my love."

As her carriage drove away, the baron's heart, long dormant, jumped in his chest, then fell silent. He rushed into his study and pulled out his log to record the incident for Dr. Tremaine.

#

Arriving at Darthmore Hall just before 7pm, Holmes rang the buzzer. He was greeted by a large, hulking figure, who inquired as to his business.

"I should like to see Baron Barlucci. My name is Sherlock Holmes." At the mention of his name, he noticed a glimmer of recognition register on the man's face. Peering into the man's deep set eyes, Holmes was sure they'd met, but just where eluded him for the present.

"Please, come in. I'll let the baron know you're here." Taking Holmes's hat, he waited for him to remove his coat.

"Thank you, but I'm afraid I'm still a bit chilly. I'll keep the coat, for now," Holmes explained as he was led into the library.

"Please wait here," Garrett said as he left Holmes alone to await the baron's arrival.

Holmes took advantage of this momentary solitude to take a quick mental inventory of the room. Items he found of particular interest included a leather-bound journal lying on the desk, a silver-handled walking stick in an umbrella stand and a small case with a locking lid, neatly tucked away on a bookshelf. As he waited, he reached across the desk, casually flipping open the journal. He read the following passage, "...the hunger continues to decline day by day, and with it I've noticed a like decline in visual sensitivity, not only to light..."

"How may I help you, Mr. Holmes?" interrupted the baron, seeing Holmes standing at his desk.

"Ah, Baron Barlucci, I presume," as Holmes simultaneously closed the journal and turned to greet the baron.

"That is correct. Did you find my medical journal interesting?"

"I apologize, Baron, it was open," Holmes lied. "I hope you'll forgive me. My curiosity is my bane, I'm afraid."

"Curiosity, they say, killed the cat, Mr. Holmes."

"Again, I apologize," Holmes moved away from the desk. "I'm here on semi-official business," Holmes said as he moved slowly toward the baron, "I'm investigating the recent spate of murders in the Whitechapel District."

"How does a thing like that bring you here?" The baron asked as he casually walked behind his desk, removing the journal from the desktop and placing it carefully in a drawer, which he closed and locked with a key he'd drawn from his waistcoat pocket.

Pretending to peruse the books on the shelves, Holmes moved closer to the locked case, noting the baron's apparent discomfort, "You have some wonderful books in your library, Baron."

"Thank you, Mr. Holmes, but I'm afraid I cannot take credit for them. They were here when I took possession of the estate." The baron began to probe with his mind, mentally reaching out towards Holmes in a vain attempt to turn his attention away from the case, but he was unable to find an entry. "Forgive my impatience, Mr. Holmes, but how do these events in Whitechapel concern me?"

"Your coach was seen in Whitechapel on the same evening that Catherine Eddowes and Elizabeth Stride were murdered."

"I do not recall being in Whitechapel recently. I am curious, though," an amused smile began to steal across his face, "have you made it your business to track down the owner of every coach reported to have been in Whitechapel that evening?"

"No, Baron, I'm afraid not. Only the ones on which the doors have been painted with a monogram of the letter 'B'."

"I see. Well...I admit to having a monogram on the doors to my coach, but I hardly think that would implicate me in murder, Mr. Holmes. I hope you have more to offer than that."

Holmes held out a linen handkerchief, "That same monogram appears on this handkerchief found clutched in the hand of one of the victims, Baron. Her name was Catherine Eddowes," quickly returning the handkerchief to his pocket.

"That proves nothing, Mr. Holmes," the baron said firmly.

"Perhaps it doesn't clinch the case, Baron, but it is a damning bit of circumstantial evidence when you consider the monogram is exactly the same as the one on your coach doors." Holmes pulled his pipe from his coat's breast pocket and asked, "Do you mind if I smoke, Baron?"

"Not at all, Mr. Holmes."

As Holmes replied, "Thank you," he struck a match on the case sitting in the bookshelf, noting with satisfaction the apprehension on the baron's face as he did so. "There is, of course, evidence which might prove conclusively who the

202

murderer is," Holmes suggested.

"Oh? And what, pray tell, might that be, Mr. Holmes?"

"The murderer is apparently a collector, of sorts." As he said this, Holmes glanced back at the case on the shelf.

"A collector? Of what?"

"Our murderer went to great pains to collect a few organs from his victims – a uterus here, a kidney there – perhaps as a memento, something he might keep locked up, preserved, which he might, when the occasion suited him, bring them out to admire the fruits of his dark work."

"My dear Mr. Holmes, I'm now beginning to believe you are quite delusional."

"Delusional? We shall see!" Holmes quickly grabbed the case from the bookshelf. "I'm taking this to Scotland Yard. We shall see who is delusional, my dear Baron."

"Stop!" leaning forward on his desk, the baron pressed a hidden button beneath the lip.

"Stay back, Baron!" Holmes warned, case in hand and pistol now out of his pocket and leveled toward the baron as he backed his way to the door. Opening it behind him, he failed to see Garrett.

"Stop him!" shouted the baron.

Holmes turned, but too late. Garrett grabbed Holmes from behind, his huge right hand crashing down on Holmes right forearm, causing the pistol to be dislodged from his grip, skittering harmlessly across the carpet. At nearly the same time, Garret spun Holmes around and his left fist connected with Holmes chin and both Holmes and the case fell to the floor. As Holmes lost consciousness, he heard the baron's clear baritone shouting, "FOOL!" above the sound of shattering glass beside his ear. Then, there was only silence.

Chapter 21

PERILOUS QUERY

November 1, 1888

Watson arose very late on Saturday and finding Holmes nowhere about, sat down to a fine breakfast of poached eggs and ham. As Mrs. Hudson was clearing away the breakfast dishes, Watson remarked, "I suppose Mr. Holmes has already taken his breakfast?"

"Why no, Doctor, he went out yesterday evening not long after you left, and hasn't yet returned. I just assumed you knew."

"Well, no matter. I'm sure he's off this morning making arrangements with the Chief Magistrate about that poor young Italian lad. He'll turn up sooner or later. He always does."

Letting out a sigh, "I suppose I should be used to his disappearances by now, but I do wish he'd let a body know when he's going to be gone."

"Yes, Mrs. Hudson, I quite agree. It is one of Mr. Holmes least endearing habits."

Chuckling, "One among many, I'd say, like shooting up the plaster."

"Why, Mrs. Hudson," Watson smiled, "you surprise me."

"Oh, please, Doctor, don't misunderstand. He's a dear, dear man and a model tenant, despite his peculiarities. It'd be quite dull around here without him. Quite dull indeed."

"Wouldn't it just. I couldn't agree with you more," Watson remarked as he settled back in his favorite chair and began to read the morning issue of *The Times.*

\#

Abigail descended the stairs when she heard the rapid knocking upon the door. As she opened it, Baron Barlucci stepped into the foyer, "This is a pleasant surprise, Antonio, and so early in the day, too."

"Is your uncle home?"

"Why no," answered Abigail, noting a look of concern on the baron's face, "he's gone to work. Is there something wrong?"

"Yes, I'm afraid so," he said as he closed the door and removed his outer gloves and coat. Looking around, he took Abigail's arm, "Let's go into your uncle's study."

"You're scaring me," Abigail said as he closed the doors to the study behind them.

"Here," motioning to the same two chairs he and Sir Charles had occupied on a previous visit, "let's sit. I have some disturbing news to tell you."

"Go on," she said as they sat down, each on the edge of the chairs, facing each other, he holding her hands in his.

"Last night, shortly after you left Darthmore, I had another visitor, a Mr. Sherlock Holmes."

"I've heard my uncle speak of him. I believe he is some sort of policeman. I don't believe my uncle cares for him very much."

"No, I don't suppose he would. He's not a policeman, not exactly. He's a detective. He's been looking into the Whitechapel murders."

"But what has that to do with you?" Even as the words were echoing in the room, she understood. Her eyes told him he didn't need to explain. "Does he know?"

"He suspects, which may be enough. Abigail, this may change our plans. I may be forced to flee, leave London sooner than we planned."

"I shall go with you."

"No. It will be too dangerous."

"But…"

"Trust me, love."

"I do…with all my heart, I do."

"Then, should I be forced to flee before our arranged departure on the ninth, you must continue as planned. I shall

205

arrange for you to be properly escorted in the event I cannot escort you myself. But should any suspicion fall upon me, you must allow your uncle to think you have unfavorably reconsidered your feelings toward me."

"But how will you…"

"Don't worry about me, my dear sweet Abby, I will be fine and we shall be together in New York, just as we planned. Have no doubts about that."

"I will do as you ask, Tonietto."

"I know that you will, my sweet Abigail. Now I must go. There is much to do in preparation regardless which way fate turns."

Walking to the door, she reached up to kiss him, "Please, Tonietto, be careful."

"I will, my love." He bent down and gave her a loving peck on the cheek, then, thinking this might be the last time he would see her until they were together in America, he embraced her and gave her a long and loving kiss.

"Things will work out, my love," he said as he climbed into his coach.

As he drove away, he called up to Garrett to head toward the Southbank area of London, near the Southwark bridge, to a warehouse in Farrington. Once there he went into the warehouseman's office to meet with Silas Fenley, proprietor of the warehouse.

"Mr. Fenley, I've heard you are a reputable warehouseman," eyeing him intently, "one who knows how to keep his business to himself."

"That's true, that's true," chuckled the diminutive septuagenarian through a mouthful of rotting teeth, "that is, for a price," he added, sizing up his customer as a man of considerable means, if a bit overdressed.

"Very well, then. I have a house full of possessions, which I need picked up immediately and stored until they can be moved onto my ship, and I would appreciate the utmost confidentiality. Do I make my meaning clear?"

"Very clear, sir, very clear indeed," he said as he rubbed

his dirty thumb against his even dirtier forefinger, "has I made myself clear?"

Satisfied the baron replied, smiling, "I think we can do business, Mr. Fenley," and he proceeded to give Fenley the details of where and when he should pick up the goods from Darthmore.

November 7, 1888

"By the order of the Chief Magistrate in the court of the Admiralty of Her Majesty's government, Carlino Gaetano, you are found guilty of the murder of Gianetta Rossini and are hereby sentenced to die by hanging for this most heinous crime. The sentence will be carried out at Newgate Prison on the morning of November 11, in the year of our Lord One Thousand Eight Hundred Eighty Eight."

As the bailiff read the scroll of judgment, Carlino Gaetano closed his eyes in disbelief.

"HE IS INNOCENT!" cried Vittorio.

"Bailiff, remove the condemned," ordered the Magistrate.

Watson and Vittorio followed along behind Carlino and as he was being put back into the police wagon for the trip back to Newgate Prison Watson tried to reassure both Vittorio and Carlino, "You must have faith in Mr. Holmes. I've never known him to disappear during an important phase of an investigation such as this not to arrive in the nick of time with a crucially exculpatory piece of evidence."

"But where is he?" asked Vittorio.

"I'm sorry to say I do not know," and having admitted his ignorance of Holmes whereabouts, he and Vittorio could only stand and watch as Carlino was taken away to await his execution.

"Don't worry, old boy," Watson said quietly to Vittorio, "Holmes will come through...Holmes always comes through." He hoped his words sounded more convincing to Vittorio than they did to him.

Chapter 22

REVELATION

November 7, 1888

The days and nights since Mr. Holmes fateful visit and the destruction of the serum passed quickly. With each day, with each hour, it seemed, the baron felt the effects of Dr. Tremaine's elixir draining away as if it were sand escaping in an hourglass. Holmes was kept bound and sedated in the wine cellar, behind the specially locked door, while the baron awaited what he assumed would be the inevitable inquiries as to his whereabouts. After the first three days had passed and no one had inquired, he began to breathe more easily. Unfortunately, the hunger, which had been so blissfully silent since Dr. Tremaine left for America, was now beginning to rage inside him like a wild animal.

Keeping Holmes alive while sedated was managed through intravenous feedings and occasionally allowing him to achieve a semi-conscious state, long enough to ingest sustenance and relieve necessary bodily functions. Garrett was instructed to maintain a watch on him whenever the baron was absent.

With no one coming to Darthmore in search of Mr. Holmes and the date of his and Abigail's departure approaching, the baron returned to Fenley's warehouse to make final arrangements for his imminent voyage.

No longer able to endure direct sunlight, he marveled and lamented at how quickly his condition had reverted. Even indirect sunlight caused his eyes to burn and his head to ache. He was also now aware he would need to quench his thirst soon and before his voyage or he might become a danger to his beloved Abigail.

He was visiting her tonight, his last visit before their departure, to explain the worsening of his condition and to give her the opportunity to forego this crossing, with the promise he would send for her when it was safe.

He had sent word ahead by post he would be visiting, but

that he preferred to meet with her in secret, in the garden, as he didn't want his appearance to give Sir Charles any cause for concern. He had Garrett stop the coach on the road intersected by the long drive of Sir Charles's estate and walked to the garden, carefully keeping to the shadows.

As he had expected, Abigail was waiting for him on the bench by the well. It pleased him to see her, and yet he still had to fight down his growing urge to feed. It sickened him to think of his own dear Abigail as prey, but a part of him could not keep this thought from creeping into his mind.

Instinctively, he approached her from behind, silently positioning himself to strike, "Abby," he said softly when he was directly behind her.

Turning quickly Abigail started at the sight of him. The absence of the serum had caused his skin to take on an ashen appearance and his face was tired and drawn. "Tonietto, you startled me," she said looking into his eyes, which were red and bloodshot, "what is wrong?"

"My darling, how can I tell you that I'm turning into a monster again," he looked away from her, his eyes welling with tears.

"No, don't," she said touching his arm to turn him back to face her, "it's all right, my love, remember? 'Things will work out'...this is what you told me and I believe it. With all my heart I believe it, my Tonietto."

"Abigail, listen to me. The serum...the serum left me by Tremaine—it's gone."

"Gone?" a flash of fear passed over her eyes briefly.

"You know what this means, don't you. You know you are in danger, even now," looking at her intensely, then turning away.

"No, I don't believe it. I don't believe you would ever, could ever hurt me, Antonio," touching his cheek.

"I don't want to believe it either, my darling, but we must be practical" he said as he looked into her eyes once again. "I cannot bear the thought of your coming to harm by my hand. I shall go on to America without you."

210

"No, Tonietto, I will come with you," she replied firmly.

"Oh, my sweet little Abby, it's better for you to wait until it is safe. Then I will send for you."

"No, Antonio, there must be another way...some way that will keep us together," she said wistfully. "If my uncle suspects you are involved in Whitechapel, he will forbid me to leave. There must be another way..." her voice trailed off as their eyes met and between them passed the secret knowledge of what the baron would need to do to keep Abigail safe, with Abigail giving her silent consent. "I know you could never hurt me."

Now clearly understanding Abigail's resolve to join him and seeing in her a strength he had not realized she possessed, the baron relented, "Very well, Abigail, but you must follow my instructions to the letter. To do otherwise would place you into great peril."

"I will, Antonio, I promise."

"You must be onboard the ship, my ship, the *Animus Lacuna*, tomorrow night. Go directly to your cabin, it's been made ready for you, and lock the door. The ship will sail at dawn. Remain there until after the ship is at sea. The crew will bring your meals to you. I will come for you when all is safe."

"Yes, Antonio, my Tonietto."

"One more thing, my love...you must not let your uncle know you are leaving. He must believe you are not going to America until later."

"Yes...you are right. I shall leave a letter for him and Aunt Bridget to find after I've gone."

"Now I must go. There is much to do to prepare for the voyage," kissing her tenderly. "You are brave, my dear, sweet Abby, I pray your courage and trust is not misplaced," kissing her lips tenderly.

"They are not, Tonietto. They are not."

November 8, 1888

Watson and Mrs. Hudson were so familiar with Holmes and his erratic behavior that they never gave his absence a second thought. But after a week, when Holmes failed to be present at Carlino's sentencing, Watson began to become concerned. Holmes had disappeared before at a critical juncture and had always shown up in the nick of time. Watson was sure Holmes would show up at any moment and with the proof required to save young Carlino.

He was, in fact, writing that very thought in his journal when Inspector Abberline came to call, late on the afternoon of November 8th. "Good afternoon, Dr. Watson, is Mr. Holmes around? I'm quite anxious to hear what you and he have discovered about our friend the baron."

"What's that? I was under the impression we were all on hold until the Home Secretary gave us an all clear on the diplomatic front."

Abberline looked at Watson quizzically, "The Home Secretary? Now I'm a bit confused, I'm afraid I don't know what you are talking about."

"Yes, the Home Secretary, in your note to Holmes last week."

"The note I sent? My note said I had been ordered to drop my investigation of Baron Barlucci, that's true, but I made no mention of the Home Secretary. I even intimated I hoped you and Mr. Holmes would continue investigating without me until I could get the moratorium lifted."

"I see, but Holmes…" Watson began to replay the events of the previous Friday evening over in his mind until, "My God! Holmes must have gone to Darthmore Hall alone…that very night."

"But why didn't you go with him, Doctor?"

"I was to meet my fiancée that evening to take her to the train station, as she is visiting relatives in the country. It was quite late when I returned and I'd assumed Holmes had already retired.

"I see now that Mr. Holmes, when he received your note saying you'd been forbidden to press the investigation, surmised—and rightly so—I would have insisted on accompanying him should he strike out on his own. Accordingly,

212

he concocted that little fairy tale about the Home Secretary thus I wouldn't have cause to break my engagement that evening."

"Then he hasn't told you what he's discovered?"

"Don't you see? That's just it. I haven't seen Holmes since that night. I'd assumed he'd gotten off on some other track, quite possibly with you, in an effort to clear the Gaetano boy, who even now is awaiting the noose, poor lad," Watson said, suddenly realizing how dire the young Italian's situation was. "But now, with you here... We must go to Darthmore at once!"

"Yes, at once. I'm still under orders not to investigate officially, but as I am on holiday for a week, there isn't much Sir Charles can say about my checking on a friend."

Watson put on his greatcoat, retrieving his pistol from his desk. On a whim, he walked to Holmes desk and checked, "Holmes has taken his pistol," he noted with some alarm. Once outside the Baker Street flat, they hailed a cab and gave the driver half a crown to make all haste to Darthmore.

The sun had set as the cab stopped in front of Darthmore Hall and Abberline and Watson emerged. "Would you like me to wait 'ere, gov'nor?" the driver asked.

"That won't be necessary," Watson replied, handing the man an additional sixpence and sending him on his way.

"Much obliged, sir," and cracking his whip over the head of his bay mare, he drove away.

Darthmore Hall was an imposing structure, surrounded on all sides by Oak and Elm trees, each over a hundred years old, inside stone walls. Between the manor and the walls was a great expanse of lawn, which was dotted with large shrubs in a pseudo-random pattern, which was symmetric about a central walkway. The building itself was in excellent repair with fresh paint, but somehow still gave the impression of gloom, an ethereal crypt-like melancholy, and although neither Abberline nor Watson gave voice to the thought, it was evident to each, the other felt its effect.

Watson rang the buzzer. He was about to ring it again when Garrett opened the door. "We'd like to see Baron Barlucci," said Dr. Watson.

213

"The baron is indisposed," the word seeming oddly out of place coming from the hulking man's lips.

"This is Dr. Watson and I am Inspector Abberline of the Metropolitan Police," Abberline said, moving forward into the doorway as he displayed his badge for Garrett to see.

"As I said, sir, the baron is indisposed."

Abberline noted a queer look in the man's eyes, as if he were frightened. He mistakenly believed Garrett to be intimidated by his authority as a policeman and decided to press the advantage, "You aren't interfering in an official investigation, are you?"

The odd, fearful look on Garrett's face was suddenly gone, replaced by a look of amused disdain as the hulking man moved toward Abberline. Before he could speak, however, Baron Barlucci appeared behind Garrett, "That will be all, Garrett," the baron said in a clear but soft tone, which had the edge of steel about it. At the sound of the baron's voice, the timid, childlike look stole back across Garrett's features and he slowly receded into the foyer. "Yes, Baron," he said, and then he was gone.

"Come in, gentlemen. Please, you must forgive Garrett. I'm afraid he's a bit rough around the edges, I believe you'd say, but he's quite loyal," said the baron while leading Watson and Abberline into the library, the only room in Darthmore, aside from the kitchen, which still had most of its furnishings. "Now, gentlemen, to what do I owe the pleasure of your company this evening?"

Watson spoke up, "Baron, on Friday last an associate of mine, Mr. Sherlock Holmes, paid you a visit, did he not?"

"Ah, yes. So you are friends of Mr. Holmes?"

"Why yes," answered Watson, a bit surprised the baron admitted seeing Holmes so readily, "then he did visit you?"

"Yes, yes, he came by, inquiring about that terrible business in Whitechapel. Nothing has happened to him, I trust."

"That is why we're here. We haven't seen him since he visited you that evening. Baron, what was the object of Mr. Holmes visit that night?"

214

"Oh dear, I hope nothing untoward has befallen him," showing what appeared to be genuine concern. "Let's see…" he continued, "Ah, I believe it was something about a monogram. Yes, that was it. He had a handkerchief with a 'B' embroidered in the corner. He was very anxious to see my coach, so we went out into my stables."

"And Mr. Holmes appeared satisfied?"

"Perfectly." Chuckling deep in his throat, "He struck me as being a bit embarrassed by the whole thing actually, as I recall."

Watson and Abberline looked at each other, then Abberline asked, "Baron, would you mind showing us your coach?"

"My, my…you wish to see my coach too?" After a moment of silence, a gruff laugh burst forth, "Of course, gentlemen, follow me, if it will satisfy your curiosity." The baron led Watson and Abberline through the house, down a long corridor, past an open cloakroom, a formal dining room, the music conservatory, the servants' quarters, and out a back door onto a covered veranda. The veranda led to a small livery stable, which housed both his horse and coach.

"There you are, gentlemen," spoke the baron as he opened the stable door.

Both Watson and Abberline looked at the coach in amazement. The 'B' on the coach door, rather than a flowing, flowery style with tails and flourishes as on the handkerchief, was instead a blocked letter 'B' with a single garland of ivy around it. "I can see why Mr. Holmes was embarrassed," said Abberline. "Other than it being a 'B', it bears no resemblance to the handkerchief whatever. I'm afraid we owe you an apology, Baron."

Watson, who'd been unusually silent since they'd left the library, said, "Yes, we are sorry to have bothered you, Baron," his eyes darted around the stable, "and if you'll excuse us, we won't take up any more of your time."

"No harm done, gentlemen, no harm done." The baron glared at Watson, as if sensing he was ill at ease.

"Very well then, Baron, if you will pardon our intrusion and if that gate," Watson turned and pointed to a low gate at the far end of the veranda, "leads to the street, we'll let ourselves out."

"Yes of course, that gate opens to a short garden path at the other end of which is a second gate leading to the street at the front of the house. Now, if you will excuse me," the baron made a curt bow and turned, leaving Watson and Abberline alone as they moved toward the gate.

Watson walked quickly down the path, his eyes darting around as if he were expecting something to jump out of the shrubbery.

"Watson," asked Abberline, "what is it?"

"Not now, Inspector," Watson said in almost a whisper, "wait till we are on the street."

As they emerged onto Westbourne Grove Place and had gotten what Watson considered a safe distance from Darthmore, he turned to Abberline, "Holmes is there."

"What? In Darthmore? How do you know?"

"His hat. As we passed by the cloakroom, I saw Holmes's hat."

"Are you certain?"

"I've been associated with Mr. Holmes for many a year and that is his favorite hat, I'd know it anywhere," he said emphatically. "What did you think about the coach?"

"I'm certain it's the same coach I saw the night of the Stride and Eddowes murders. He must have had it redone; the paint looked very fresh."

"My thoughts exactly. What do we do?"

"I'm afraid we are on our own, Doctor, I am unable to draw on Scotland Yard for support until we have something more concrete. If you earnestly believe Holmes is there, and I have no reason to doubt your intuition, I recommend we watch the estate closely until the baron leaves, then search the house."

Chapter 23

CONFRONTATION with a VAMPIRE

November 8, 1888

Despite the near complete absence of light in the small chamber, the baron had little difficulty seeing the slow, rhythmic rising and falling of Holmes's chest as he awaited his return to consciousness. Notwithstanding the danger he posed, the baron found himself admiring the sleeping detective for his intellect and his boldness. Perhaps if he knew the baron's unusual circumstance he could gain in him an ally. After all, it would be in both their best interests for the baron to be cured of this ailment. It would make no more sense to arrest the baron and see him hanged than it would for the baron to extinguish the life of Sherlock Holmes. He felt an odd sort of kinship with the detective, a man he considered to be of an intellect nearly as great as his own.

He'd seen men like Holmes before, men whose intellect allowed for a certain amount of forbearance in line with unusual circumstances. The trust of a good many men such as Holmes had been gained by him in the past and there was no reason for him not to believe he could gain Holmes's trust as well. He'd learned that noble men with the intellect and courage to see beyond the bounds of the commonplace could often be persuaded to enter into a symbiotic relationship.

As he watched Holmes's breathing become shallower as the drugs he'd been given wore off, the baron contemplated how quickly the absence of the serum had caused a reversal in his own condition. His senses, which had become less acute—a fact that alarmed him at first—as the serum worked its magic, were now hyper-acute. He could not only see Holmes chest rising and falling, but he could hear his heart beat as well as his breathing, smell his breath and feel the heat radiated from his body, noting its rise as he began to regain consciousness.

As his senses returned to him, Holmes maintained the

presence of mind to display no external signs of doing so as he gradually became aware of his surroundings. That he was bound and hooded, as well as blindfolded was his obvious first impression. The second thing he noticed was a slightly musty odor to the air, air that was somewhat damp and cool as well. Acoustically, he had the impression of a somewhat small room with walls that absorbed sound. From this he deduced he was being held prisoner in a cellar or basement chamber.

Lastly, the blow rendered by Garrett upon his chin made itself known in a distinctly painful way. It was then he made the connection to where it was he had met Garrett previously.

It had been a bit more than six years ago and Holmes was working on another case. This case involved the theft and smuggling of a rare and priceless antiquity known as the Scarab of Cleopatra, a solid gold clasp purportedly used by Cleopatra to fasten her robe across her breast. The scarab had an image of Mark Antony struck upon it with the letters S*P*Q*R beneath the image, a gift from her lover.

Holmes, during the course of his investigation, assumed the disguise of an antiquities smuggler while investigating in some of the rougher areas along the docks of London. It was here where, as a disagreement erupted into a pub brawl, he made the acquaintance of Garrett, who mistakenly clipped Holmes on the chin. He believed Holmes to be a part of the pack of thieves he was investigating.

Thankfully Holmes was able to avoid a direct hit during the assault that night and was met with merely a glancing blow instead. Garrett had occasion to realize his mistake when during the course of the brawl Holmes saved his life. When one of the smugglers drew a knife across Garrett's face, a wound that would leave a lasting scar, Holmes disarmed him before he could finish the job by stabbing Garrett through the heart.

After the brawl was broken up, the local constables came in and arrested three others in the fight who Holmes identified as the smugglers. Unfortunately for Holmes, in this latest encounter with Garrett, he was taken unaware and knocked cold from a direct blow from his massive fist.

As Holmes listened carefully, he was soon satisfied, by the absence of any other sounds in the room, that he was quite alone. The only sound he heard was of his own breathing, slow and regular. After a few minutes of patient waiting to ensure no one was about, Holmes began to systematically test the strength of his bonds.

"I see you have awakened, Mr. Holmes," the baron intoned in an almost soothing manner.

"Baron, I didn't hear you come in. Do pardon me if I don't get up."

"That's quite all right, Mr. Holmes, I hope you aren't too uncomfortable."

"Very snug, thank you," Holmes answered as he tested the bonds, "but not painfully so."

"I apologize for the necessity, but your insatiable curiosity has greatly inconvenienced me in two ways. First, you are quite correct, I am responsible for the recent deaths in Whitechapel, though I'd hardly term them murder and when you've heard my tale, I trust you will have a different opinion also."

"I'm curious, Baron, if not murder, how would you describe them?"

"Why, as two of your own countrymen might, Mr. Holmes, 'survival of the fittest' I believe is the phrase used by your Mr. Spencer and Mr. Darwin. You see, Mr. Holmes, nature's imperative is adapt or perish."

"You're mad! How can you equate the butchery you've perpetrated with survival? How can a man's survival be dependent upon senseless slaughter?"

"How indeed, Mr. Holmes, unless the 'slaughter' of which you speak isn't senseless or isn't perpetrated by a man. If senseless murder were my aim, Mr. Holmes, how do you explain the fact that you are still alive?"

"I said you are mad, Baron, not stupid," replied Holmes attempting to display a confidence he didn't quite feel. "Surely you know that my coming here tonight was no secret, and as such you must be aware my compatriots will soon be looking for me."

"I must admit that thought crossed my mind at first, Mr. Holmes, but after two days had passed and still no inquiries were made on your behalf...," the baron observed Holmes head snapping about as he mentioned that at least two days had passed. "Ah, I see that surprises you. That's right, Mr. Holmes, you've been my guest for a full week now, which brings me back to the subject of inconvenience.

"I am neither madman nor butcher, Mr. Holmes. I am as much a victim of my condition as are those poor women, perhaps more so. For them, the nightmare of their existence is over. For me, it stretches timelessly forward, as endless as it is hopeless. You see, Mr. Holmes, I am a vampire, neither man nor beast, neither alive nor truly dead, but rather, one of the undead." As he spoke, he walked around Holmes, noting how Holmes followed his movements instinctually. "My condition, with which I've been afflicted for over 600 years, is not unknown in history, although it is not commonly accepted."

"Your superstitious rendering would be more convincing if read in a 'penny dreadful' beside a roaring fire on a dark, stormy night, Baron. You speak as though you actually expect me to believe you."

"You doubt me, Mr. Holmes? I assure you, I am quite serious."

"Baron, I am a man of science, not superstition."

"Of course, yes, of course, a man of science. I am most familiar with men of science. I've known many during my existence—men of great knowledge and ambition. Copernicus, Descartes, Da Vinci, Keppler, I've known them all. Before Galileo became embroiled in a controversy with the Holy See, I had financed some of his experiments." The baron watched in the darkness as Holmes sat silent, listening. Perhaps he was getting through to him. He continued, "It was through associations such as these and countless others I came to realize that one day, if I were patient, and careful, science would eventually evolve to a point where it could serve to free me from my suffering. As you can appreciate, Mr. Holmes, affliction makes the intelligent man wise, not remorseful." The baron paused to gauge Holmes's reaction. "But I get ahead of myself. I've twice alluded to the inconveniences you've caused me. Let me explain. It is your life that is the first inconvenience. Believe it or not, I have no wish to be the instrument of your demise; quite the contrary, I've taken extraordinary measures, including intravenous feeding, to keep you alive, captive to be sure, but very much alive."

"I'm terribly sorry to be a bother, Baron; if you'll be so kind as to loosen these bonds, I'll be on my way."

"You jest, Mr. Holmes, but this is no laughing matter. While you've been a guest here at Darthmore, I've read up on your varied exploits. Your biographer, Dr. Watson, who by the way was here this evening at last to inquire as to your visit a week ago, is apparently a great admirer of yours. If only half of what he has written about you is true, you are an extraordinary man with exceptional talent and intelligence. I too admire men with both talent and intellect. It would be a true pity to end your life without just cause.

"But what to do with you...? That is the question. That is the first inconvenience. I promise you, Mr. Holmes, if at all possible, I will spare your life."

"Baron, I'm touched. But we both know what you are, just as we both know you cannot let me live. You've admitted your guilt to me. My testimony will ensure they put a rope around your neck."

"How naïve you are, Mr. Holmes."

"Not naïve enough to be taken in by your tale of being a victim. Nor am I the fool you apparently take me for, Baron. Do you sincerely believe you can convince me you are a vampire and that by being such you are a victim, thus I should not bring you to justice? Madness!"

"Justice?!" the baron suddenly raised his voice in enraged indignation, "What do you know about justice? I've lived a dozen lifetimes, seen wars waged by men such as you who seek justice. I've seen entire villages burned with all inhabitants slain, man, woman and child; babes in arms ripped from their mothers' breasts and crushed under the heels of soldiers' boots, all in the name of justice. I've seen the loves of my life repulsed by what I am—what I've become, seen my entire family grow old and die before my eyes. I've watched as nations have risen and fallen. You dare speak to me of justice?!"

On his feet, the baron closed the distance between himself and Holmes, towering over his seated captive, "Was it justice when I fell in battle waged to purge Christendom of heretics only to have God condemn me to walk the earth for eternity, undead? Cursed to live in darkness, seeking sustenance through the destruction of others, having to bear the guilt of so many lives taken?

"And what of you and your <u>enlightened</u> society? The very district in which my victims were taken is evidence that damns it. The squalor in which they live, scraping for pennies tossed to them by your elites who use them, then cast them aside, is an indictment on that same society. Whole generations are lost to the abortionist's knife for the price of a few guineas, while the elites of your so-called society venture into the nether world for an evening of sport. No, Mr. Holmes, speak not to me of justice! You haven't the right!"

"Surely, Baron, you cannot equate what you have done, the murders you have committed, with the natural selection, to use a term you are undoubtedly familiar, of societal norms. The poor, I've heard it said, will always be with us.

"As I said, Baron, I'm a man of science. You must understand that to me your story is no more credible than if you were to tell me you'd walked on the moon."

"Ah, yes, of course," said the baron, fighting to regain his composure, feeling the heat of hunger rising within. "You are the second to tell me as much in as many months, which brings me to the second inconvenience you've caused me. I said before that my condition is hopeless, and so I've believed for over six centuries, until very recently."

"Oh? And what has changed your mind?"

"Three months ago I met a doctor. I believe he has the ability and the skill to cure me at last of my malediction."

"And in meantime, you murder innocent victims. Not

exactly an even exchange, is it, Baron?" Holmes laughed under his breath.

"You are amused, Mr. Holmes?"

"Only by your insistence on continuing this fairy tale. Tell me, Baron, who is this physician, or should I say magician, who's come to your aid?"

"I fear giving you too much information would be a mistake, Mr. Holmes, particularly in the eventuality I should decide to allow you to live. Let it suffice to say that a cure for my condition is, or should I say was, in the offing. You see, my dear Mr. Holmes, when you came to see me, I was under treatment for my condition, the symptoms of which had been much diminished. My need for fresh blood was in check. The streets of London, as I'm sure you noted from the lack of new victims, were safe from my predations."

"You speak in the past tense, Baron."

"That is because, my dear Mr. Holmes, in your clumsy attempt to capture a prize proving my guilt, you destroyed the serum that kept my symptoms in check. Thereby, you've unleashed the hunger within me once again. Even now I can feel it stirring. It grows with the darkness, urging me to the hunt."

"Madness!" Holmes said dismissively.

The derisiveness in Holmes's voice incensed the baron. He could feel the hunger welling up inside him. The beast, which had been sedated under the influence of Dr. Tremaine's serum, raged within him. Standing over Holmes, he railed, "Madness? You would do well to think so. Remember this, Mr. Holmes, it was your meddling that has released the beast within me to walk the streets of London once again." With his voice rising to a thundering crescendo, he concluded, "Tonight's blood is on your hands, Mr. Sherlock Holmes!"

"It is the darkness in your soul that urges you on, Baron...Baron.........Baron!" Holmes sensed rather than heard the baron's movements, then felt a rush of cool air as a door opened, then closed. Finally, he heard a metallic scraping, followed closely by the click of a lock spring. Holmes began to work loose from his bindings, but his progress was maddeningly slow.

Taking long strides, the baron threw on his greatcoat and cape, retrieving his walking stick from the umbrella stand. Before leaving he gave Garrett instructions, "Keep a close eye on the house and the grounds. Should anyone approach before tomorrow's dawn, you are to go to the wine cellar," handing him the key, "and dispose of Mr. Holmes. Do I make myself clear?"

Garrett's eyes widened when he heard the baron's orders, "Yessir," then fearfully he asked, "and if no one comes before the dawn, sir?"

"Then you may release Mr. Holmes at dawn." Donning his hat, the baron exited the house by way of the stable.

Troubled, Garrett placed the key the baron had given him into his pocket and took up his post at the front bay window. Soon after he saw the baron's coach careening out of the drive, he observed two figures stealthily making their way across the grounds. With a resigned obedience, Garrett headed for the wine cellar.

#

Shortly after midnight, the baron's coach issued from Darthmore's gate at full gallop, with the baron at the reins. Watson and Abberline waited until it was out of sight, then moved from their hiding place and slowly approached the house across the expanse of grounds, attempting to remain within the shadows. At last reaching their goal, they tried the large front door and were cautiously surprised to find it unlocked. Mindful Garrett might be prowling about, they moved from room to room in a quiet, careful search, pistols drawn.

They soon discovered they needn't have worried about Garrett. When they came to the formal dining room they found him. He was hanging from a bell cord, which was wrapped around his neck on one end with the other attached to an ornamental cornice piece above the entryway. A chair, on which he'd apparently stood to fasten the cord, was carelessly turned over beneath him. Together, they wrestled to get the body of the big man down from the makeshift gallows. Once he was on the floor, Watson examined him for signs of life. Finding none, he pronounced him dead.

They pressed on in their hunt through the other rooms, Watson retrieving Holmes hat from the cloakroom. When they'd reached the kitchen, they encountered their first locked door. With both men applying their shoulders to it, the door, which was never meant to be much of a barrier to begin with, gave way and they discovered stairs leading down into a wine cellar. Cautiously, they made their way down the stairs. The cellar was dark and apparently well-stocked with an assortment of expensive wines, undoubtedly served at the baron's many parties.

At the far side of the cellar, they discovered another locked door. This one, though, appeared substantially sturdier than the one at the top of the stairs. The lock was of an unusual design and the door itself appeared to be newly installed, made of the strongest teak. Watson tested its strength with his shoulder, then called, "Holmes...Holmes, are you there?"

From the other side of the door they heard, "Watson, is that you?"

"Yes, Holmes...thank God you are all right."

"Where is the baron and his manservant?" shouted Holmes.

"The baron is gone," Abberline relayed. "He drove off in his coach not twenty minutes ago. As for his man, I'm afraid he's dead. Hanged himself."

"Do you see a lock on the door?" Holmes inquired.

"Yes, we see it," answered Watson. "Are you able to pick it, old boy?"

"I'm afraid it hasn't an opening in which to place a pick on this side, merely a blank surface. You'll have to do it, Watson. I'll try and talk you through it." Holmes instructed, "You'll need a stiff piece of wire or two."

Looking around the cellar, Watson retrieved some wire from a packing crate, "I have it," he cried. "There appears to be a lever on the face of the lock," and as he was saying it, Watson pressed the lever. The lock face swung out of sight with a scraping sound, being replaced instead by a blank plate. "Oh dear," muttered Watson.

"Good work, old boy," shouted Holmes from the other side.

Watson and Abberline looked at each other quizzically and Watson, believing Holmes's remark to be a rather sarcastic admonition, started to apologize when they heard a metallic click, followed by the door swinging open.

Holmes charged out, leaving the room, which was black as pitch, behind him. "The game's afoot; we must get to Whitechapel at once," Holmes glared at them alarmingly. "The baron is on the hunt!"

The trio departed Darthmore in great haste, flagging down a coach on the street. On the way to Whitechapel, Holmes related the story of the baron's bizarre confession as well as his belief that the only rational explanation was that the baron was quite insane and actually believed himself to be a vampire.

It was agreed Abberline would part company with Holmes and Watson at the Bishopsgate Police Station, where he could make his report to Scotland Yard as well as alert the Whitechapel area stations, relaying a description of the baron and his coach by police telegraph, then join the beat constables patrolling the streets. Watson and Holmes would go on to the areas Holmes had previously identified as possible future murder sites on his map whereas to begin their search.

Chapter 24

ESCAPE

November 9, 1888

The hunger caused the baron to drive the coach harder than perhaps he would otherwise. Despite his concern this could cause him to be noticed, he knew this would be his last night in London and he needed to ensure all preparations were made before he could unleash the beast once more. The pursuing hounds, he knew, were closing in on him. Holmes was proof of that, yet the baron allowed him to live knowing he would certainly escape confident he would be detained long enough for the baron to satisfy his hunger as well as make good his escape.

His first stop was the warehouse on the south side of the Thames, which by now should be empty of his belongings. Slowing to a trot as he crossed Southwark Bridge, he angled east to Briar Crossing and the South Farrington Warehouse. "Mr. Fenley," the baron bellowed at the office from his perch on the coach. "Wake up, Fenley," he called as he leapt to the ground.

Inside, a light flickered on in the small, cramped office and the disheveled old warehouseman emerged, tucking his nightshirt into his trousers, "Aye, Baron, she's all aboard now. Nothing left inside, save the rats," smiling a grotesque and nearly toothless smile.

"And the hansom?"

"I'll fetch it right away, sir," taking the dapple's harness and leading her in back of the warehouse, only to reappear leading a sorrel pulling a hansom. "Here you are, sir, just as we spoke of."

"And as we spoke, you will find the rig on the south dock at St. Katherine's on the morrow," climbing up into the seat of the cab, "and you can keep both for your trouble. As for the cargo housing," reaching beneath his cloak, "as promised," the baron shouted as he threw down a small bag of gold coins, then cracked the whip wheeling the cab toward his next stop.

A light rain began to fall on this cold night and the sorrel gelding was skittish, but the baron drove him hard, plumes of white breath from his mouth and nostrils getting lost in the fog and drizzle. The baron crossed back to the north side of the Thames over London Bridge. On he drove, to St. Katherine's Docks, where his ship was moored.

He'd purchased the *Animus Lacuna* while he was still in Italy and the ship was carrying rum from the West Indies. She was a sound and swift ship with a competent captain. The baron rode hard right up to the dock, then stopped abruptly as he sprang from the driver's seat to the dock, bounding up the gang plank.

"Captain!" the baron called as he crossed the deck to the Captain's cabin, the rain now beginning to fall in earnest.

"Ahoy, Baron," called the captain of the ship from the hatch of the forward hold.

The baron wheeled round to face him, eyes flashing and even in the low light, through the rain, the captain could see a fire in those eyes that chilled his blood colder than a North Sea gale, "We sail on the morning tide!"

"Aye, Baron, all is ready. I was just in the hold making sure all is secure. Will ye be stayin' aboard now?"

"I shall return before the dawn. Has my cabin been properly prepared?"

"Aye, sir, all is ready per your instructions," handing the baron a brass key. "Your lock's been installed and this is the only key."

"Excellent, Captain, you'll know I'm aboard when the lock is turned," taking the key from the captain. "I expect you to set sail before first light."

"Aye, Baron, as you wish. The other passengers have been made aware and all are onboard, as is the crew," gruffed the captain against an increasing wind.

"And the lady Abigail? She is onboard and in her cabin?"

"Aye, sir, don't worry, there'll be no delays."

"See to it there aren't, Captain, I'm paying you well for your discretion and dependability," he said as he made his way down the gang plank.

"Aye, and you have my word, Baron," the captain called down to him, but he was already in the coach and cracking the whip.

The baron traveled along St. George Street to Cannon Street Road, following it up to Commercial Street. He drove the horse more lightly as he made his way to Whitechapel. Just before turning onto Commercial Street the baron spotted a young woman walking in the same direction, alone in the rain. He slowed the rig, following her closely up the street.

"It's not a fit night for a young lady to be about alone," the baron called down from his perch atop the hansom through the rain, "climb in, Miss, and allow me to see you safely home."

"Go on wi'ye, I got no money for a hack. Who do I look like to you, the bloody Duchess of Devonshire?"

"I ask no fare, Miss, just a bit of conversation on a cold, wet evening."

Mary Jane Kelly stopped and looked up at the driver. In the darkness she was unable to see the fire in his eyes as they sat well back within the collar of his greatcoat he'd turned up against the cold, "Well, I am a bit tired and wet," she said, tempted. "You sure you ain't after nothin'?"

Reaching for the lever to open the coach door, "We're all after something, Miss," he replied, "but just now I only wish to see you safely home." Smiling, "Which way shall I go, Miss?"

"Up by Spitalfields Market," she said. As she climbed into the coach, she spied an unopened bottle of Jameson Pure Pot Still whisky, "Well, now, this'll knock the chill off the bones," she called up through the transom.

"Help yourself," returned the baron, "'twas left by my gov'nor," as he busied himself scouting the by-ways for a convenient place to park the rig and take his fill.

After taking a long pull on the bottle, "Whew! That's good Irish, Gov'nor. When we get to my place, you might bring it in for a swig," and she began to sing a little melodic ditty.

"I'm sure your house-mates wouldn't care for that, Miss."

"Oh, that's not a problem, my girlfriend is off this week up-country, we'll have the room to ourselves, we will."

Upon hearing this gratuitous bit of news, the baron increased the cadence of the horse's hooves on the cobblestone street and forsook his inspection of the side-streets and by ways.

This was exactly what the baron desired, uninterrupted license to take his fill of this woman. He could hear her happily singing in the cab of the hansom below him. He opened the trap-door, "Coming up on Spitalfields Market soon, Miss...the address?"

"26 Dorsett, number 13," she sang, "26 Dorset, 13, 13, 13..."

The rain had lightened a bit and the baron parked the cab in a small, dark alley, tying the horse to a gutter spout. Opening the door to the cab, he grasped Mary's arm as she spilled out, steadying her. She affectionately leaned against him as he wrapped her in his cloak against the rain.

"That's it, m'lady, this way to your door," as he guided her along.

"I'll bet I know what it is you'll be wantin' when we get inside," she said in a laughing, playful singsong voice as she fished her keys from her small, tattered handbag, "you'll like as not get it too, you will. You've been a perfect gentleman," fumbling for the lock.

"Allow me," he said, taking the key from her fingers and turning it in the lock. "After you, m'lady."

Upon entering and locking the door behind him, and as Mary took another drink from the now half-empty bottle, the baron began undressing to the waist.

"There now, I knew we'd get around to that," Mary laughed as she plopped down hard on the small bed against the rear wall of the dingy gray apartment. She unfastened the buttons of her dress bodice and kicked off her shoes. The baron was struck by how young she was, not much more than twenty was his guess, though hardly with the blush of youth still upon her cheek, such was her life. She continued undressing before him, half in stupor, humming a happy melody.

The baron watched as she bared herself and only when she was at last completely naked, still sitting on the edge of the bed, did he approach her. Sliding his arms around her small waist, supporting her back with his hand, he gently laid her down and kissed her, his cold lips moving from her mouth to her cheek, then down her neck. He could feel the warm blood pulsing just beneath the surface of her throat as he bit.

\#

Throughout the night, Holmes and Watson patrolled through the rain the streets of Whitechapel in search of the baron, his coach or any sign of his handiwork. Abberline joined in the hunt soon after making his reports and briefing the London Police and the chief inspectors of the various divisions. He patrolled the streets from the Bishopsgate station working his way eastward.

Shortly after Abberline made his report, a police van with two extra officers were dispatched to Darthmore Hall. The body of Garrett was removed and the officers stayed on in the event of the baron's return.

The long hours on patrol yielded nothing. Surprisingly, after the baron's indictment of Holmes for what he was about to do, no deaths were reported nor was there a single sighting of the baron's coach. It was as if the night and the rain had swallowed him whole.

At about eight in the morning the rain stopped. Holmes, Watson and Abberline rendezvoused at Aldgate station. From there they traveled to Whitehall to discuss their next move. A description of the baron was communicated to all posts and stations in London and extra constables were positioned at the train stations should the baron try to escape the city.

Abberline had coffee and breakfast sent in to his office for Watson and Holmes as they waited while he went to give a verbal report to Sir Charles. He felt the report was necessary to explain how he came to be at Darthmore, when Sir Charles had given him orders to the contrary.

As he approached Sir Charles's office, he noticed the door was wide open. Sir Charles was within, packing personal items into a crate.

"Beg pardon, Sir Charles," Abberline said as he rapped upon the door.

"Ah, Abberline, come in, come in. I suppose you've heard."

"Heard, sir?"

"Yes, I'm out, Abberline, sacked! Matthews says this was the last straw. Appears he's been looking for an excuse to get rid of me, and now you've given it to him."

"I, sir? I...I..."

"There, there, Inspector, I don't blame you. Only doing your job and all that, eh? And doing it in a splendid manner, I should say," looking downward into the crate of accumulated artifacts, "I should have trusted your instincts more, I suppose." Then he mumbled to himself, "...and to think I was going to allow Abigail to travel to America with him..."

"Beg pardon, Sir Charles?"

"Hmmm..." Sir Charles asked, distractedly, "...oh, nothing...nothing at all, my boy." Taking a deep breath and appearing to shed his melancholy, Sir Charles stiffened his back and said, "I expect you've come to make a report?"

"Yes, sir."

"Well, you can make that report to Monro. I'll be making the official announcement later this morning, but he's the Commissioner now," then softly, "God help him, and good luck to you, my boy."

"Yes sir, thank you." As he turned to leave he stopped at the door and turning around, asked sincerely, "Is there anything I can do for you, sir?"

"Yes, you can capture that damned Ripper, Inspector."

"Yes sir!"

Abberline went directly to Monro's office and made a full report, omitting any reference to vampirism. Afterward, he learned Sir Charles was asked by the Home Secretary to step down from his post as commissioner. The official reason was that he had embarrassed the Home Secretary with his increasingly frequent and incendiary outbursts in the press of being undermined as commissioner by his detectives reporting through other channels to the Secretary.

The truth was that he simply could not keep up with the pressures of the job and was beginning to crack under the strain. These last two months had been particularly difficult. Now, with the added news he may have impeded an active investigation due to personal entanglements, the Home Secretary had no choice. Owing to his impeccable record up to the present time and his venerable military record, he was allowed to retire quietly with full pension.

It was some time before Abberline returned to his office. Holmes and Watson had been going over the facts of each of the murders, hoping to discover additional clues that might lead them to finding the baron. Each fact needed to be re-examined in the light of knowing who the perpetrator was. They were in the process of updating Abberline when a commotion occurred outside his office causing them to pause. A detective sergeant knocked on the door, "Inspector Abberline, there's been another murder."

"In Whitechapel?" Abberline asked, looking quite shaken.

"Yessir, and it's a nasty one, I'm afraid."

Abberline, Holmes and Watson grabbed their coats and hats and ordered a police van to take them to the scene, a single room, number 13, at 26 Dorsett Street, Spitalfields. The victim was a young woman named Mary Jane Kelly.

When they arrived, they were met by Inspector Beck, who was the first policeman on the scene. Ghastly didn't begin to describe the carnage inside the room. The young woman's body lay naked upon the bed, throat cut cleanly with a handkerchief placed over the cut, an embroidered handkerchief of fine linen. Her abdomen was gaping, intestines draped about her body and, as they would not discover till later, her uterus and kidneys were removed, apparently drained of blood and discarded beneath the bed. Her heart was missing entirely.

Holmes made a painstaking investigation of the room, then stepped outside. "Beastly," Watson commented, obviously

233

shaken despite his military medical background.

"To be sure, but there's little more to be learned here," replied Holmes. Then casually, "The handkerchief was a rather cheeky touch."

A messenger handed Abberline an envelope as he emerged from the murder scene.

"What is it, Inspector?" asked Holmes.

"We must go to the docks at once," answered Abberline as he handed the note to Holmes, "they found this," holding up a small silver key, "on the body of the baron's manservant, along with a note," reading:

> "'Mi lif aint for liven no mor. I couldnt stop the uther myrders. The baryns gon frum St Kates to New York. I cant do his bidin no mor. He cant tuch me til we meets in hell I expek. God hav mercy on my soel.'"

As they arrived at St. Katherine's Dock, the coach pulled up to the dock master's office and Abberline went in. In just a few moments he returned. Holmes and Watson were standing on the pier looking down river.

"One ship bound for New York left this morning in time to make the tide," reading from his notebook, "a barque named *Animus Lacuna*, four passengers, a crew of 12 and the Captain and Mate, Italian flagged and owned by," pausing as he looked up at Holmes and Watson, "Baron Barlucci."

"Then he has escaped." Holmes remarked, looking wistfully down the Thames.

"Yes, we wired Gravesend to see if she'd yet passed. They wired back that the *Animus* passed in time to make the tide," adding in a grave tone, "We must cable the authorities in New York."

"Yes," mused Holmes, "if New York is indeed his destination. I'm afraid he's free to wreak his wicked havoc wherever there's a port in which to land. New York may well be his next port of call, the London of the New World. God help them if he comes to port unnoticed."

234

"We'll make sure they at least know he's coming, Mr. Holmes. If he makes port anywhere along the eastern seaboard, he'll be caught."

As they turned to depart, Holmes saw the *Lira* had just docked. "Watson, there is the ship that brought the baron to our shores."

"My God, Holmes, I'd almost forgotten. While you were held hostage, young Gaetano was sentenced to hang. He's to walk the gallows steps on Monday morning. How fortuitous that we should discover the *Lira* here, just when the baron has fled."

"One door closes, my dear Watson, as another opens. Let's go aboard and have a chat with the Captain, shall we?" Turning to Abberline, "Inspector, as this matter is far removed from your jurisdiction, we shall excuse ourselves from your company."

"Of course, Mr. Holmes, I have reports to make and I must prepare the cables for the police officials in America. Good luck."

"Thank you, Inspector. Come Watson."

Chapter 25

FREEDOM

November 12, 1888

"Mr. Holmes, I don't know how to thank you," Carlino was close to tears as the gaoler released his chains and presented him with his personal belongings. "How were you able to convince the authorities to release me?"

"Go with Watson and wait for me in the administrative offices. There are some papers for you to sign; I will explain all in the cab," replied Holmes as Watson led Carlino out of the gaoler's office.

After Watson and Carlino had departed, Holmes spoke quietly to the warder who had so poorly used Carlino, "Your name's Collins, isn't it?"

"Yea, what of it?" he growled at Holmes.

"You'll be interested to know I've been doing some checking and have discovered certain irregularities regarding the funds sent to care for the prisoners here at Newgate from their benefactors."

"What's that you're saying," grizzled the warder through clenched teeth.

"Yes, I'd say it's a fair bet you'll be wearing new stripes very soon," Holmes remarked. "Tell me, warder Collins, did you notice anything unusual occurring in the last month?"

"Unusual? What do you mean, unusual."

"Oh, not much. Perhaps some discoloration of your fingers," Collins eyes widened as Holmes went on, "turning bright blue as you tried to wash it off with soap and water?"

"'ere now, what sort of mischief are you talking about?" Collins asked as he moved around the desk, his hand clenching a cricket bat he normally reserved for inmates.

"What was your cut in the arrangement? Five pounds, ten per transaction?"

"You ain't got no proof of nothin'," he said as his face

236

grew redder.

"Think again, Collins, why do you think your hands turned blue? The money you took, or rather, the money you stole from the prisoners was tainted."

"Tainted?" Collins asked, his curiosity staying his hand for the moment.

"Yes, tainted. Tainted with a small amount of powder, which when it comes into contact with liquid, either acidic or base, reacts to it by changing color."

"Why, you..." and he drew back the bat as he advanced on Holmes.

"Inspector!" called Holmes, upon which three burly constables and an inspector came through the door from the adjoining room.

"I'm afraid you've been turned in by the head gaoler, Collins."

"Bloody 'ell you say," realizing the stew in which he now found himself, "I ain't goin' to prison, not for the lousy few quid I got for me trouble. It was Clancy what got most of the money, 'im and that banker friend of 'is. That's whose idea it was too. Said as long as we kept 'em bruised and achin' they'd never complain."

"Take him away," ordered Inspector Lestrade, of Scotland Yard. Then, turning to Holmes, he said, "in another minute, he'd have middled you, Mr. Holmes."

"Yes, lucky for me, I had Scotland Yard as my MCC," replied Holmes referring to the Marylebone Cricket Club, which acts as the custodian of cricket laws. "I trust you have enough evidence now to seize the lot of the Newgate conspirators."

"Quite enough, Mr. Holmes. Since you put us on to this crew last month, we've been keeping a keen eye on them. All told, there's a dozen in on this caper. A nice haul, if I do say," said Lestrade, obviously well pleased. "Oh, and thanks," looking round to make sure no one was in earshot, "for allowing me to take credit for breaking up this ring."

"Nonsense, Lestrade, you've done me a few good turns. It was only fair of me to repay in kind."

237

"I guess I have at that, Mr. Holmes," grinned Lestrade.

"Inspector, please see to it the money I told you about is delivered to the account of Carlino Gaetano in the Bank of England, won't you?"

"Of course, Mr. Holmes, you can depend on me."

"I'm sure I can," Holmes replied on his way out of the door to the gaoler's office. He caught up with Watson and Carlino just as they were finishing up the paperwork. "Ah, here you are. Shall we go?"

"Yes, Mr. Holmes, I cannot wait to get out of this place," Carlino said, looking around.

Vittorio was waiting near a landau cab as they emerged from the prison, "Carlino!" he exclaimed as he ran to greet his friend.

"Vito! How good it is to see you, my friend."

"I told you everything would be all right, Carlino, and now you are free, at last."

"Yes. Free…thanks to Mr. Holmes and Dr. Watson."

The four men climbed into the cab of the landau and Holmes gave the driver instructions. Once inside, Carlino again asked, "Mr. Holmes, how did you do it? How did you convince them of my innocence."

"Very simple, really. I believe I mentioned we were in pursuit of the mystery passenger onboard the *Lira*…"

"Then you have captured the man who murdered my Gianetta?" asked Carlino excitedly.

"No, I'm afraid he has eluded us. He sailed to America two days ago," answered Holmes.

"Then, I do not understand," Carlino said, confused.

"It was during our pursuit of the mystery passenger, who as it turns out is actually Baron Antonio Barlucci, a well known and quite wealthy financier, when we realized the *Lira* was back in port. Dr. Watson and I went aboard to question Captain Madison about his passengers on that fateful journey from Italy."

"And he told you about the baron?"

"No, I'm afraid the former captain of the *Lira*, Josiah Madison, is quite dead. But the new captain, Brady's his name, confirmed Barlucci was a passenger on that crossing. He also confirmed the manifest had been altered by the now deceased Captain Madison."

"But this could not, in itself secure your freedom," interrupted Dr. Watson.

"Quite so," continued Holmes, but two pieces of evidence I was able to find inside the Captain's cabin proved to the authorities that your story was true and that our Whitechapel murderer was indeed the man who killed Gianetta."

"Evidence? After such a long time? What is it you found, Mr. Holmes," asked Vittorio.

"Blood remains detectable, with the proper techniques, even after a considerable amount of time has passed and despite attempts to wash it away. I found several traces of blood inside the cabin and on the railing of the deck immediately aft of the cabin."

"Gianetta's?"

"Yes, we believe so. It is our theory the baron murdered Gianetta inside the Captain's cabin, then disposed of her remains into the sea, over the railing of that deck."

"But that is only, as you say, a theory. How did you convince the authorities it is true?"

Reaching inside his vest pocket, Holmes pulled out a ring, "With this," he said as he handed Carlino the ring he had given Gianetta the night before she disappeared.

"This is my ring…how?"

"Gianetta was apparently wearing that ring when she was murdered. Since it is obviously too large for a woman's finger, it must have slipped off her hand unnoticed by the baron and lodged in the decking beneath a large desk. I found it there after a thorough search of the cabin," Holmes related matter-of-factly.

"This, along with the blood stains and the fact that Baron Barlucci is suspected of the Whitechapel murders, has convinced the maritime authorities that you, my boy, are innocent," Watson said, patting Carlino on the shoulder.

"Doctor, Mr. Holmes, how can I ever thank you?"

"No need. In fact, you can thank Gianetta. It is she who left the crucial bit of evidence that freed you."

"My Gianetta," Carlino said in a sad voice, "I will never forget you," as he clutched the ring tightly in his hand, then, opening his hand he placed the ring on his finger and touched it to his lips, "This is all I have to remember her."

"Here, I believe we've arrived," Holmes declared as he opened the door to the cab.

"Arrived? This isn't my apartment, Mr. Holmes," Vittorio said looking out at the three story edifice with the words, "*THE TIMES*" in four foot letters near the top.

"Not your residence," said Watson, "but your new place of employment."

"Employment..." repeated Vittorio.

"Here?" asked an incredulous Carlino.

"Yes, I took the liberty of asking an acquaintance of mine if he could use two apprentice typesetters. I believe that was your intent when you began your voyage, was it not?"

"Mr. Holmes, Dr. Watson," said Carlino, overcome with emotion.

"You are most generous, Signore Holmes. Carlino and I are very grateful. How can we ever repay you."

"By being useful citizens of your new home here in England. That will be payment enough," clapping the two young men on the shoulders. "But here, there is someone else who wishes to see you."

Carlino turned to see a man walking towards him. Recognizing his father, he ran to meet him. Standing together in Printing House Square, they threw their arms around each other, kissing each other on the cheeks, "Papa, how...why...?"

"Carlino, Signore Holmes wired me last month you were in prison and due to a ring of thieves you had received neither the money I had sent for your care nor the wires. I came immediately."

"Papa, you sent money?" Turning to Holmes, "what he says, Mr. Holmes, the money? What happened?"

"The man who beat you in the prison, along with being

240

among the lowest level of human being, was also the lowest level of a crime syndicate who prayed on the weak and hopeless, especially foreigners. The ring extended from the prison to the Bank of England. They were stealing money from the accounts of those who tried to ensure their loved ones were treated better while in prison."

"Mr. Holmes, I want to thank you for what you and Doctor Watson did for my Carlino," said Cesenza Gaetano.

"Signore Gaetano," replied Holmes, "you should be very proud of your son. From all I have witnessed, both he and his friend, Vittorio, here, are young men of high honor."

Epilogue

November 30, 1888

Holmes and Watson were enjoying breakfast approximately three weeks later when they received a visit from Inspector Abberline.

"Come in, Inspector, have you had your breakfast?" Holmes inquired congenially. "If not, allow me to invite you to share ours."

"No thank you, Mr. Holmes."

"Are you quite sure? Mrs. Hudson has prepared some excellent German sausage for us this morning. I highly recommend it."

"That's quite all right, I only came by to give you some news about our friend, the baron."

Turning in his chair, Holmes responded, "The baron?"

"Has he been caught?" asked Watson.

"I'm afraid not, and there's reason to believe he won't be. Our man in New York received a wire from the coastal authorities in Newfoundland."

"That would be Inspector Andrews, would it not?" asked Holmes.

"Yes. He reports they recovered a longboat and some debris. It appears to be from the *Animus Lacuna.* The longboat, which still had the canvas topping lashed across it, bore the name painted below the gunwale and contained the body of a young woman, presumably a passenger. We think it may be Miss Abigail Drake, Sir Charles's niece."

"Ah yes, I'd heard he had a bad time of it after discovering she left with the baron. Terrible business," noted Holmes.

"My understanding is the news of her fleeing with the baron has given him a stroke," added Watson, "I've heard he's begun to recover somewhat of late."

"Hopefully this latest news won't cause a relapse," offered Holmes.

"I sincerely hope not. Despite our differences, I always admired the man," replied Abberline. "He was quite accomplished, you know."

"Yes, so I've heard," responded Holmes. "Did you have more news of the baron's ship, Inspector?"

"Yes, pieces of the ship have been washing up along the shoreline in Newfoundland, where the longboat was discovered. It's believed she may have hit an iceberg and sank. The condition of the longboat suggests they didn't have time to launch it properly as a lifeboat."

"The sea can be most unforgiving this time of year," offered Watson.

"Of course we can't be certain, and the authorities will still be on the watch, but that appears to be the end of Baron Barlucci."

"Yes, it appears so, doesn't it," said Holmes. "By the way, Inspector, it may interest you to know this may conclude a murder investigation in two of Europe's great cities."

"Two cities, Mr. Holmes?"

"Do you recall the string of similar murders I mentioned when you first visited Baker Street?"

"Why, yes, I do. Please go on," Abberline urged.

"Yes, well it seems Paris may have fallen victim to the baron's sinister machinations before London. Before my, ahem, guest stay at the baron's, I'd made some inquiries. It appears at that time, in Paris, an American, a Dr. Alan Tremaine, was giving a series of lectures at Paris's Academy of Science, which coincides quite nicely with the fairy tale the baron alluded to during our discussion the night before he sailed."

"I'm not sure I understand," Abberline replied.

"Ah, perhaps you were unaware that the baron had thrown a gala for the doctor upon the event of his final lecture here in London and that the doctor was a guest—a willing guest—at the baron's estate," concluded Holmes. "In his invective to me, the baron insisted the doctor was devising a cure for his _vampirism_."

"Crazy as a loon! Then you believe the baron must have

been in Paris and while there committed the Parisian murders," interjected Watson. "You might have let me know, old boy."

"Since you've promised the Home Secretary not to chronicle this little adventure, I didn't feel it was of sufficient import. Besides, as I recall, you rather poo-pooed the theory."

"All the more reason, I'd say."

"Perhaps, perhaps," Holmes replied with an introspective look crossing over his face. "A singularly curious case, this Baron Barlucci. One cannot help but wonder what could drive a mind to such machinations as to totally convince itself of this most preposterous condition in order to rationalize its own diabolical actions. So complete was his delusion that he constructed around his fiendish deeds a framework to support his wild imaginings."

"You're speaking of vampirism, Mr. Holmes?"

"Yes, haven't we come further as a society in our scientific reasoning than to still harbor such superstitious beliefs to the point where they can infect the mind and become a sort of reality for some."

"It was certainly real enough for him, I'd say," said Watson. "I wonder what this Dr. Tremaine would say if he knew of the baron's assertions."

"As a man of science, I'm sure he'd be a bit amused, as well as repulsed, that the baron could have included him in his mad tale."

"Mad, certainly," agreed Watson, "but without the baron's neck to fit into a noose, I'm afraid the common Jack and Jill of London would not be so convinced."

"Exactly, old boy, and it is precisely because we are unable to produce the baron and dispel the myth that we cannot, I think, advertise the method nor the motive behind his madness. Better leave the murderer go down in history as 'Jack the Ripper', such as he is portrayed in the newspapers, than to entice the collective imagination with the tale of a more novel menace. At least the populace can understand that sort of murderer, depraved as it may be. As time goes on without further incident, they will forget. But give them the specter of a vampire, a beast who never dies, to haunt their dreams, and they'll see one in every dark corner of the night."

"I believe you are right, Mr. Holmes. The world is better off with demons it can understand than ones it cannot."

"Well said, Inspector, well said.

Acknowledgements

My thanks go first and foremost to my wife, without whose patience and willingness to read chapter one over and over again, this book would not be possible.

I also want to thank those who read my novel and gave me the feedback I needed to make it stronger. In particular I want to thank Theresa McGirr, Adrienne Jones, and Peter Rodill.

In researching Victorian London one of the books I found most useful was *Dickens's Dictionary of London, 1888.* For information on the Jack the Ripper murders I relied heavily on the website Casebook: Jack the Ripper, at www.casebook.org, Stephen Ryder, Executive Editor. My vampire was modeled from the king of vampires, Count Dracula.

I would also like to thank Jon Lellenberg, American representative of the Conan Doyle Estate, for his encouragement and patient with a novice author. I would be remiss if I did not thank the multitude of agents who rejected my novel, not wishing to represent it. I'm quite certain the majority of them did so wisely, as with each batch of rejections, I went back, researched some more and came out with a much better book.

Lastly, I want to thank Steve Emecz and all the other fine people and other authors at MX Publishing for showing faith in my work. Writing this book has been a true labor of love for me, and an opportunity to add my small contribution to the lasting legend of Arthur Conan Doyle and that of his great detective.

Also from MX Publishing

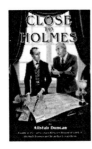

Close To Holmes

A Look at the Connections Between Historical London, Sherlock Holmes and Sir Arthur Conan Doyle.

Eliminate The Impossible

An Examination of the World of Sherlock Holmes on Page and Screen.

The Norwood Author

Arthur Conan Doyle and the Norwood Years (1891 - 1894) – Winner of the 2011 Howlett Literary Award (Sherlock Holmes book of the year)

www.mxpublishing.com

Also From MX Publishing

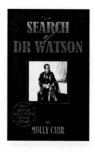

In Search of Dr Watson

Wonderful biography of Dr. Watson from expert Molly Carr – 2nd edition fully updated.

Arthur Conan Doyle, Sherlock Holmes and Devon

A Complete Tour Guide and Companion.

The Lost Stories of Sherlock Holmes

Eight more stories from the pen of John H Watson – compiled by Tony Reynolds.

www.mxpublishing.com

Also From MX Publishing

Watsons Afghan Adventure

Fascinating biography of Watson's time in Afghanistan from US Army veteran Kieran McMullen.

Shadowfall

Sherlock Holmes, ancient relics and demons and mystic characters. A supernatural Holmes pastiche.

Official Papers of The Hound of The Baskervilles

Very unusual collection of the original police papers from The Hound case.

www.mxpublishing.com

Also From MX Publishing

The Sign of Fear

The first adventure of the 'female Sherlock Holmes'. A delightful fun adventure with your favourite supporting Holmes characters.

A Study in Crimson

The second adventure of the 'female Sherlock Holmes' with a host of sub-plots and new characters joining Watson and Fanshaw

The Chronology of Arthur Conan Doyle

The definitive chronology used by historians and libraries worldwide.

www.mxpublishing.com

Also From MX Publishing

Aside Arthur Conan Doyle

A collection of twenty stories from
ACD's close friend Bertram
Fletcher Robinson.

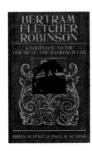

Bertram Fletcher Robinson

The comprehensive biography of the
assistant plot producer of The Hound
of The Baskervilles

Wheels of Anarchy

Reprint and introduction to Max
Pemberton's thriller from 100 years
ago. One of the first spy thrillers of
its kind.

www.mxpublishing.com

Also From MX Publishing

Bobbles and Plum

Four playlets from PG Wodehouse 'lost' for over 100 years – found and reprinted with an excellent commentary

The World of Vanity Fair

A specialist full-colour reproduction of key articles from Bertram Fletcher Robinson containing of colour caricatures from the early 1900s.

Tras Las He huellas de Arthur Conan Doyle (in Spanish)

Un viaje ilustrado por Devon.

www.mxpublishing.com

Also From MX Publishing

The Outstanding Mysteries of
Sherlock Holmes

With thirteen Homes stories and
illustrations Kelly re-creates the
gas-lit, fog-enshrouded world of
Victorian London

Rendezvous at The Populaire

Sherlock Holmes has retired,
injured from an encounter with
Moriarty. He's tempted out of
retirement for an epic battle with
the Phantom of the opera.

Baker Street Beat

An eclectic collection of articles,
essays, radio plays and 'general
scribblings' about Sherlock Holmes
from Dr.Dan Andriacco.

Also From MX Publishing

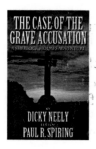

The Case of The Grave Accusation

The creator of Sherlock Holmes has been accused of murder. Only Holmes and Watson can stop the destruction of the Holmes legacy.

Barefoot on Baker Street

Epic novel of the life of a Victorian workhouse orphan featuring Sherlock Holmes and Moriarty.

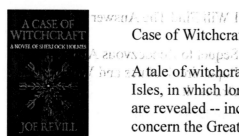

Case of Witchcraft

A tale of witchcraft in the Northern Isles, in which long-concealed secrets are revealed -- including some that concern the Great Detective himself!

www.mxpublishing.com

Also From MX Publishing

The Affair In Transylvania

Holmes and Watson tackle Dracula in deepest Transylvania in this stunning adaptation by film director Gerry O'Hara

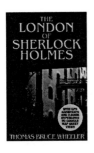

The London of Sherlock Holmes

400 locations including GPS co-ordinates that enable Google Street view of the locations around London in all the Homes stories

I Will Find The Answer

Sequel to Rendezvous At The Populaire, Holmes and Watson tackle Dr. Jekyll.

www.mxpublishing.com

Also From MX Publishing

The Case of The Russian Chessboard

Short novel covering the dark world of Russian espionage sees Holmes and Watson on the world stage facing dark and complex enemies.

An Entirely New Country

Covers Arthur Conan Doyle's years at Undershaw where he wrote Hound of The Baskervilles. Foreword by Mark Gatiss (BBC's Sherlock).

Shadowblood

Sequel to Shadowfall, Holmes and Watson tackle blood magic, the vilest form of sorcery.

www.mxpublishing.com

Also From MX Publishing

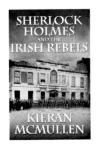

Sherlock Holmes and The Irish Rebels

It is early 1916 and the world is at war. Sherlock Holmes is well into his spy persona as Altamont.

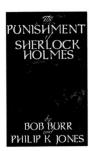

The Punishment of Sherlock Holmes

"deliberately and successfully funny"

The Sherlock Holmes Society of London

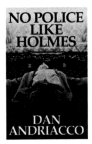

No Police Like Holmes

It's a Sherlock Holmes symposium, and murder is involved. The first case for Sebastian McCabe.

www.mxpublishing.com

Also From MX Publishing

In The Night, In The Dark

Winner of the Dracula Society Award – a collection of supernatural ghost stories from the editor of the Sherlock Holmes Society of London journal.

Sherlock Holmes and The Lyme Regis Horror

Fully updated 2nd edition of this bestselling Holmes story set in Dorset.

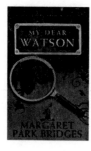

My Dear Watson

Winner of the Suntory Mystery Award for fiction and translated from the original Japanese. Holmes greatest secret is revealed – Sherlock Holmes is a woman.

www.mxpublishing.com

Also From MX Publishing

Mark of The Baskerville Hound

100 years on and a New York policeman faces a similar terror to the great detective.

A Professor Reflects On Sherlock Holmes

A wonderful collection of essays and scripts and writings on Sherlock Holmes.

www.mxpublishing.com

Lightning Source UK Ltd.
Milton Keynes UK
UKOW041307260712

196610UK00005B/3/P